ALL ABOUT VEE

ALL ABOUT VEE

C. Leigh Purtill

razOr
bill

All About Vee

RAZORBILL

Published by the Penguin Group
Penguin Young Readers Group
345 Hudson Street, New York, New York 10014, U.S.A.
Penguin Group (USA) Inc., 375 Hudson Street, New York, New York 10014, U.S.A.
Penguin Group (Canada), 90 Eglinton Avenue East, Suite 700, Toronto, Ontario, Canada M4P 2Y3
(a division of Pearson Penguin Canada Inc.)
Penguin Books Ltd, 80 Strand, London WC2R 0RL, England
Penguin Ireland, 25 St Stephen's Green, Dublin 2, Ireland (a division of Penguin Books Ltd)
Penguin Group (Australia), 250 Camberwell Road, Camberwell, Victoria 3124, Australia (a division
of Pearson Australia Group Pty Ltd)
Penguin Books India Pvt Ltd, 11 Community Centre, Panchsheel Park, New Delhi – 110 017, India
Penguin Group (NZ), 67 Apollo Drive, Rosedale, North Shore 0632, New Zealand (a division of
Pearson New Zealand Ltd)
Penguin Books (South Africa) (Pty) Ltd, 24 Sturdee Avenue, Rosebank, Johannesburg 2196, South Africa

Penguin Books Ltd, Registered Offices: 80 Strand, London WC2R 0RL, England

10 9 8 7 6 5 4 3 2 1

Library of Congress Cataloging-in-Publication Data

Purtill, C. Leigh.
 All about Vee / by C. Leigh Purtill.
  p. cm.
 Summary: When her father finally sets a wedding date, eighteen-year-old Veronica convinces her
best friends to head for Los Angeles to try to make their dreams come true, but her weight and inex-
perience make it hard for the aspiring actress even to get auditions.
 ISBN 978-1-59514-180-4
 [1. Actors and actresses--Fiction. 2. Overweight persons--Fiction. 3. Interpersonal relations--Fiction.
4. Self-actualization--Fiction. 5. Remarriage--Fiction. 6. Los Angeles (Calif.)--Fiction.] I. Title.
PZ7.P9793All 2008
[Fic]--dc22
                              2007023946

Printed in the United States of America

For my mother, Rosanne

chapter 1

Applause, applause, applause. Glorious, thundering, appreciative applause. From the base of the footlights to the top of the balcony, three hundred mouths sent waves of admiring "bravo, brava!" across the stretch of auditorium that was the home of the Chester Community Theater.

It must have been The Dip, Veronica mused, as she brushed back a wig full of long black ringlets and waited offstage for the heavy velveteen curtain to rise. It was her own creation, she would tell anyone who asked. A slight incline of the chin toward her ample bosom, a flutter of butterfly lashes, a subtle smile dancing on her full lips.

But it was her eyes more than anything else that made The Dip memorable: violet, like Elizabeth Taylor's. Would the local press deem them *luminous* this time? Or *provocative*?

A sweaty hand grabbed hers. She recognized it as belonging to Romeo a.k.a. Gerald Jackson—or Biff, as everyone called him. *Not the brightest bulb in the marquee,* she thought. All through the rehearsals, he insisted on saying "Monta-goo" instead of "Monta-gyu," like everyone *knew* it was pronounced. He yanked her onto center stage, where the entire company stood in one long line.

Veronica glanced right and left, could see in the dark several ladies-in-waiting hopping from slippered foot to slippered foot. "Don't be so anxious," she wanted to tell them. "Don't look desperate or, God forbid, needy. No one's going to applaud *pathos.*"

She felt a squeeze being passed from actor to actor, hand to hand, down the line. She knew it was coming, could sense it before it arrived, would be expected to pass it down to Biff on her left. *These yahoos,* she thought, *the squeeze came before the performance, not after. It was a sign of support, of togetherness, a symbol of a team effort—all-for-one, etc.* Well, she would not squeeze Biff's hand; no sir, the squeeze stopped here. She didn't need a clammy claw to assure her. She was Veronica May, after all. She could keep her cool, she could maintain her composure, she could—oh! The curtain was going up! She squeezed.

The roar as the curtain lifted to reveal the entire cast on stage seemed deafening. Yes, it was a cliché, but clichés were born of truth, *n'est-ce pas?*

The first to step forward were the background extras—the atmosphere, as they said in the movies. This group consisted mostly of what Veronica termed "Virgins." Virgins were new to the border town of Chester, Arizona, new to the theater, but usually old, like around thirty-five or so. They never had any lines or much to do. Sometimes the director would tell them to whisper "peas and carrots" over and over again. He claimed it sounded like casual conversation from the audience, but Veronica could never tell since she was always onstage. And sometimes the Virgins would lift things, like parts of the set, or even this one time when Veronica played Cleopatra, the Virgins had to carry her throne across stage while she leaned back against pillows and smiled seductively at the audience. (That, by the way, was probably the best use of The Dip in Veronica's career thus far—the press raved!)

Next to trot downstage were the ladies-in-waiting and the bozos who played Romeo's friends. Veronica called this group "Two-Timers" because they usually hung around for two plays and then stopped coming. Probably because they weren't very good actors and only got to say things like "Hark!" or "Very good, ma'am." Not like Veronica, who always got the lead and always had the big monologues.

And now it was time for Romeo's and Juliet's parents to stumble forward for their bows. *"Sundowners,"* Veronica thought kindly. Much nicer than calling them "old." They weren't bad, really, when you considered the Virgins or the Two-Timers. In fact, she thought generously, it was good to see these people, some of them grandparents many times over, onstage and at rehearsals, interacting with others instead of cooped up in some nursing home. It was, she thought magnanimously, almost like a public service the community theater was performing by allowing these folks to tread the boards.

Suddenly the applause grew louder. Biff was tugging on her arm, pulling her toward the footlights in his uncouth, desperate, needy manner. Veronica tugged back, as if she were forcing a dog to heel, and Biff obediently complied, permitting her to slow their pace and bask in the adoration of their fans.

Veronica turned her violet eyes on the crowd, Dipped her head to her chest and curtsied. Beside her, Biff bent double at the waist stiffly, but she doubted anyone even noticed him.

A single red rose was tossed onto the stage. Then a bouquet of yellow and white carnations with baby's breath. Lilies, wildflowers . . . was that a pair of underwear? How gauche and yet . . . Veronica cast her eyes down toward the Jockeys—nope, just a soggy white paper towel wrapped around violets in a clump of earth.

She felt Biff's hand slip out of her grasp as she continued forward downstage. Gliding, she daintily lifted her voluminous skirts and, toes-first, edged closer to the apron of the stage. Again, she curtsied, and again, the applause grew louder, if that were even possible. She reached a delicate hand toward the single rose and, careful not to prick herself, brought the perfect flower to her nose for a dramatic sniff. *C'est magnifique.*

Oh yes, they loved it. And her.

All 217 pounds of her.

chapter 2

"Veronica! Veronica! Over here!"

A shrill voice, one unaccustomed to shouting across rooms and over other people's heads, called to Veronica as soon as she emerged from the backstage dressing room.

She peered through and around the mass of bodies in front of her, knowing full well who that voice belonged to: Daddy's girl-friend, May. *Fiancée, fiancée,* Veronica reminded herself. *They've been engaged for . . . well, forever almost.*

"Excuse me," Veronica heard beside her, "Veronica?"

Veronica looked down to find a petite Sundowner next to her. "Hello, Mrs. Jackson."

"Oh, my dear," the tiny lady gushed, "you were marvelous tonight."

"Thank you," Veronica responded to Biff's grandmother, as expected. "You were good too."

"Really?" The old woman brought a bony hand to her throat. "Honest to goodness, my gown is so long, I was afraid I would trip when I made my entrance. I could barely remember my line. You'd never do something like that, I know. But you thought I was okay?"

"Well, sure," Veronica smiled patiently while casting a glance around for her friends. Where were the Vees anyway?

A spindly hand appeared on Veronica's forearm. Veronica looked down into Mrs. Jackson's hazy, cataract-covered eyes. "Your mother would have been so proud."

Veronica swallowed and thought about that. Her mother. *Would* she have been proud? She had no way of knowing and really, couldn't they leave it at that?

"Veronica!" May called again from the other end of the hallway.

"Oh," Veronica said, "would you excuse me, Mrs. Jackson? I have to meet my father."

Mrs. Jackson demurred. "Of course, dear."

Veronica stifled an involuntary chuckle as she strode toward May and her father. What an odd pair! Looking at the two of them together was like watching that old cartoon, the one with the big fat dog and the tiny little dog with the black bowler hats who were always palling around.

May and Daddy were like those two dogs: big, fat Daddy and tiny, little May. Except neither of them wore a hat.

"Hi, May May," Veronica said when she got a few steps closer. No reason to look like a fool yelling down the hall. May was always May May, even though she hadn't married Veronica's father. It was a private joke the three of them shared for as far back as Veronica could remember. She supposed the joke would be less funny once May and Daddy eventually *got* married and May Sanchez legally became May May, but Veronica doubted any of that would ever happen.

"Well, my baby girl's done it again. Brought the house down." Veronica's father reached out and enveloped her in a comforting bear hug. Veronica could smell his Head & Shoulders shampoo and the cheese tacos he had for dinner when he leaned in.

"You were beautiful," May May murmured. She had a whisper of a voice, perfect for her career as a librarian. "Those ringlets . . . like Olivia de Havilland in that movie, *Gone with the Wind*."

May wore her own lustrous black hair in a long braid down her back. The style, combined with her lack of height, made her look much younger than her thirty-seven years. When she was a little girl, Veronica liked to play with May's hair, pretending she was a life-size doll. She would take May's tortoise-shell glasses off and on and paint her unblemished skin with rouge. May never seemed to mind.

"Wasn't she, Moose? Wasn't she just like Olivia de Havilland?" May May always called Veronica's father Moose, the nickname he earned playing high school football. He wasn't ever any good, but he was big and people just assumed he was mean so they stayed out of his way. In fact, no one—including Daddy—could ever remember him tackling anyone. But Moose he was and Moose he would remain, even after he became the head of the town's library.

He let Veronica go and placed his arm back around May May's shoulders. "Yes, dear, she was just like Olivia. And you died remarkably well, sweetheart, remarkably well."

"Thanks, Daddy."

"Vee! Over here, Vee!"

Finally, Veronica thought. Her friends had arrived backstage.

Veronica turned to the voice calling her: It belonged to Valeria Maria Carmellita Padilla y Lopez, a mouthful of vowels her friends had long ago shortened to Val. Val was a former beauty queen with a mane of thick, nearly jet-black hair offset by impossibly smooth skin and a glow-in-the-dark smile, a Miss Chester three years in a row. At the age of fifteen, Val's reign as the town's sweetheart ended when she reached her full height of five feet three inches—but continued to grow. In one long Arizona summer, Val turned into her mother, gaining more than twenty-five pounds, all of it in a curvy hourglass shape. Her resulting figure was, needless to say, very popular among the boys in their school.

Standing next to Val was the third member of the Vees: Virginia Cooper. Ginny was an unassuming young woman, the kind who rarely got noticed. With her sandy blonde hair pulled back in a ponytail, she always seemed to blend into the background, as if she deliberately didn't want to stand out. As the girls walked toward her, Veronica could see Ginny's spiral bound notebook poking out of her purse. She was always writing, jotting down something for the town's paper—probably a few words about Veronica's own magnificence this evening. She was pleased to see Ginny wearing the silk print blouse that she had handed down to her from last season. It was a bit tight around the chest, as it had been on Veronica, but Ginny had smartly unbuttoned the top three buttons to give herself a little more breathing room.

The fourth member of the Vees, Vivian Reed, was there in spirit only. Vivian had graduated six months early and flown the coop to Los Angeles where she was certain to be a famous movie star. Veronica thought of her and felt a pang in her heart. Ah, petite Vivian—Little Vee to Veronica's Big Vee. Veronica wished she were here to celebrate this moment.

The second Vivian settled herself in L.A., she had emailed invitations for Veronica and the rest of the Vees to visit. Veronica had promised she'd see Little Vee once *she* had graduated from CHS, but that was more than a month ago and so far . . . well, there was way too much going on for her to leave just yet.

"Veronica, smile!"

Veronica turned to May who had her digital camera raised. She quickly Dipped her chin and smiled brilliantly as the flash went off. Not that she was a pro or anything, but posing for the camera just seemed to come naturally to Veronica.

"Move closer to your father," May May quietly instructed. "Moose? *Por favor?*"

Moose made a face and ran a hand over his hair, blond and thick, which he still wore in a football player's crew cut, and across his freshly-shaved cheek as if he were considering the request.

"Come on, Daddy," Veronica said, wrapping her arm around her father's waist. "You know she'll just keep on us if we don't." She grinned at May who merely waved father and daughter closer together.

"*Uno, dos . . .*" And the flash went off on May's "*Tres.*" She pulled the camera back and stared at the tiny screen with a frown. "Moose, *querido,* you blinked."

"I always blink," Moose replied. He bugged his eyes, opening them wide and making May and Veronica giggle. "Take it now."

"Our turn!" Val arrived with Ginny in tow, over-smiling, ready for their close-ups.

"*Que ninas bonitas!* Smile!" May snapped a picture of the Vees as Veronica took note of the glasses of white wine in their hands. She knew what Daddy would say before she even looked at him. Something along the lines of, "I know you're eighteen, Veronica, but I don't like you drinking and—"

"Designated driver!" Veronica blurted out.

Her father looked dumbfounded. "What's that?"

"The cast party? You remember. I know Ginny and Val are drinking, but I can be the designated driver."

"Let's go, Vee! Join the fun!" Val called as she scooted away. She and Ginny raised their glasses in Veronica's direction, trying to wave her over.

"You know Daddy, it's a special occasion," Veronica put on the little pout she had been perfecting since she was a little girl. Unfortunately, it never got her very far when it came to alcohol. "I can call a taxi and—"

"I'll pick you up. What time will you—"

"No, Daddy!"

May May blanched slightly at Veronica's outburst. Veronica lowered her voice.

"I'm old enough to take care of myself. You have to trust me." She turned to May May who demurred, her head slightly bowed, the floor suddenly of immense interest. She was, after all, only Daddy's fiancée. Her say in the matter was limited.

Veronica's father held her gaze. His forehead creased and his jaw jutted forward. It was his "when-pigs-fly-Veronica-and-possibly-not-even-then" look.

Veronica sighed. "Fine, Daddy, I won't drink. Not even a sip. You win."

"It's not a matter of winning or losing," he replied, although clearly it was.

"Have a good time, dear." May May brushed her lips against Veronica's cheek, then dug a subtle elbow into Moose May's ample stomach. He leaned forward and pecked his daughter on the forehead.

"Don't stay out too late, sweetheart. We love you."

As May May and Daddy wandered away, Veronica joined up with the Vees. She rolled her violet eyes dramatically and intoned, "I thought they'd never leave."

In the music room, Chester Community Theater's director Jim Neece took his place in front of the blackboard and raised a plastic cup of beer with a grin.

"Does everyone have a glass of something?"

Cheers arose as everyone held their glasses aloft.

Veronica glanced down at her cup of Sprite with dismay. Beside her, Val and Ginny were giggling and refilling their glasses of wine.

"Welcome, one and all," Jim Neece began. "Castmates, family, board members . . ." A dramatic pause and then, "Friends."

More self-congratulatory applause. Veronica stage-clapped noiselessly.

"Gentlemen, gentlewomen, Shakespeare never had a company as dedicated, energetic, and talented as I," Jim pronounced. "Our run of *Romeo and Juliet* was the best I have ever witnessed, and believe you me, I have seen the best."

Blah, blah, blah. Veronica had heard this all before. This was the "California to Connecticut, Alaska to Alabama" section of Jim's speech. Jim wouldn't be praising her for a while.

She glanced around the band room, at all the Virgins and Two-Timers and Sundowners. She knew just about every person in this room, she realized happily. Not that Chester was miniscule, but after eighteen years in the same town, you got to know it.

She thought again of Vivian in L.A. Each week, it seemed, Little Vee was regaling Veronica with tales of Life in Los Angeles, of night clubs and hot actors, of auditions for movies and television. She was meeting new people and seeing new faces every day.

And why wasn't Veronica there? It wasn't as if she couldn't handle the big city. She most definitely could. It was Daddy. Leaving Chester would mean leaving Daddy, and frankly, *he* couldn't handle it. Under those three hundred pounds of gruff exterior beat the heart of a sad and lonely man—a man whose spirit would be crushed if his only child left home. Sure, there was May May, but she was just a girlfr—*fiancée*. As much as Daddy loved May May, Veronica was his own flesh and blood. She kept the family functioning and together. Nope, Daddy would die if she went away, and she simply couldn't break his heart that way.

"—the many wonderful people I've met and come to love, in this town," Jim was saying.

Right. "Never been so happy and satisfied." Yadda yadda. Compliments arriving in another minute or so.

Besides, there was every opportunity for success right here in Chester. Hadn't Jim Neece talked about scouts from big theater companies coming to their productions? And wasn't CCT in the midst of raising funds to make the company a more professional one? It could happen. Any day now. It could.

"Veronica May?"

She looked up, surprised when she heard her name called. She hadn't been monitoring the speech as closely as she thought.

"Would you join me down here?" Jim asked.

She heard a warm gentle applause as she took the short walk to the front of the room beside Biff and Jim. Would she never tire of hearing that sound? Veronica smiled up at her castmates and friends. This was where she was meant to be.

Jim took both Veronica's and Biff's hands and squeezed. "Let's have a round of applause for our leads, okay?"

The room roared and Veronica felt a sudden kinship with each and every one of the people in it. *I'm here for you,* she thought. *I am your star.*

"And now, I'd like to announce our summer production," Jim went on.

Here it comes, Veronica thought gleefully. He was going to talk about *Cat on a Hot Tin Roof,* the Tennessee Williams play. She had already started memorizing Maggie's lines.

Maggie the Cat. *Mmm*aggie . . . she savored the name. Not only was she the logical choice for the role, there being virtually no other woman the right age or with the talent, but—and this point sealed the deal—it was a role immortalized by Miss Elizabeth Taylor on the big screen. Elizabeth Taylor, she of the distinctive violet eyes (just like Veronica's!) and feminine figure (just like Veronica's!). Veronica felt it an honor to do the same for Chester, Arizona.

"Our summer production is—Glengarry Glen Ross!" Jim finished triumphantly.

Wait. What did she miss?

A chorus of *oohs* and *ahhs* rose up from the assembled.

Wait. *What?*

"A terrific play by one of our country's most distinguished playwrights, David Mamet," Jim gushed.

"But Jim—" Veronica started.

Jim Neece turned to her, his face a question mark.

Veronica started again. "What happened to—"

"Jim!" A hand shot up in the back of the room, attached to . . . someone's body, Veronica wasn't sure whose.

"Yes, Roscoe?"

"That's that Al Pacino movie, right, Jim?" The disembodied voice pronounced the actor's name with a soft "s," *Passino*.

"Why yes, it is. Did you like it?"

"Well, yeah, but, Jim, there's lots of, well, bad language in that, isn't there, Jim?"

The director took his time answering. "I prefer to think of it as edgy, Roscoe." He curled his hand into a fist with a well-practiced dramatic flair. "Edgy."

Agreeable murmurs wafted through the crowd. Was Veronica the only one who had a problem with this? She felt her inspired kinship with the group rapidly diminishing.

"All right, everyone, all together!" Jim raised his glass and the crowd followed suit.

"Eat, drink, and be merry!" The room toasted as one. "For tomorrow we may die!"

As the cheers died down and everyone returned to eating nachos, drinking cheap wine and being generally jolly, if not entirely merry, Jim Neece turned to Biff. "I've been thinking you'd be perfect in the role of—"

Veronica slammed her plastic cup onto the table in front of her. "I'm supposed to be Maggie the Cat!" she cried. Jim turned with a shocked expression. She leaned in closer to him and lowered her voice, excluding Biff from the conversation. "You told me we'd be doing *Cat on a Hot Tin Roof.* I've been studying my lines. I have the whole play practically memorized. And Tennessee Williams is totally edgy!"

"I'm sorry, Veronica." Jim did sound sorry. "Believe me, I was absolutely stunned when the board approved the Mamet play. I mean, come on. *Mamet?* In *Chester, Arizona?*"

Veronica felt her chin quiver. "But Jim—there aren't any girls' roles."

"I know, Veronica, I know." Jim placed his hands on her shoulders and sighed. "Don't worry," he continued, his tone brightening. "We can do your play next." He smiled and walked away with Biff, leaving Veronica openmouthed before the entire Chester Community Theater company.

But I'm your star, Veronica thought sadly. *Or at least, I was.*

chapter 3

Outside the high school, Veronica searched for Val's Oxford green BMW 325i coupe, a gift from Papi three years ago for Val's *quinceañera*.

"Where did you park, Vee?"

Val and Ginny stumbled a few yards behind, giggling and sloshing their cups of white wine. Val stopped and gestured vaguely with a flip of her wrist. "It's somewhere here . . . Ginny?"

"Hmmm?"

"Big Vee wants to know where we parked the Papi-mobile."

That was just like Val, nicknaming her car after her father. Although Veronica and Val were both only-children, they couldn't have been raised more differently than if they had been born on two separate planets. And while Veronica often felt a mite jealous of her friend, she reminded herself that deprivation and struggle were good—if not for her social life, at least for her acting career. Plus, it would certainly add depth to her *E! True Hollywood Story*.

Suddenly, Val called out, "There it is!" She pointed at the BMW, parked not twenty feet from where they were standing. "Shotgun!" she yelled and tossed the keys to Veronica.

"Where are we going now?" Ginny asked as she stuffed herself into the back seat.

Veronica started the engine and aimed the car out of the lot.

"Oooh, let's cruise past Charlie's and see who's there," Val suggested.

"Yeah, good idea, Vee," Ginny cheered.

Veronica kept the car on its path down Main Street.

"Vee, *chica*, you're going the wrong way," Val noted. "Charlie's is on Las Cruces."

"We're not going to Charlie's." Veronica maintained a firm grasp on the steering wheel. She glanced in the rearview mirror and saw Ginny batting the bouncy head of a toy Chihuahua which was mounted on the top of the back seat.

Alarmed, Val leaned forward and grasped the tan leather dash with her hands. "*Coño!* You're taking us home!"

Veronica sighed and shook her head. "I promised Daddy. No drinking and home by eleven." She steadied her hands on the wheel and looked straight ahead, pointedly ignoring her friends' entreating faces.

"Oh, come on. One drink?" Val asked. "He'll never know."

"He never has before," Ginny mumbled.

"I'm trying to be good," Veronica insisted.

A muffled chirp came from somewhere in the car.

"That's mine," Val said and shoved a hand into the glove compartment. A dozen Burger King ketchup packets fell out onto the floor.

"Mami? *Si, si. Bueno.*" Val nodded. "No, I'll be home later. Okay?" She rolled her eyes at Veronica. "*No se . . . si, claro, claro.* Bye." She tossed the phone into her purse. "*Ay, dio.* Mothers. They can be a pain in the ass, ya know?"

Veronica glanced at Val, who immediately colored. "Sorry, Vee, I didn't mean that."

"I'm lucky," Veronica shrugged lightly. "It's pretty hard for a dead mother to be a pain in your ass."

Ginny met Veronica's eyes in the rearview mirror. Ginny snorted in amusement.

"*Dios mio*! A dead mother is nothing to joke about!" Val quickly crossed herself. "It was a tragedy that she died so young and left you alone."

"My mother drank too much and drove her Buick off a bridge," Veronica paused as she remembered something her father once told her. "If you don't laugh, you'll never stop crying."

She let her foot off the brake and drove slowly through the intersection. There was silence in the car until Ginny gently cleared her throat.

"Hey, I've got two mothers," she piped up from the back seat, "and they're both a pain in my ass. I'd gladly give one away." She forced a laugh and Veronica smiled into the rearview mirror. Ginny's family consisted of multiple stepmothers and stepfathers and half-brothers and sisters, all living across the street from each other. It was a complete mess, if you asked Veronica.

"Come on, Vee," Veronica said softly to Val. "It's okay. We can laugh."

Gradually, the scowl faded from Val's pretty face, and she allowed herself a smile.

"Hey," Ginny tapped Veronica on the shoulder. "You know, it's not *that* late. I don't think your dad would mind if you broke curfew just a little. You don't have to work at the drugstore tomorrow, right?"

Veronica shook her head. She didn't—and she didn't really want to go home yet; it was just . . . she was still stinging from Jim Neece's news. How could he change plans like that? They were called plans for a reason: because people—certain people like Veronica—*planned* their lives around them. You weren't supposed to alter the course of people's lives on a whim. It simply wasn't fair.

Veronica cocked her head to one side and considered Ginny's suggestion. "You know, neither of you told me how marvelous I was tonight."

Instantly, the girls began burbling, their compliments tumbling on top of one another.

"Oh, Vee, you *were* marvelous!" Ginny exclaimed.

"You were just like that girl . . ." Val snapped her fingers a few times. "The one with Leo."

"Claire Danes!"

"Yes! Claire Danes!"

"What about Claire Danes?" Veronica asked.

"She was in that Shakespeare movie, Vee! You were just like her!" Val insisted, oblivious to the fact that Miss Danes was of the petite variety, about one-third the size of Veronica. And there were differences so tremendous in their depictions of Juliet, Veronica couldn't even begin to list them.

"Oh, Vee!" Ginny agreed. "You were better than Claire Danes!"

Veronica rolled her eyes, but the thought cheered her up immensely. Her Vees knew exactly what she needed to hear. She smiled pleasantly and hooked a U-turn at the next light. "All right, one drink. Charlie's?"

"Charlie's!" Ginny and Val cried in unison.

One drink, Veronica told herself. *Daddy would never even notice.*

Two hours later, when Veronica finally arrived at the pale-peach split-level with the white picket fence she and Daddy called home, she was surprised to see May May's Hyundai in the driveway.

"Hello! I'm home!" she yelled. Just in case she was interrupting something, *bien sûr*. She did a quick breath check and cursed herself for not having a tin of Altoids with her. It was only the one drink— really, half of one when she considered the many sips Ginny took from it. Hopefully her father would be so absorbed with other things, he wouldn't notice.

In the narrow kitchen, May May was perched on one of the stools at the center island, a pen fluttering in her dainty hand, her daily planner open in front of her. Daddy was sitting across from her, a grin on his face. They both looked up when Veronica entered.

"Hi, guys. What's up?"

May May closed her planner and hugged it to her chest. "Your Daddy and I were just talking about how wonderful the play was tonight and how amazing you were in it."

"Well, thanks, sweetie. I'm glad you had a good time." Veronica reached into the cupboard for a coffee mug and thought she saw Daddy and May May exchange a glance.

Ech. Elderly flirtation. Repulsive.

"How was the party?" May May ventured. "Did you meet anyone?"

"At the cast party? Not me. But Val collected a few numbers, like she usually does." Veronica poured herself a cup of coffee and threw in a handful of sugar cubes. She took a long slurp and grimaced.

Oh god! This was horrible. In fact, it was a particular kind of horrible. It was May May's.

Her father was supposed to warn her when May had fixed the coffee. Veronica tried to catch his eye, but he was too busy fiddling with something on the counter. She discreetly poured the cup into the sink.

"Something wrong, *querida*?" May asked, a concerned smile twisting her lips.

"Huh? Oh no, no. I just realized it's kind of late for coffee." Now she caught Daddy's glance. His eyes widened slightly and he mouthed, "*Sorry.*"

"Oh yes! It *is* late," May May said. She alit from the stool and slid the canvas planner into a hard leather clasp purse, the same purse she had carried all of Veronica's life. Strangely, that fact seemed to comfort Veronica. "I really should be going."

"I'll walk you out," Moose offered.

May and Veronica exchanged good-night kisses at the kitchen doorway, and then May gave Veronica an extra squeeze. "I was so proud of you tonight," she whispered.

Veronica's face flushed at the compliment, and she immediately felt guilty for dumping the coffee. But it was *really* bad. May just didn't have the touch. "Thanks, sweetie. You'll email me your pictures?"

May smiled. "Tomorrow."

As soon as Daddy had escorted May May out the door, Veronica turned her attention to the coffee pot. She emptied its contents into the sink and began preparing a new one. Honestly, it was never too late for coffee, in her opinion.

While the pot was brewing, she sifted through some papers on the counter: a phone bill, a gas bill, a coupon for $5 off carpet cleaning. She straightened up, placing the bills in a pile, throwing the coupons in the trash, putting caps back on pens, tossing paper clips in a clear plastic container and . . . what was this? She hefted the circular gold object in the palm of her hand.

Daddy's wedding band.

Veronica turned it over, inspecting it carefully. Inscribed inside in thin block letters: *Diana & Moose 11/30/89.*

Daddy had switched the band from his left hand to his right years ago, shortly after May Sanchez began work as the assistant librarian. But he had never taken it off, never in the eighteen years that Veronica had known him. So why was it sitting here on the counter?

The front door clicked shut, and Veronica quickly stuffed the ring back among the papers. She hastily dumped the container of paper clips on top, along with a couple of pens, and swirled the whole mess around on the counter.

"That woman is never gonna get a simple cup of joe right, is she?" Moose said as he took a place at the island. "Maybe you'll give her a few pointers."

Veronica set a fresh mug of coffee in front of him and then turned back to her own coffee, immensely interested in the manner in which the sugar cubes were dissolving and how the cream formed a little foamy ridge. "Sure, I can do that."

"May's a good woman, Veronica. She likes you very much."

"I like May May," Veronica said, a little more irritably than she had intended. She took a sip of coffee and wondered if she should bring up the small matter of finding the ring among the junk on the counter.

"She had a wonderful time at your show."

"That's nice," she said. Surely there was a reason the ring was left out that way, she thought. Unconsciously, her eyes darted toward the counter.

"Daddy, did you—"

"Mmmm. Now that's a good cup!" her father interrupted. "Why don't we have a little something sweet with our coffee?"

Veronica immediately felt cheered. Yes, between Jim's announcement and this wedding ring weirdness, a little something sweet was just what she needed. She opened the cupboards and peered inside. "Good idea. What shall we have?" She took down a handful of boxes and held each one up in succession. "Vanilla cupcakes?"

Her father shook his head.

"Oatmeal raisin bars?"

Her father wrinkled his nose and frowned.

"Coffeecake?"

Her father considered it, then asked, "Do we have any of those pecan cookies you made last week?"

Veronica stuck her head in the cupboard, looking far in the back beyond the cereals and crackers. "Nope. I think we finished them."

"Oh. That's too bad." Her father looked dejected.

"I can make some more if you want," Veronica offered.

"That's too much trouble and it's so late. . . ." Daddy said, but his voice was hopeful.

"It won't take long."

"Well, okay. If you're sure."

With the efficiency of a diner prep cook, Veronica set to making the cookies. Her father relaxed, a contented smile on his face. Now that May May was gone, he removed his tie and unbuttoned the collar of his Oxford cloth shirt.

"Ah, the start of the weekend."

"Hardly a weekend, Daddy," Veronica said as she turned the oven on. "You only get one day off." Her father kept the library open from nine 'til nine every weekday (ten to three on Saturdays).

He had a duty to the good people of Chester, he frequently said, even if that meant he only had a day and a half off each week.

"You should take a break," Veronica suggested. "You've probably got about a year's worth of vacation time coming to you."

"Eighteen weeks and three days," Moose admitted.

"Geez, what are you saving it for?" Veronica emptied a bag of pecans into a bowl.

Her father sighed and looked up at the ceiling. "Tell you the truth, I have been thinking about it." He dropped his gaze back to Veronica and smiled. "Where should I go?"

Veronica cracked the third of four eggs into the bowl. "If it were me and I had all that time, well, I'd go to a beach in the Caribbean and lie on the sand for a month." She gazed out the window as she stirred the batter, a dreamy look in her eyes. "I'd go where the water is clear and blue, and men in white jackets would bring me fancy drinks all day long." She stole a glance at her father and added quickly, "Non-alcoholic, of course."

He smirked. "That's what you'd do if you were me, huh?"

"Well, no, if I were *you*, I'd take two days off, spend one of them fixing the fence in the back yard and the other one reorganizing the books in your den." Veronica laughed.

Her father laughed too. "We'll see, Veronica. We'll see. I might just surprise you one of these days."

Veronica measured out two cups of flour and dumped them into the batter.

"You gonna put any chocolate chips in there?" Moose asked.

Her father liked chocolate in just about anything.

Veronica reached for a bag of semi-sweet chips and poured half of it in the batter. "Is that enough?" She showed him the contents of the bowl.

"That's good. Or maybe just a few more."

She dropped another cup of chips in and vigorously stirred.

"Maybe you can teach May May that recipe."

Veronica felt a flush in her cheeks. "Um . . . yeah . . . it's not really a recipe."

"Well, how do you know what to put in if it's not a recipe?"

Veronica hesitated, a little uncomfortable with this topic of conversation. "I guess I just know. I've been making them for a long time now and I just know."

"But you could show her how to do it. She could watch you and learn—"

Veronica placed the bowl down on the counter. "No, Daddy, I can't teach her."

Moose stopped, surprised. "But why not?"

"It's not—" Veronica said sharply, then paused and softened her tone. "It's not my recipe."

"Whose . . .?" Moose May met his daughter's eyes and understanding dawned. He smiled gently. "I'd rather have you make them for me anyway. It'll be our special treat."

"I *will* show her how to make coffee," Veronica offered.

"If you'd like."

"She should know how to make a pot of coffee, don't you think?"

"If it's not too much trouble."

"Tomorrow. I'll show her tomorrow."

Her father smiled benignly. "That would be very nice of you." He brought a finger to his lips. "But don't tell her I asked you to."

24

Veronica zipped shut her lips. "Our secret."

Exactly twelve and a half minutes later, Moose May bit into a warm pecan cookie and sighed with pleasure.

"Veronica," he smiled, chocolate coating the corners of his mouth, "what on earth would I do without you?"

chapter 4

The first day after a play ended, Veronica relished sleeping in and not having to get up early for work or rehearsals or any other play-related activities. On this Sunday, she luxuriated under the longest, hottest shower she could stand, then wandered, with her hair and torso wrapped in thick purple towels, into the guest bedroom, where a full-length mirror hung on the back of the door. She stared at her reflection, starting at the bottom, with a pair of nice calves and shapely thighs. She liked her legs. They were *feminine*. She turned around and lifted the bottom of the towel, craning her neck to take a look at her butt. It, too, was shapely and altogether female. Two crescent moons separated by a curvaceous dimple. She placed her palms below her buttocks and shook them up and down. Nice wiggle.

Facing the mirror again, she slowly lowered her gaze to her chest. Even beneath the flattening towel, she could make out the mounds that were her booblies. By the time she was thirteen, they were a 40D, which earned her the envy of lesser-endowed girls who nevertheless had *her* envy. She would have much preferred to wear those silky 34A bras with the pretty lace patterns and delicate spaghetti straps than the painful underwire and wide elastic bands she was cursed with.

Veronica sighed. *But then,* she reasoned, *everyone always wanted what they couldn't have. C'est si vrai.*

One of these days—very soon she hoped—she would find someone who would appreciate what she did have. It hadn't happened yet but it would. She was certain of it.

Veronica walked on her tippy toes into her bedroom, then swooned dramatically onto her bed. She lay back against her pillows, hands behind her head. She hadn't anticipated having the next three months free. She had just assumed she would move on to the next play, as she had done throughout her years of high school. In fact, she had counted on it now that school was over and she had only her job at the drugstore to keep her busy.

Possibly the best thing about working at Rosenbloom's Apothecary was that Mr. Rosenbloom, the store's elderly proprietor, allowed her to switch shifts, arrive late, or leave early as necessary to pursue her acting. Much as she disliked standing for hours at a stretch in front of a cash register, it was worth it if it allowed her to follow her dreams.

And she was good too—at the acting thing, that is, not the cashier thing. Aside from all the rave reviews she had been collecting since she was an itty-bitty floret in the Veggie Parade, she had taken home the Chapman Prize—the award given to the most promising actor at her high school—the last three years in a row. The award was named for Leslie Chapman, the only graduate of CHS to ever become a famous actor—or famous *anything*. That was nearly thirty years ago and he was dead now. There had been no one since.

Veronica took her time dressing in a pair of light blue capris and a CCT T-shirt that the board had been selling to raise money. She had a drawer full of them.

She couldn't believe she would be spending all her time at the drugstore—at a regular job!—at least for the time *Cat on a Hot Tin Roof* was *not* being put up. She refused to mention the name of the Mamet play, even to herself.

Without acting, she was just a regular person with a regular life. The thought depressed Veronica beyond words. Deflated, she turned on her computer, a tiny laptop Daddy had given her as a graduation gift. She located the folder where she saved Vivian's letters and clicked it open. Here was one from the first week of *Romeo and Juliet*, when Veronica sent her the opening night's review:

"Big Vee! Congrats on a wonderful review! You are such a star!"

Veronica smiled. Vivian was fond of exclamation points.

The letter lifted her spirits immediately. She found another dispatch from a couple of weeks ago:

"I can hardly believe some of the idiots in my acting classes! They are totally delusional, like *American Idol* delusional! None of them are anywhere near as good as we were at CHS. Even Biff could kick their butts."

And then the most recent one, a few days ago:

"Sorry I can't make the last show, sweetie. Busy busy here! Auditions galore. It feels like everyone in town wants to see me."

Veronica stared at the screen. She dearly wished Vivian had been able to make at least one of her performances. It wasn't as if L.A. was so far away. It was only a six-hour drive, four if one drove like Little Vee.

The Vees, after all, were a tight-knit group. They had been since the fourth grade when they decided to band together—a group of girls comprised solely of those whose names began with "V" (first names only, not last, which meant that, as much as Joanie Van Meter wanted to join, the most she could hope for was auxiliary membership, and even that was doubtful as she had a tendency to smell like bad cheese).

Veronica remembered how the girls had codified the rules for being a Vee with a list they called, *naturellement*, "The ABCs of Being the Vees." Among them:

1. Everyone is each other's best friend equally.
2. Whoever gets to the lunch room first will save seats for the rest, no matter how hard it is to keep non-Vees, like Stinky Joanie, from stealing the chairs.
3. If any Vee hates someone, the other Vees hate them too.
4. Everyone has to go to the school dances at the exact same time so no Vee stands there alone or is forced to dance with either of the Carls.
5. All the Vees will go to the movies every Saturday, no matter what's playing.

That last rule had been the hardest for Veronica to follow. Daddy simply would not let her out every Saturday afternoon.

Veronica remembered one Saturday, not long after the Rules were instituted, when she paid a visit to Daddy at the library. It was about a year after the accident. The walls of Daddy's office were covered with movie posters and celebrity photographs: Rita Hayworth in a thick-strapped bikini and John Wayne with his holstered six-shooter. Daddy liked old romantic comedies, like *The*

Philadelphia Story, as well as war movies, such as *The Dirty Dozen.* He had eclectic tastes, he liked to say. *Eclectic* was a library word.

On that day, when eight-year-old Veronica burst in on her father, she had found him staring at his posters. He was smoking a Camel and staring. That was all. He didn't even turn around when she entered.

"Daddy?" Veronica had approached carefully, always considerate of her father at work.

Moose May didn't move, didn't swivel in his swivel chair. Veronica heard a long sigh, saw his wide back heave up and down. "Yes, Ronnie?"

"It's time for the movies. Can I have five dollars?"

A long pause. Veronica wondered if her father had even heard her.

"No movies today, honey."

"But, Daddy, I have to. It's a rule. All the Vees are going." Young Veronica couldn't understand this behavior of her father's. Why, he *adored* the movies.

"Well, not you. Not today."

"But why not?"

"I said so, that's why not."

"Val's going."

"Valeria's parents are too permissive."

"Ginny's going."

"Virginia's family won't even notice she's gone."

"Vivian's going."

"Vivian's not you."

Her father was really being a sourpuss, she thought. But she knew how to get to him. She raised her voice, "If Mommy was here, she'd let me go! Mommy would—"

Her father whipped his head around. "Enough, Veronica May!

This is a library; there is no shouting here. I said no movies today and I mean no movies today. If you want to shout, go outside." He stared at her, his eyes red. Finally, she wheeled around and stomped out the door, slamming it behind her.

Once outside, she stood on the bottom step and opened her mouth for a big scream. "Ahhhhhhhhhhhhhhhhhh! I hate you!!!!!"

She closed her mouth but the scream continued to ring in her ears, deafening her to the noises of the outside world. Cars drove by in silence; people passed her, their lips moving soundlessly.

Then she turned around and slowly started back up the library steps.

Her father was behind the reference desk, looking over the shoulder of a young woman Veronica didn't recognize. It was Ms. May Sanchez, the new assistant librarian. With downcast eyes, Veronica took a couple of steps closer to the desk.

"This is your daughter, Mr. May?" May smiled at Daddy. "Why, she's lovely. Looks just like you." Her voice was barely above a whisper. At the time, Veronica assumed that was because she worked in a library. Later she would learn that that was the way May always talked.

Daddy crooked a finger and waggled it at Veronica. Veronica took another couple of steps closer. He leaned down to her. "Is there something you'd like to say?"

Veronica glanced sideways at May Sanchez, who busied herself with some periodicals. She whispered in her father's ear. "I'm sorry, Daddy."

"Ms. Sanchez could use some help pasting labels on the new magazines. If you spend the next hour helping her, I will personally take you to the movies tomorrow."

Veronica considered the offer. It wasn't the same, and it would be breaking the brand new Rules of the Vees, but it was better than nothing. "I could do that, sure."

Moose smiled, reached into his pants pocket and pulled out two fun size Snickers bars—one for each of them. Veronica unwrapped hers and popped it into her mouth. She felt better almost instantly.

"Well, all right then." Her father led her back to the desk. "Ms. Sanchez, my daughter Veronica would like very much to help you."

May looked up with a friendly grin. "*Que bueno.*"

Veronica stuck out her hand, like her father had taught her. "How do you do, Ms. Sanchez?"

May solemnly took Veronica's hand in hers (they were nearly the same size at that time) and shook it smartly. "Very well, thank you. It's a pleasure to make your acquaintance."

Daddy pulled over a stool and gestured to Veronica, who took a seat next to May. May slid a copy of *Newsweek* across the desk. "Let's see, first thing we do is . . ."

After all these years, Veronica couldn't remember the proper method of periodical-labeling or anything else May May told her during that first meeting. She could only recall her father watching the two of them working together, observing them. . . .

Veronica shook away the memory. Just as she placed her fingers over the keyboard, about to type Vivian an email, her cell rang. She checked the I.D.: ROS APO. It was Mr. Rosenbloom. Veronica hesitated. This would probably mean a day of work. Mr. Rosenbloom was, no doubt, calling her in to cover a shift. She sighed.

The only other good thing about working at the drugstore was the public adulation. After a show ended, nearly every customer in the store complimented her on her performance.

That might be worth it, she thought. She could use a little praise.

"Hello, Mr. Rosenbloom," she said.

"Good morning, Miss May. Would you be able to come in today?"

"No problem," she told her boss. "One hour okay?"

"That's fine, Miss May. See you then."

Veronica clicked off her cell and returned to her email.

"Hi Little Vee!" she typed. "The show ended with a bang last night. A standing O for yours truly. And the house was packed! Tell me more about your exciting life in L.A."

Things in Chester might not be 100 percent hunky-dory, but Little Vee would help her focus on the bright side.

Fifty-five minutes later, Veronica pulled her Escort into the employee parking area behind the squat brick building that housed Rosenbloom Apothecary. Perhaps Constanza Garcia, the store's other cashier, had called in sick, she thought. That girl was germ-trendy: She always seemed to catch the latest in colds and flu and plague.

Veronica was surprised to see Constanza's mini-van pull into the lot just two minutes after she did.

"Hey," Veronica said to the girl as they met up at the back entrance, "what are you doing here?"

The two were dressed twin-like in the Rosenbloom Apothecary uniform: white polo shirt with the RA logo, navy skirt and chunky orthopedic shoes. Constanza's glossy black hair was wrapped in a tight bun at the base of her neck, and her bangs were swept across her forehead and secured with a metal clip. Veronica had only had time for a ponytail.

"You were great last night!" Constanza said and let loose with a vicious cough. She covered her mouth with a ragged Kleenex that looked to Veronica like it had been peeled from the bottom of her shoe. "Did you see us? We stood up at the end."

Hack, hack. Veronica flinched. It sounded like Constanza was coughing up a lung.

"Thanks." Veronica held the door open for her coworker.

"*Gracias.*" *Hack, hack.*

"Are you okay?" Veronica asked, following at a distance. "You sound—"

"I'm fine." *Hack, hack.*

There goes lung number two, Veronica thought.

"Good morning, ladies," Mr. Rosenbloom called from his office. "Would you come in here for a moment?"

Veronica was startled to see her boss dressed in a pair of denim slacks and a distinctly non-RA-approved T-shirt. He had the wiry frame of a vegetarian marathon runner, and his clothes hung off him like they were on a hanger. Most shocking of all, though, were the prickly white hairs on his chin and upper lip. He hadn't even shaved!

"Sit down, please," Mr. Rosenbloom said, gesturing to two chairs in front of his small, cluttered desk.

Constanza and Veronica exchanged a glance before they eased themselves onto the chairs.

The druggist placed his hands flat on the desk and stared down at them. After a long moment, he lifted his eyes to the girls. "I'm selling the business."

"You're . . ." Veronica stared at the man's hands too, as if they would explain things.

"Tomorrow morning, the southwest regional marketing manager for Drug Rite will be coming to assess the store for remodeling." Mr. Rosenbloom turned his hands over and stared now at the palms. As far as Veronica could tell, they weren't saying much.

Mr. Rosenbloom chuckled hollowly. "I thought this would be easier. I mean, I'm selling the business, I'll be able to retire finally but . . . I never thought about you two."

"Well, what about us?" Constanza demanded. "Are you selling us too?"

Mr. Rosenbloom shook his head. "No, Miss Garcia. I'm . . . letting you go."

The girls gasped.

"You can't fire us!" Constanza protested. "We need these jobs!"

"They promised me you'll get first consideration for jobs at the new store," their boss assured them, although to Veronica's ears, he didn't sound so certain.

"First . . ." Constanza turned to Veronica. "What does that mean?"

"I think it means they'll give us preference over other people who apply," Veronica said vaguely.

But—this was so not fair, she thought. *This was just not right.* A Drug Rite in Chester? The town prided itself on its quaintness, on its small-townness, on its lack of Wal-Martness. What was a corporate drugstore doing replacing the old-fashioned apothecary?

And what of *her*? What would become of her now that she had no job, no income? Her paycheck didn't put much in the bank, but she had been able to kick in for groceries and coffee every week. Plus the occasional splurge with the Vees.

Veronica felt a hollow pit in her stomach. No CCT, no RA. Her life was quickly becoming DOA! She slumped down in the chair and let her knees rest against the lip of the desk. The metal felt foreign and cold against her skin.

"*Coño*," Constanza muttered. "This sucks."

"I'm sorry, ladies," Mr. Rosenbloom said, resigned. "I should have warned you this might happen but I, well . . ."

"You didn't have the guts," Constanza finished for him.

"Connie!" Veronica hushed her coworker. "He's worked all his life. He wants to retire." She glanced at her boss. "You gotta do what you gotta do," she told him.

"Not fair," Constanza mumbled. "Just not fair." Veronica saw the girl's face redden; any second now, she would explode in a coughing frenzy. *Run away!* Veronica thought wildly.

"I'm staying closed today," Mr. Rosenbloom said. "Why don't you two take the day off?"

"With pay!" Constanza pointed at the druggist. "We came in when you asked us to."

"Of course, of course. With pay."

Veronica stood uncertainly and shook out her skirt. The desk's edge had creased her knees, giving her fat red indents below her kneecaps.

Mr. Rosenbloom stood as well and shook each girl's hand. "I'm so sorry," he said.

The girls filed out of the tiny office, visibly dispirited.

"Oh, Miss May?" Mr. Rosenbloom called.

Veronica turned. "Yes, sir?"

"I saw your show last night," he said warmly. "You were a wonderful Juliet."

Veronica felt her lips turn up in a smile. She couldn't help it; praise was a glorious, uplifting thing. "Thank you."

"Good luck, Miss May."

And that, Veronica thought as she left the drugstore, *was that*. She and Constanza shared a hug and separated moments before Constanza erupted into another coughing frenzy. Veronica watched as her former coworker's mini-van swerved from side to side exiting the lot, as Constanza's hands shook the wheel. She wisely waited a moment before heading out herself.

* * *

Veronica wasted away the afternoon, traversing Chester in her car. From Charlie's Bar to the electrical plant. From the water tower to the parade grounds downtown. As she drove, hesitant to return home and face Daddy with the bad news, she thought about things that would cheer her up.

Food, of course, always topped the list, although eating by her lonesome had never been Veronica's *modus operandi*. It was the communal aspect of food that she appreciated, the act of sharing a meal, of breaking bread with loved ones, which pretty much meant Daddy and the Vees.

She was never tempted by a Dunkin' Donuts Boston Cream or a Baskin Robbins Banana Split but by the dinners she and Daddy shared each evening.

In their years together Veronica and her father had fallen into a pattern—a rhythm of meal making—that gave each day of the week a different flavor, a different smell.

Friday, of course, was the best day, it being at the end of the week and the start of the weekend. Friday smelled like pizza topped with sausage and peppers and a layer of milky mozzarella. Daddy and Veronica would split an extra large with double meat, which was not a choice on the regular menu, but the Mays were preferred customers. Friday was a quick meal that someone else made for you and that you could wash down with a cold root beer before heading out with the Vees to cruise Main Street and check out the cars in the lot at Charlie's.

Saturday was Veronica's second favorite, as it was the exact middle of the weekend. Saturday had the flavor of the tacos her father picked up at the Burrito Machine on Flores Street. It was a meal to be savored while discussing the rest of the weekend's plans at the kitchen's center island.

Wednesday was a good day, falling as it did in the center of the week. Once a Wednesday was over, you knew the second half of the week was upon you. Wednesday tasted like a thick steak, perfectly cooked with just a tiny spot of pink in the middle. If the weather was right, you could grill the steak on the barbecue in the backyard along with a potato, and the whole neighborhood would smell Wednesday and smile.

Thursday, ah, Thursday, heralding a Friday and a new weekend. The possibilities were limitless on Thursdays, and Moose's philosophy was that omelets were the way to go. You could do so much with an omelet: stuff it with three kinds of cheese, layer it with mushrooms and spinach, or go crazy with ham and onions and tomatoes. The options, like Thursday, were endless.

Once you reached down into the dregs of the week, you found Monday. A Monday had the flavor of a salad—and not a Caesar salad that you could enjoy if you dumped a boatload of creamy dressing on it and covered it with parmesan and anchovies. Monday was just a plain old house salad, the kind with bland iceberg lettuce and store-bought tomatoes and hard croutons with a dusting of garlic that barely made up for the fact that it was a salad. Tuesday was just Tuesday, a day that was neither here nor there. But the worst, the absolute worst day of all was Sunday. Sure, every Sunday started out great with plans to sleep late and have a nice brunch on the deck and maybe laze around the lake for a few hours before coming home and getting ready for the start of your week— and that would seem to be enough. But the day would wind down and no matter how tightly you grasped, time would slip through your fingers, until there was nothing left except Sunday dinner and an early bedtime.

On Sundays, the only taste that would soothe Veronica and her father was macaroni and cheese. A comforting smell of melted American and cheddar would fill the house, and your mouth would water, anticipating the soothing down-home meal.

Well, at least she could look forward to that.

At five o'clock, Veronica parked her Escort in the driveway behind May's Hyundai and glanced up at the split-level. What a day she had had, she thought.

She paused just inside the foyer. A delectable odor of cooking meat wafted across her nostrils. Delicious—but wrong, very wrong. She followed the scent through the hallway to the kitchen where she found a pot of artichokes steaming on the stove. She opened the oven door and saw a loaf of bread wrapped in tin foil. What in the world was going on?

In the dining room, the table was set for three, with Grandma May's fine linen napkins, the heirloom silver, and good lord, china plates. Veronica surveyed the table with a discerning eye. Beside each plate was a water glass, complete with a slice of lemon floating atop the ice cubes. She counted the forks—three of them at each setting! Two knives—one serrated, one butter—and two spoons. What *was* this?

Muffled laughter drifted through the house. Veronica pulled aside a lace-trimmed curtain and saw Daddy and May May standing at the barbecue outside on the patio. Daddy was wearing an apron over his polo shirt and khakis. In one hand, he held a bottle of nonalcoholic beer, and in the other, a metal spatula. May May, dressed in a floral-patterned skirt and matching blouse, held a plate, but Veronica couldn't tell what it was from this distance.

She was certain only that it was not macaroni and cheese.

"Uh, hello," she said shyly from the edge of the patio, acutely sensing she was interrupting something.

They both turned to look at her, still smiling, ever so relaxed.

"Good evening, Miss May," Daddy said.

"Would you like something to drink?" May May asked.

Veronica frowned. Was she suddenly a guest in her own house? "No, thanks. I can get something myself if I want it." She paused. "I guess."

"Did you happen to see what was cooking on the stove?" Daddy asked with a mischievous grin.

"Artichokes?"

"Correct, Miss May!" Daddy stabbed the air with the spatula. "May May and I were out by the lake this afternoon, and we found this great produce stand—"

"Patty's."

"Why, yes, Patty's Produce," Daddy said in amazement. "You know it?"

"Duh," Veronica cleverly quipped. "Me and the Vees go there all the time."

"You do?"

"It's been there for years, Daddy."

Daddy and May May shared a glance as if this newfound knowledge about local produce would dramatically change their lives. Geez. Was she talking to pod people?

"So you went to Patty's?" Veronica prompted.

"Yes, yes," Daddy said. "There were these wonderful artichokes—"

"Just begging us to buy them—" May May interrupted.

"That's right, begging us—"

"Saying, 'Eat us, eat us'—"

"If they could talk, that is—"

"Not that they could, of course—"

"No, of course not!"

Daddy and May May burst into laughter. Veronica began to wonder if the beer in her father's hand really *was* nonalcoholic.

"No, they can't," Veronica stated firmly. "Artichokes cannot talk."

The laughter subsided. Daddy gestured to the grill. "May May picked out the steaks, what do you think?"

Veronica stepped between the two of them and studied the grilling meat. She nodded. "Looks pretty good." Then under her breath she added, "For a *Sunday*."

When she turned around, Daddy and May May had linked their arms and were gazing lovingly into each other's eyes. She cleared her throat. "A-hem."

"Veronica, maybe you can help me in the kitchen while your father finishes up here," May May suggested, taking Veronica's elbow and leading her toward the house.

"Uh, I guess." Veronica took a last glance back at her father, who was happily turning over the slabs of meat. She would have sworn she even heard him whistling.

She'd be sure to check the label on his beer later.

At the stove, May May lifted the cover off the pot of artichokes and stabbed one delicately with a fork. "Just a couple more minutes, I think."

Veronica slid onto a stool at the center island and observed May May bustling about the kitchen, looking more at home than she ever had before.

"Did you enjoy your day?" May May asked as she reached, without hesitation, for the paprika. Veronica noticed that she seemed to know exactly where everything was located.

"Um, well . . ." *How to broach the current unemployment situation,*

Veronica wondered. "I didn't really do too much." That part was true. Driving around town and thinking sad thoughts about the future had indeed been uneventful.

"*Bueno*. The Lord wants you to rest on His day."

Veronica rolled her eyes internally. She forgot at times, perhaps conveniently, that May May had grown up in a convent in Mexico.

Yes, until the age of fifteen, May Sanchez had lived and studied in a secluded nunnery, her parents having determined that she would serve God and thus ensure their own places in Heaven. But on a visit to a tiny and disorganized public library one day, young May discovered the world of secular books. She had a sudden urge to reorganize the shelves, to separate, to alphabetize!

At that precise moment, May Sanchez experienced an epiphany: She would become a librarian. Her calling was not the convent but the Dewey decimal system. The nuns were kind, she said, having lost other oblates to the land of sex and books. Her parents, on the other hand, banished her from their home forever.

May then set out for the United States, where she believed her organizational skills would be better appreciated, and that's how, after obtaining her MLS at the University of Arizona, she happened to land in Chester. Every once in a while, though, she would inject a "Lord willing" or a "Jesus said" into a conversation which otherwise would not have had a religious connotation.

Truth be told, it drove Veronica a little bit nuts.

May May opened the oven door and withdrew the bread wrapped in tin-foil. "What do you think? I found this cookbook," she said, holding up a photograph of the exact meal Veronica saw being prepared in front of her: artichokes, steak and garlic bread, not to mention the place settings in the dining room. *Entertaining for Dummies* or some such. Still, she was impressed by May's thoroughness.

"Wow," she said.

"I hope 'wow,'" May replied, chuckling. "This was more work than I imagined!" She opened a drawer and rooted around inside.

"Looking for something?"

"A bread knife. I thought I—"

"Second drawer from the left. Next to the sink." Veronica was startled at the satisfaction she felt in pointing out the knife drawer. She supposed May May would have found it eventually.

May May began slicing the loaf of garlic bread—on a diagonal, Veronica observed. She and Daddy never ate their bread that way. How unusual.

"Can I help you with something?" Veronica asked. That's why May May wanted her in the kitchen in the first place, wasn't it?

"No, no," May May said. "I just wanted some company. I thought we could talk."

Veronica slumped forward on her elbows. "Whadja wanna talk-abouw?" she slurred.

"Oh, you know," May May tittered. "Girl stuff."

"You mean like periods?"

May May's cheeks colored. "Well, no—"

"Gotta strange discharge or something?"

May May gasped. "Veronica, *por favor*!"

Veronica smiled. "Sorry, May. I was just having a little fun."

May May sliced the bread roughly. Crumbs spattered all over the cutting board. "I just thought it might be nice if you and I spent some time together."

"But we've spent *plenty* of time together. You and Daddy have been dating for ten years."

"I meant, time without your father. I feel like there's so much about you I don't know." May May's eyes sparkled. "You've grown up so fast. You're an adult now, not a little girl anymore."

"Yeah . . ." Veronica replied uneasily.

"You have hopes and dreams. There must be dozens of things a young woman like you wants to do in this world." May May stared at Veronica with an encouraging smile. "Maybe there's something you'd like to talk about that you can't tell your father."

"Uh, thanks, May May, but I already have the Vees. We talk about pretty much anything."

May May's shoulders slumped and she looked crestfallen.

"I didn't mean—" Veronica began, but May interrupted her.

"No, no. You're right, you're right. You don't really need me." She bent her head over the pot of artichokes and poked at one with a fork.

"Um," Veronica said, "I think I'll go, uh, wash my hands before we sit down." She ran out of the kitchen and upstairs to her bathroom before May May could protest. The conversation, she thought, had grown increasingly awkward.

Better to end it than to prolong the torture.

The steaks were cooked perfectly, the artichokes were chewy not soggy, and the garlic bread was evenly toasted, although it was hard to overlook the extreme diagonal-ness of the slices. All in all, a fine Sunday dinner, especially since Moose and May May had ceased their embarrassing mooning once the food was on the table.

"Let me go put the coffee on," May May suggested as she cleared the table of plates.

Daddy cast a glance at Veronica and gestured with his head toward the kitchen. She jumped up from her chair and followed May May. "Why don't I help you with that?" she offered. "The coffee maker's been acting up lately." Daddy smiled approvingly.

While Veronica took care of the coffee, May May brought out a foil-covered plate.

"What is it?" Moose asked, his eyes wide.

"A little something I made."

May May had never brought a homemade dessert before. Veronica vaguely recalled a burnt pumpkin pie one Thanksgiving and some watery lime Jell-O with floating pineapple slices last summer, but that had been it.

Veronica left the coffee to watch May May lift off the tin foil with a flourish and smile proudly. On the plate was a log about a foot long, covered in white cream. She sliced a knife through the log and showed off the inside: layers of chocolate alternating with the white cream.

"It's a chocolate icebox cake," May said quietly. "It was in my cookbook." She cut two-inch thick slices of the cake and set them on plates.

Daddy and Veronica each took a bite simultaneously. Daddy's eyes widened further. "Mmm! Outstanding, May. Absolutely outstanding."

Veronica took a second bite. Mmmm…The chocolate was moist but not soggy and the filling was whipped cream, not the canned stuff.

May May watched Veronica expectantly. "Do you like it, *querida*?"

Veronica let the sweet treat dissolve over her tongue. Did she like it? She wanted to take a bath in it, be buried up to her neck in it, scarf it down for breakfast, lunch and dinner.

"It's fine, May," Veronica said.

May May beamed and then she, too, placed a dainty forkful in her petite mouth. "It's not bad, is it?"

"Don't be so modest," Daddy said as he shoved his plate across the table and gestured for a second slice. "It's wonderful."

Chocolate was always a sure bet in the May household.

"Well, then," Daddy said, looking from Veronica to May May. "Well, then."

May May pursed her lips, hesitated. "Veronica . . ." she finally began. Moose engulfed her petite hand in his and squeezed gently. "Your father and I would like to talk to you about something."

Veronica forked a larger bite of cake and nodded. "G'head."

May May glanced at Daddy again. "We've set a date for the wedding."

Veronica swallowed. What was that? *What was that?*

"You what?"

"A date, we've set a date."

"Um," Veronica stuffed another bite of cake in her mouth. "When?"

"December twentieth."

"Of *this* year?"

"Yes, of course this year," Daddy interjected.

"It'll be a small ceremony," May May added. "And a small reception."

"Out in the backyard is what we were thinking," Daddy said.

"But—that's so close to Christmas," Veronica said, stating the obvious.

"Exactly. We'll close the library for the holidays so we can have the wedding and then take a honeymoon." Daddy smiled at May May.

"You're taking a honeymoon too?" Veronica asked, as she polished off the slice of cake on her plate.

"We think we might cruise to Mexico," May May said demurely.

"It's been more than twenty years since May May's been back there," Daddy added. "She might even try to see her parents."

"But it's so . . . soon," Veronica stated again. She sliced herself another piece of cake. "Wouldn't it be nicer to have it in June? *Next* June? Everyone gets married in June, don't they?"

Daddy shook his head. "We've put it off long enough."

May May nodded in agreement. "It's the right time."

Veronica ate the next piece of cake in four quick bites, nodding, trying to assimilate this new information. "Okay," she said, "okay."

May May reached for Veronica's hand. "There's something else," she whispered, so low that Veronica had to lean forward to hear her. "I'd like you to be my maid of honor."

"Me?" Veronica squeaked. "Why me?"

"It's not just your father I'm marrying, it's you too. We'll be a family." May May's eyes shone wetly.

Veronica blinked. "Can't I just take pictures or decorate the backyard?"

"Veronica, don't be rude," Daddy said. "This is obviously something very important to May May. It would behoove you to be gracious and accept her offer."

"Don't push her, Moose," May May said. "She doesn't have to answer right now."

"Hush," he said, then turned back to Veronica. "Out of the kindness of her heart, May May has generously opened herself up to you in telling you how much she cares about you. Do you think it's easy to lay bare one's emotions, to wear one's heart on one's sleeve? You didn't know that she had this dinner planned for days, did you? She practiced all week because she wanted it to be perfect when she asked you."

"Moose, don't," May May fidgeted with her napkin. "There's no need to—"

"And you rudely dismissed her as if her feelings didn't matter in the least."

Veronica sat openmouthed. She had no idea how things had gotten to this point. Her father and May *getting married?* An actual wedding, here in this house where she and Daddy had made their home for nearly two decades?

Where her mother had lived, however briefly?

Sure, May was okay to have around and she didn't make too much of a fuss most of the time, but the nicest thing about her, in Veronica's opinion, was that she went home every evening. To her *own* apartment. *Would she be living* here *now?* Veronica wondered.

Why, this was absurd! She stared at her father, pleaded with wide open eyes. "Daddy, don't I get a say in this?"

"You?" Her father blurted out.

"Yes. Me . . ." she lowered her voice, excluding May May. "It's been you and me for so long. Shouldn't we talk about things?"

Moose May shook his head. "I've made my decision, Veronica. We *will* be a family."

Veronica felt suddenly nauseated by the cloyingly sweet chocolate of the icebox cake. The air was thick and heavy, and when she stood up, she felt as if she were moving through frosting.

Her hands trembled by her sides. "I thought we already *were* a family," she said.

As she ran up the stairs to her bedroom, Veronica felt hot tears welling in her eyes.

First CCT had cruelly kicked her to the curb, and then Mr. Rosenbloom shuttered his doors to her, and now—well, she was no longer needed here, either. And after everything she'd done for Daddy!

Replaced! She was being replaced in her own home. *How had it come to this?* she wondered. *How had things come to* this?

Quelle horreur.

chapter 5

Veronica was up early the next morning, having never truly fallen asleep the night before. Daddy was at the library and she had the place to herself. But only temporarily, of course.

Veronica needed to do something. She needed to fix things, hatch a plan, take action. But where to begin?

First and foremost, she couldn't stay in Chester anymore—that was certain. Just look at the situation: She was clearly being pushed out. No CCT show, no job, no place in her own family—what was next? Would the Vees dissolve their friendship? Would the sky literally fall and knock Veronica on the head?

What would Daddy and May May turn her bedroom into, she wondered, once she was gone? A sewing room for May? An exercise room for Daddy? Or maybe just a catch-all space for all the leftover junk that accumulated when two people combined households?

She unscrewed the top of an aspirin bottle and dropped two pills into the palm of her hand. She washed them down with a swig of water from the tap in the kitchen. She had a massive headache this morning. Her eyelids looked like miniature eggplants, all puffy and shiny and purple, and her hair stuck up in all directions.

She was a wreck and she didn't care.

Hadn't life been good the way it was? she wanted to know. Hadn't they been happy, she and Daddy? For that matter, hadn't CCT been better off *with* her around than not? Why did so many things have to change so fast?

Veronica plopped herself down onto the couch in the living room and threw her legs over a soft pillow, one that they had owned for about seven or eight years. Was it time to kick this pillow out the door too?

Or maybe . . . maybe this was a cue from the Universe. A message to Veronica from above: Time to leave, Vee! Time to pack up and head for . . .

Where? New York? Chicago? London? Paris? She needed to go where she would be appreciated—a place where she could become the great actor she always knew she could be.

Veronica's eyes lit upon a collection of photographs on the top of the bookcase that she called her Row of Roles. Each one was a portrait of Veronica's many parts throughout her long and illustrious career.

As a tiny Vee, she had played a stem of broccoli—the star of the Veggie Parade! Later on, she was Mrs. Claus, Alice from Wonderland, Martha Washington—all the way up through her tour-de-force turn as Juliet. Imaginary, fictional, or historic, she could perform them all! A scrapbook upstairs in her room held various clippings of reviews and newspaper articles, all praising her performances and heralding her awards.

Veronica sighed. Yes, she had to leave. The Universe was definitely giving her a sign. The only question was where to go.

Start packing now, she told herself, *decide later.*

Not a bad idea.

Veronica made her way to the hallway outside the guest room where she tugged on the pull cord for the attic stairs. She hadn't been up here in a while, but she remembered a set of faux Louis Vuitton luggage from her trip to Grandma May's in Minnesota when she was ten. Gosh, had it been that many years since she had traveled? She really had to get out more.

The attic was not much more than a crawl space. Hunched over and stepping carefully, Veronica climbed over old shoeboxes filled with mementos and trunks of winter clothes. She spotted the luggage under an eave and kicked her way free to it. A little dusty, yes, but it was still in pretty good shape.

Veronica dislodged the luggage, dragged it to the stairs and shoved the pieces through the opening where they landed with a soft thud on the carpeted hallway below. As she turned around to go back down the ladder after them, her eye caught sight of a small box behind a worn-out rocking chair.

It was only about a foot square, made of blue matte cardboard. Its color, originally vibrant and cheerful, had been dulled by age. Its top fit snugly and was secured in place by a taut string; once white, it too was now stained by time. Despite the discoloration, Veronica recognized it immediately.

Eleven years ago, Daddy had brought this box to her bedroom and asked her to place inside it all her photos of her mother.

"So we won't cry anymore," he had told her. He promised he would place all his photos in there too, every scrap of Diana May that had ever existed in the house. The box would then go up in the attic, its contents never to be viewed again.

So I won't cry anymore, Veronica told herself as she put old Polaroids of her mother inside the box.

Since then, she thought of it as the "forbidden box," like something out of a cheesy PG-13 horror movie in which creepy things popped up into frame and musical cues warned you when to close your eyes. She never went near it again.

But she was older now, she reasoned, no longer a child. She shouldn't be afraid of a stupid box. She reached across the floor for it and took it down to her bedroom.

The string slipped off surprisingly easily, and when Veronica took off the top, she knew why: It had recently been retied. Because Daddy's ring, the one she had seen sitting on the countertop a few days ago, was sitting on top of a pile of papers.

Veronica removed the ring and pulled a yellowed newspaper article from underneath. Very carefully, using only the tips of her fingers, she unfolded the paper.

"Spotlight on Musicals," the headline read. "Are we seeing the return of the big budget movie musical? These dancers think so. The subject of a daring new film called *Forever Dancing* is a group of fledgling Hollywood newcomers willing to make it big at any price." Veronica's eye scanned the page. She caught this farther down: "'I don't consider myself strictly a dancer,' claims Diana Shepherd of Arizona. 'I'm an actor, first and foremost. I act, I sing, I dance. I do it all. That's what it takes in this town.'"

"Oh my god . . . " Veronica whispered as she read the article a second time. Shepherd, she knew, was her mother's maiden name. Could it be? She felt her heart quicken. Could this be her mother's voice? Speaking to her from—where? She spotted the notation at the very bottom of the page—*Los Angeles Daily News. September 27, 1989.*

So Diana had been an actor! And she had been in Los Angeles less than a year before Veronica herself had been born!

Veronica needed to know more. She dove into the box. Aside from the pictures she and her father had placed there long ago, the only other item inside was a stack of envelopes, yellowed and secured with a rubber band—actual letters from when people wrote those things instead of emailing. The return address on them was a post office box in Los Angeles, California.

Veronica removed the one on top. The postmark in the right hand corner had smudged but the date was clear: June 30, 1989. Today's *date*, she noted with a start, *exactly nineteen years ago.*

Inside, Veronica discovered her mother's slanted scrawl covering a couple of double-columned, green-hued steno pages.

Dearest Moose, the letter began, *I'm here! The bus was a bumpy ride and I lost my favorite pair of sunglasses, but everything is fine. The weather is beautiful. I love it already!*

The girls I'm staying with promise they'll help me meet some people and get me auditions. You're going to be so proud of me, Moose. I just know I'll be someone special in L.A.!

We have to pay to use the phone here, so I'll try not to use it too often. Instead, we can write to each other. It will be so romantic, like love notes!

I miss you.
Yours, Diana.

Veronica read the letter three times, and her heart was still beating rapidly by the time she had folded it and put it aside. She was tempted to read the remaining ones, to gobble them up like a box of chocolate-covered cherries, but she restrained herself. Too many sweets, after all, could spoil one's dinner.

She took a deep breath and slowly exhaled.

She didn't know much about her mother. That was true. Hadn't asked much. That was true too. It was just . . . easier not knowing. Easier on her. Easier on Daddy.

From what Veronica could remember, Diana May simply didn't fit in. She had no desire to be a PTA member, and she didn't like to cook. She hated to be called "Mommy" in public; "Diana" or "Di" would suffice, thanks very much. Her sole contribution to the neighborhood potlucks was always a plate of her pecan cookies. She loved her cocktails in a tall, frosted glass with a matching stirrer, and she loved the movies.

From the moment Veronica was old enough to walk and could be trusted not to run up and down the aisles—long before the Vees existed—her mother had taken her to the movies every Saturday afternoon. It was a special time, a mother-daughter time that began with a leisurely bath and breakfast. Diana would put Veronica in her best smocked dress and patent leather Mary Janes, with a matching grosgrain ribbon in her hair. Then, with Veronica at her side, she would carefully dress: first a layer of pantyhose and then a slip and a pair of high-heeled sandals.

"Pink, today? Are we in a pink mood?" Diana might ask, as she stood before her closet. "Or powder blue? Maybe it's a powder blue day. Go look outside and tell me what today looks like."

Veronica would climb on her mother's queen size bed and crane her neck toward the clouds. "The sky is blue, Mommy."

"And are the flowers blooming, sweetheart? Look outside and tell me what flowers are in bloom."

"Yellow flowers, Mommy."

"Yellow? That must be the wild daisies under the hedge. All right, then," she would say, reaching a hand into the closet. "I think it's a blue dress with yellow flowers sort of day."

And like magic, a blue dress with tiny yellow flowers would appear in the closet.

If Diana was in a truly good mood, the kind of mood that Veronica could never predict but was always happy to witness, she might even ask Veronica to brush her hair while she stared at her reflection in the vanity mirror. On those days, Veronica would be very careful not to pull or snarl her mother's shiny brunette mane, because the slightest pain might cause her good mood to disappear.

Then they would walk hand-in-hand to the theater, and Diana would say to the cashier, "One adult and one child." And she would hand her daughter the adult ticket and keep the child's ticket for herself.

And that's where Veronica found herself every Saturday afternoon: cuddled next to her mother in the dark, a bucket of greasy popcorn and a super-size Coke between them, staring up at the screen.

Veronica looked down at the letter in her hand, and a smile slowly spread across her face. She knew exactly where she was going. Where her mother belonged—and where she, too, would find her place . . . without her father.

Hollywood.

chapter 6

"This isn't goodbye," Veronica said. "It's *au revoir.*"

Val sent a glass of iced tea down the table. "What's the difference, *chica*? It's still *hasta la vista.*"

Ginny laughed, shaking her head. Veronica watched her friend pull her spiral notebook from her back pocket and dash off a few words—probably fodder for her next short story.

That was the price of befriending a writer, Veronica thought. *You never knew which new sentence you might pop up in.*

They were in Val's house, in the kitchen. A glance to Veronica's right provided a view of the natural rock pool Val's *papi* installed last year and the hot tub he added for the cold desert nights. On the patio were red, white and blue decorations Val's *mami* was putting up for their coming Fourth of July party.

"There's nothing for me here," Veronica said. "Besides you two, I mean. No play, no job, no place to live."

Val's eyes grew wide. "Daddy is kicking you out?"

"Drama queen," Ginny said with a good natured grin. She looked straight at Veronica. "Your father isn't kicking you out, is he?"

"No, but a newly married couple needs privacy," Veronica explained.

Val agreed with a knowing nod. "Three *might* be kind of a crowd."

Ginny turned to Veronica, ignoring Val. "So why are you going to Los Angeles?"

"Hollywood," Veronica corrected. She looked down into her tea, swirling the cubes and lemon around and around until she created a hypnotic yellow pinwheel.

"What's in Hollywood?" Val wanted to know.

"Acting jobs," Veronica replied.

"You mean movies?"

"And TV and commercials."

"Oooh . . . maybe you'll get on that dancing-with-celebrities show, and you can dance with one of those really cute guys." Val did a sexy salsa, kick-stepping and turning in her three inch heels. "And you can bring me and I'll teach you."

Ginny rolled her eyes. "I'm not even gonna begin to tell you what's wrong with that scenario." She looked at Veronica. "What are you gonna do for money? Do you have a job?"

"I have some savings," Veronica said. "Graduation money and a little from the drugstore."

"Uh-huh."

"I won't need much," Veronica insisted. "Just enough to last 'til the cash starts rolling in from acting."

"Vee, sweetie, acting jobs are kind of hard to get," Ginny said, adding quickly, "from what I understand."

Veronica shrugged. "Little Vee gets tons of them."

"She does?" Ginny sounded skeptical.

"What's with that face?" Veronica asked. "She's always emailing me about her auditions and stuff."

Val poured some more iced tea into Veronica's glass. "I haven't seen her in *anything*. And I watch a *lot* of TV."

"Well, she says she is, and if Little Vee can do it, then so can I," Veronica said. "Besides, she'll help me learn everything I need to know."

"Vivian?" Ginny asked. "I doubt that."

Veronica sighed, exasperated. "Why wouldn't Vivian help me?"

Val and Ginny exchanged a glance.

"Have you forgotten what she's like?" Val asked.

"You're talking about one of our best friends," Veronica warned. "What's wrong with her?"

"Don't tell me you've *Eternal-Sunshined* the whole Jason Dietrich thing," Ginny said, frowning.

"When *you* crushed on him for two years, and then *she* went to Homecoming with him?" Val added.

Veronica crossed her arms. "*I* crushed on Jason? No."

"Are you kidding me?" Ginny asked, incredulous. "You were in total love."

"With Little Vee's guy?" Veronica shook her head. "No way."

The girls became silent. Veronica used the pause as an opportunity to change the subject. She pulled Diana's letter and the *News* article from her pocket and placed them on the table.

"This is it, girls—my legacy," Veronica said proudly.

Val gasped. "Is this it? Is this the letter?" She gingerly handled the envelope as Ginny snatched up the newspaper and began reading it.

"Wow," Ginny breathed.

"Hollywood is my destiny!" Veronica clasped her hands together. "*Real* acting. Not just community theater where no one notices you."

Ginny looked up from the paper. "You're right. You should go."

"Really?"

Val patted Veronica on the shoulder. "We are 100 percent behind you."

"You are?"

"Absolutely." Ginny got up from her chair and stood next to Val. Behind them the red, white and blue streamers flew in the wind. "Acting's your thing. You gotta do your thing."

Veronica had told Mr. Rosenbloom nearly the same thing days earlier, yet she was surprised by the twinge of disappointment she felt hearing it from her Vees. "Don't you want to convince me not to go?"

"Why? Are you afraid to leave us?" Val asked, her brow creasing in concern.

"Afraid? Oh. No, no," Veronica said quickly.

"We'll miss you, Vee," Ginny said. She and Val wrapped their arms around Veronica.

Veronica grasped the girls tightly. "I'll miss you too," she said, and a flock of butterflies hatched in her stomach.

chapter 7

Shortly after the Padillas' Fourth of July blowout, Veronica began packing the old Ford Escort. With the Vees' help, she was done a week later.

"Would you do something for me?" Veronica asked Val and Ginny on the day she left. She handed them the packet of Diana's letters from the forbidden box. "Would you send these to me?"

"They'll fit in the car, *chica*," Val insisted. "Give them to me. We'll squash them in with your shoes."

Veronica shook her head. "No, no. That's not what I meant. See the postmarks? I want you to send the letters to me—one at a time—on those dates. I want to know exactly where my mother was and what she was thinking on those exact dates. Please?"

Veronica wanted to experience Hollywood right along with her mother—step by step. If she had all the letters with her, she'd be too tempted to read ahead and spoil any surprises that were in store.

She never read the last pages of mystery novels first, like other people did, so she was always shocked to learn the butler did it. Why should this be any different?

Ginny took the letters and nodded. "Of course, Vee. You can count on us."

May May exited the house then. She gave Veronica a small cooler filled with her favorite snacks and sodas, and a phone card with 100 minutes on it.

"In case you want to call," May whispered. "But don't feel like you have to."

Veronica frowned. Did that mean they wanted her to call? Or just May did? She wasn't sure of anything anymore. "Thanks, May."

They finished their goodbyes, and Veronica cast one last glance at her house. Her father remained inside, stubborn and old-man–like. Since their blow-up on the evening she was fired, the two of them had tiptoed quietly around each other, careful to limit their interaction. And then last night, as his daughter finished packing, Moose May had just one thing to say about her choice to leave and follow in her mother's footsteps.

"Your life will still be here when you come back."

Ooh, did that frost her cookies! Veronica had no intention of coming back—certainly not to this life. When—no, *if*—she returned, it would be as a successful, professional actor.

It was a promise she had made to herself. Failure was *not* an option.

May May gamely covered for Moose. "Your father's got a headache, I think. He wishes you luck."

Veronica turned from the house like a delinquent tenant. *Forget it, Vee,* she told herself. That was her past, Hollywood was her future!

Veronica gathered her friends for one last hug and then climbed into the Escort to head west toward the Golden Coast. This was it. She was going! She was doing!

A thrill of excitement ran up her spine, and she smiled as she crossed the border of Chester, Arizona.

Veronica rolled the windows down and let the wind whip through her hair.

Goodbye, old life, she thought.

Fulfilling one's destiny was *très* exhilarating.

chapter 8

"You're here!" Vivian Reed threw open the apartment door before Veronica had made it up the steps. She wrapped her tiny little arms around Veronica and buried her tiny little face into her shoulder. Veronica wondered if her friend had somehow gotten tinier and littler since she'd last seen her.

Vivian Reed was unlike the other Vees in nearly every way. The most obvious difference was her size: She was petite with a heart-shaped face and a pair of pale bee-stung lips. As opposed to the Vees with their long manes, Vivian's honey blonde hair was fashioned in a flippy pixie cut. She had a nervous, hummingbird quality about her as she tended to bounce lightly from foot to foot when she talked.

"So, where'd you park?" Vivian asked.

"Um, on the corner near Nichols Canyon?"

"Hmm . . . you might get towed. But I'm sure it's okay for a second. Here, come in, come in!"

Veronica entered and found herself in a single, moderately sized room. It held a couch, a chair and a coffee table. Several multicolored throw rugs and matching curtains from Target added interest, along with a standing lamp with a paper shade. Through a sliding glass door, Veronica spied a miniscule balcony facing the building's courtyard.

"Are you hungry? Or thirsty? I have some snacks." Vivian stepped through a doorway into a mini-kitchen and was still entirely visible to Veronica.

Veronica made the short journey through the apartment. "Your place is lovely. Can I have a tour?"

Vivian's laugh bounced around the kitchen alcove. "Sure." She spread her arms wide. "This is it, hon."

Veronica blinked. "But . . . where's the bedroom?"

"The couch folds out."

"And closets?"

"Across from the bathroom."

Vivian turned around and was instantly within the main room. She carried in a tray of baked and glazed goodies. "Krispy Kreme donuts," she announced. "An L.A. specialty!"

Veronica clapped with joy. "Yummy!" She placed a sugar-sprinkled donut on a napkin.

"Coke?" Vivian handed a soda to Veronica.

"Thank you." Veronica took the can and then gestured to a short juice glass filled with a thick green liquid. "What's that?"

"Pure wheat-grass juice. I don't do soda anymore." Vivian held her glass up in a toast. "Welcome to Hollywood, Vee!" She tossed back the juice like she was doing a shot as Veronica sipped her soda.

Veronica took a bite of the donut and silently rejoiced as it melted on her tongue. "Oh my god. This is fantastic."

Vivian nodded. "I know, right? When I first got here, I couldn't get enough of them."

"Aren't you having one with me?"

"Oh, I will."

"So, Vivian," Veronica said, taking another delectable sugary bite, "tell me everything. What exactly have you been up to?"

Vivian licked the remains of the green juice from her glass and set it on the coffee table. "Well, first of all," she said, "no one calls me Vivian out here. It's Reed."

"What? But that's your last name."

Reed nodded. "I met this guy at a party when I first got here. The music was loud, I guess, and he must have misunderstood me because the next thing I knew, I was Reed."

"You didn't correct him?"

Reed shrugged. "It's easier this way. Plus, I think it sounds kind of cute."

Veronica was astonished. If Vivian didn't want to be Vivian, did she not want to be a Vee? She pushed that ridiculous thought out of her head. Who *wouldn't* want to be a Vee?

"You never told me," she scolded.

"I'm sorry, sweetie. It never came up."

"Reed. *Reed*." Veronica repeated the name softly over and over again. *Adaptability is key in a new place,* she thought. Then she smiled. "I like it! So, *Reed*, tell me all about your grand adventures in Hollywood."

"Well," Reed said confidently, "I had four callbacks just this week, and next month, I think I'll finally get a manager."

"But you said you had an agent."

Reed stared at Veronica for a long moment and then grinned, her hazel eyes twinkling. "Oh Big Vee, you have so much to learn about L.A."

Veronica remembered one show Reed had done with the Chester Community Theater, a night of one-acts by Eugene O'Neill. They had been studying lines together at Veronica's house on the back patio, sipping grape Kool-Aid from wine glasses and playing at sophistication. Veronica had innocently suggested Reed memorize the entire play, not just her own lines, so that she would know what to do if someone flubbed on stage and couldn't remember her cue. Reed got herself into a snit about it and refused to study with Veronica anymore. And she was caught with her mouth hanging open when someone did indeed flub his lines.

But the stage was not the movies, and Veronica probably did have a lot to learn from Little Vee.

"Will you teach me?" she asked Reed in a hopeful voice.

Reed's grin grew wider. "I'll teach you everything I know." She tucked her legs under her on the chair. "Starting tonight. We have plans. My friend Bianca is this amazing model, right? She got us on the guest list for this really *chi-chi* party up on Las Palmas. There'll be *loads* of celebrities."

"Oh yeah? Do you suppose Paris Hilton will be there?"

"Maybe," Reed teased. "You never know."

"She's so skinny," Veronica observed with a shudder. "It's unnatural."

"I gotta tell you, Vee," Reed confided, glancing over at the plate of donuts, "everyone is that skinny here. Size zero, if you can believe it."

Veronica scoffed. "Zero is not a size. It's the absence of size."

Reed laughed and recrossed her legs. "Exactly."

"But," Veronica said with a frown, "you have to eat . . . don't you?"

Reed shook her head. "Not really. There're tons of ways to avoid eating if you're smart. Bianca knows all about it. You should ask her." The phone rang and Reed jumped up off the easy chair to answer it. "Excuse me, sweetie."

When the girls had been in high school acting class together, Veronica remembered, the difference in their sizes had been notable, *bien sûr*, but in the other direction. Jim Neece had complained that Vivian Reed was too petite for the stage, she had no *presence*, while Veronica was just the right size. And Vivian's voice, small as she was, did not project as well as Veronica's did.

But again, Veronica reminded herself, the movies were *not* the theater. Cameras could go where an audience could not. And film actors were notoriously small in stature. Perhaps Reed had the edge out here.

No matter, Veronica thought. She'd simply win jobs with her exceptional talent.

"Good news!" Reed yelped as she hung up the phone. "I've got an audition before my acting class this afternoon."

"That's great, Vee," Veronica said. "What's it for?"

"I'm not really sure, but this guy in my class told me he had a friend who was casting for an indie short and I would be perfect for one of the lead roles."

Veronica clapped and bounced a little in her seat. "That is *so* exciting!"

"He wants me to go over to his place so his friend can meet me."

"Is that how they do it here?" Veronica asked. "I mean, casual like that?"

"Lesson number one: It's all who you know," Reed said with a wave of her hand. She threw open her closet and surveyed her wardrobe.

Veronica stood behind Reed and was amazed at the brightly colored crop tops, mini-skirts and slinky high heels in her friend's closet. She couldn't remember Little Vee wearing anything like this back in Chester, Arizona. Veronica pulled out a pair of bubble gum stretch pants and held them up to her waist. They might cover *one* of her own legs—but just barely.

"Not those," Reed said. "This is better." She grabbed a purple and green striped A-line minidress and a pair of lime green platforms. Very mid-seventies.

It certainly wasn't an outfit Veronica would have worn for a CCT audition. The plays Jim Neece put up had gravity—O'Neill, Miller, and of course, Shakespeare. Lime green simply did not fit into the equation.

Acting in L.A. sure would take getting used to.

Veronica turned away from Reed while she changed and focused instead on the pool below the kitchen window. "Should I come with you?" she asked.

"You'd probably be bored, sweetie. Maybe you should take a drive to the beach, and we can meet back here before the party."

"Oh, okay."

Reed must have heard the disappointment in Veronica's voice because she said, "I'm not trying to get rid of you, Vee. I just, well . . . I'm kind of used to doing things on my own now. Besides, you might make me nervous."

"Me? But I'm . . ."

"You're the best, Vee. The best actress I know." Little Vee gave her a hug. "Wish me luck?"

"Sure!" Veronica nodded and grabbed her purse. "No worries. I wanted to see the beach anyway." She paused at the door. "Will we have time to grab a bite to eat before the party?"

"You mean dinner?"

"My treat. Do you have a favorite restaurant?"

Reed gave her a half-smile, as if Veronica could hardly be expected to know the ins and **outs of** Hollywood at this point. "That is such a nice idea, Vee, but it's really hard for me to eat out. I have special dietary needs."

"We don't have to eat steak or tacos or anything. We can have what you want."

"Thanks, but I think it's easier for me to eat at home. I'd love it if you joined me. You'd really get a lot out of this new plan I'm on."

"Oh, okay, sure," Veronica said. "That sounds great." She glanced over at the Krispy Kremes and noticed that, aside from the one she had eaten, they remained untouched.

Reed caught her glance. "Did you want to take them with you to the beach? For a snack?"

"Oh, no, thanks."

Reed smiled. "Okay. You can have them later. They'll all be here when you get back."

Then she hugged Veronica around the waist again. "Welcome to Hollywood, sweetie!"

chapter 9

While traveling west on Santa Monica Boulevard, Veronica noticed with pleasant surprise, there was a point when the road ahead seemed to simply disappear into the vast expanse of ocean.

It was like the end of the world. *A modern day Columbus could discover his paradise in Santa Monica,* she thought. It was a wonderland lined with imported palm trees and white sand, with amusement rides and sushi bars.

But moving to the sun-kissed coast of Southern California from a land-locked state like Arizona, Veronica didn't care about any of that. She had never before seen an ocean, except in a Coppertone ad or on *Survivor,* and she wanted to do just one thing:

Dip her toesies in the Pacific.

Veronica ripped off her sandals and dashed across the beach, luxuriating in the feel of the tiny grains of sand against her uncalloused feet. She could hardly believe the sight before her: nothing but water as far as she could see. She bent down and sifted the warm white sand through her fingers, letting it cascade across her palms.

She looked up and down the coast: Families with children were building sand castles, couples were walking hand-in-hand, groups of teens were bathing lazily in the sun. *This* was Southern California. This was Paradise. She was reminded of her conversation with Daddy about vacation on the night of her show. Now, all she needed was a chaise and a man to bring her a fruity drink.

Veronica's feet sank into the wet sand, and the bright midafternoon sun caressed her face with warmth. She couldn't move, didn't want to move, just wanted to stop time so this moment would live on and on.

A rogue wave slapped against her ankles and pulled her out of her reverie. She stepped farther into the ocean. The cold water was shocking at first, but after a moment or two, she didn't even notice it. The contrast of the burning sun and the crisp water was refreshing, exciting. Oh, she was a long way from Chester, indeed.

Nearby, a couple of kids whizzed past her on boogie boards, the gentle surf carrying them toward shore. Veronica gasped as one of the boys toppled over into the water, knocked head first by a surge of wave. She was relieved when he emerged unharmed and hopped back on his board for another ride. He caught her glance.

"These waves suck," he groused.

Oh no, they don't, she thought. These waves were *good*. They were, why, they were a gift from Heaven itself. She felt at one with the universe at that moment. Like the billions of grains of sand, she felt small next to this immense ocean, and small, in this instance, felt just right.

She turned then and faced the shore, back toward Santa Monica and far, far beyond it, the desert of Arizona, six hours and six life-times away. She was a different person already.

A group of Size Zeroes in tiny bikinis slinked down the beach before her. Veronica noted their gaunt frames, their protruding ribs.

She glanced down at her midriff and thighs, and then, crossing her arms over her chest, she stepped out of the water.

Yes, she felt different indeed.

chapter 10

Veronica could hear the jazz combo long before they rounded the tight corner halfway up Las Palmas. Little Vee had volunteered her car for the evening since Veronica's Escort was still packed. She took the hills like a pro in her metallic silver BMW.

"This looks just like Val's car," Veronica had marveled when Reed led her to the 325i in the parking garage below the apartment building. "Except for the color."

Reed smiled primly. "Not quite. Val's is ancient. Mine is brand new."

"Brand new?" Veronica was shocked. Little Vee's family, as far as she knew, wasn't rolling in it like Val's was; as Vivian Reed, she had driven a second hand Civic to class every day. "You must be doing really well with the acting jobs."

Reed slipped behind the wheel and started the ignition. "It's leased. No one owns cars in L.A. They just borrow them."

"Kind of an expensive loan." Veronica ran her hand along the leather interior. Unlike Val's dashboard, with its fun and funky toys, Reed's was devoid of any personality; perhaps that was the price one paid for leasing a car. "If I had the money, I think I'd rather spend it on a bigger apartment."

"Who sees *that*?" Reed asked and peeled out of the parking garage.

The party was being held at a three-story Spanish style stucco-covered home perched on the edge of a steep cliff. Every window had a balcony; every balcony had a single, cream-colored sconce.

After parking the car four blocks away and trudging up the incline in high-heeled boots, Reed pushed through the heavy oak door, and the muted jazz came alive, along with a crush of bodies. Veronica squeezed through as best she could, following Reed to the center of the ground-floor living room.

"Whose house is this?" she yelled down into Reed's ear.

"I don't know," Reed shouted back. "But we should find Bianca."

Veronica noticed a middle-aged man, shorter than herself, who was wearing Gap khakis and a denim shirt. Rectangular glasses framed his blue eyes. She nudged Reed and pointed discreetly at him. "He looks familiar, doesn't he?"

"He does."

"Do you think he's a movie star?" Veronica asked, and a trill of excitement tickled her spine. Movie stars, TV personalities, and music bigwigs—*oh my!*

"Could be," Reed replied, then confided, "Movie stars look different in real life."

Veronica felt an overwhelming desire to giggle, surrounded as she was by anonymous celebrities. Was that Sienna Miller in the cowboy boots and skinny jeans? Could that be Sophia Bush behind the rhinestone-studded sunglasses? She thought she saw a desperate housewife, a survivor, a hero and a refugee from *The OC* sharing a laugh near a giant plasma screen television. Although she couldn't quite place their names, there was the *potential* for celebrity wherever she looked.

"There she is," Reed said. "Come on."

They passed a bar manned by a white-jacketed server. "Ooh! Fancy drinks!" Veronica exclaimed. "Let's get Manhattans."

"Reed, dear, where have you been?"

Veronica turned and saw a blonde Amazon pose herself next to Reed. *That must be Bianca,* she thought. Six feet tall, a size one. Who else could she be? Her brows had been plucked to the thinnest of lines, and her Kohl-lined eyes were heavily mascara-ed. She wore fashionably torn and bruised jeans that hung several inches below her hip bones and a cami top that clung to her braless breasts. The overall effect was dramatic and otherworldly, like she had just stepped off a runway.

"Hi, I'm Veronica," Veronica said, holding out her hand for the giant to shake. Next to Bianca, she felt short and dumpy in her jeans, flip-flops and layered tanks. And these were her *good* flip-flops too.

"You're . . ." A stunned Bianca recovered nicely: "A pleasure."

"We were just talking about drinks," Veronica said. "Maybe a Manhattan?"

"Or a Cosmopolitan?" Reed added.

Veronica wrinkled her nose. "I don't like the fruit in those things. Why do they put stuff you have to eat in something you have to drink? If it's going to be anything, it should be chocolate."

Bianca shook her head firmly. "Do you know how many calories are in a Cosmopolitan?" She stared down at Veronica, who wasn't sure if this was a rhetorical question or if she was expected to spit out an answer.

"So I take it that checking out the buffet table is out of the question," Veronica mumbled to herself.

Bianca brushed long layers of platinum hair off her shoulders. "It's stuffy in here. Let's go out back and see who's there." She pivoted on her spike heels and headed toward the back of the house.

The "back" was a huge redwood patio overlooking downtown. On the west side she could see Griffith Park, a natural preserve that brought a little bit of country to the sprawling metropolis. Veronica stood at the edge of the wall and marveled at the lights of the city. From this distance, she could see the configuration of streets, the criss-cross pattern laid out neatly and squarely, like jewels scattered on black velvet. It was breathtaking.

Something else caught her breath too, and it wasn't the smog. It was the dense cloud of cigarette smoke from the patio's visitors. Through the haze, she saw Reed and Bianca posing next to a trio of smooth-skinned twentysomethings.

Bianca brought a long white cigarette to her thick lips and took a delicate puff.

Veronica noticed that Reed, too, held a cigarette twixt her fingers. She bent and whispered in her ear. "Vee! You don't smoke."

"Just at parties. Keeps me from eating." Reed held out the pack. "Have one."

Veronica studied the pack Reed was offering and shook her head. "No, thanks."

Reed shrugged and hopped onto the concrete wall, arranging herself behind Bianca. Veronica studied her friend studying the model. They moved their hands in the same manner, as if they were drawing pictures in the air with their cigarettes. When Bianca laughed, Reed laughed too. When Bianca frowned, Reed frowned as well. They spoke only to each other.

They were even dressed similarly, although Little Vee's outfit was cute while on Bianca, it was striking.

"Why are we here again?" Veronica wanted to know. If it wasn't to drink or eat or engage in flirtatious conversation with, say, the opposite sex, what then was the use of this party?

"We're here to meet people," Reed replied, never taking her eyes off Bianca. "You never know where you could get a job or from whom. Someone here might know someone, and you hit it off and the next thing you know, you're on a TV series."

"Really?" Veronica asked doubtfully. "That seems sort of—"

"Case in point," Reed said, nodding at Bianca. "Pay attention. You could learn something."

Veronica turned. One of the slick young twentysomethings had approached and was chatting with Bianca. "So," he said, "you'd be perfect for the new video I'm shooting."

"A music video? Please," Bianca puffed at him with disdain. "For whom?"

"Only an international *superstar* named Keith Urban," the guy said proudly.

"He is so country," Bianca said. "I don't square dance."

Reed grinned at the girl's sly wit.

"You wouldn't have to square dance," the guy explained, and Veronica noticed he was probably a lot older than he appeared. From her vantage point, she could see a telltale ring of thinning hair. "You'd be the girl Keith lusts after. *Totally* sexy."

Bianca glanced over at Reed. "What do you think?"

"You should do it," Reed said. "Nicole would kill you." The girls shared an evil glance.

"You know Nicole Kidman?" Veronica gasped.

Bianca smiled and blew a puff of smoke at the music-video producer. "I'll think about it. You can leave now." She wiggled her fingers in farewell and turned to the girls. "This party blows." Then she led the way off the patio. Reed quickly followed.

"Lesson number two . . ." Reed said authoritatively.

"No music videos?" Veronica asked.

"No music videos for country singers. That's *so* NASCAR." Reed raised a pair of eyebrows, tweezed just like Bianca's, Veronica noticed. "Bianca taught me everything I know. She's amazing."

Veronica watched the Amazon with reluctant respect. It would be hard for her to take a woman that skinny—who seemed so obsessed with her appearance—seriously.

But if Reed said Bianca was amazing, well, who was she to judge?

At six the next morning, Veronica found herself wide awake and cranky. They had gotten in too late to blow up the inflatable bed, so she had pulled the easy chair over to the coffee table and slept half-upright.

And now, with every muscle in her neck cramping, she was desperate for a cup of coffee. In Reed's kitchenette, she found beans and a French press. But no sugar or regular cow's milk.

As she tried to quietly grind the beans, she was struck by a sense memory. An image of her father drinking his heavily sweetened and creamed coffee floated into her mind. It was seven in Daddy's kitchen, and she suspected he would be up by now, perhaps just out of the shower, rubbing his hair dry with one of the striped towels he refused to replace even though the nap was nonexistent and there were holes in the corners. It was Sunday, which meant he could enjoy a leisurely morning breakfast, perhaps a fried egg and toast.

Since Veronica wasn't there, he probably wouldn't be having an omelet or pancakes or waffles.

Did he even remember how to fry an egg? she wondered. *Did he know about the trick with the toaster?* She studied her cell phone on the counter. It had been a while since Daddy had to fend for a meal on his own.

She started to dial. It wouldn't be to talk, *naturellement.* She was still angry with him. It was strictly a matter of practicality: The toaster jammed if you used the whole wheat bread.

It was true, she thought as the phone rang once. If you weren't aware of it, and used the wheat bread and then, for instance, went back to your bathroom to wipe a dab of shaving cream off your chin, the whole kitchen could erupt in flames.

The phone rang a second time.

Or maybe he wasn't on his own, she thought, hesitating. Perhaps May May was there. Perhaps she had moved in already. Maybe she was frying Daddy an egg or scrambling it or poaching it or whatever her magic cookbook told her to do with eggs. Maybe she was toasting English muffins instead of wheat bread, thus avoiding the whole toaster debacle.

Fine, she thought as the phone rang a third time. *Fine and dandy. He's got May May and her muffins, and he doesn't need any help at all. He made that abundantly clear.*

Veronica clicked off her phone then finished making the coffee. She poured herself a cup. Hmm. No sugar or milk, but she would have to make do. She stirred in a small yellow packet of Splenda and *ugh* . . . Black coffee, even sweetened artificially, was still black coffee.

She quietly opened her laptop on the kitchen counter and searched for a wireless signal. Quickly accessing her email, she found a letter from Ginny. Not surprisingly, Ginny the writer favored well-composed emails while Val preferred clicking out short text messages on her cell.

Hi Vee! I miss you! Have you met any fabulous stars yet? Have you been to any parties? Tell me everything so I can live vicariously through you. Did I say I miss you???

Veronica smiled at the email and clicked "reply."

My sweet Vee! I miss you too! I've only been to one fab party so far, but the week is young! Reed has all sorts of plans to teach me the ins and outs of H'wood. We're going to take yoga and movement classes—and acting classes, bien sûr. *And she's going to set up a photo session for head shots. Yay! The jobs will start rolling in, and you'll see me on* Extra *in no time!*

"Hey," Veronica heard and turned to see Reed stumbling through the living room in hot pink boy shorts and a sports bra. She closed her laptop and made a mental note to text Val later so she wouldn't feel left out.

"Morning."

"Mmmm . . . coffee," Reed said, eyeing the press. She poured some into a mug and took a careful sip. "Ahhh, that's just what I needed." She moved a couple of steps closer to Veronica at the counter. "Whatcha doing up so early?"

"Checking email." Veronica swiveled to face the window behind her. "The sun's coming up. Isn't it beautiful?"

Reed stared at the golden orb rising above the trees. "I love this time of day. Before everything gets going, when it's quiet and still."

They took their coffee onto the balcony, where there was barely room for both of them. Veronica could smell the fresh morning dew coupled with the yummy scent of frying bacon in a neighboring apartment.

"Do you remember," she said, "when we were twelve and you and Ginny and Val were staying at my house and we rented *A Nightmare on Elm Street*?"

"Ooh! Scary! I still have bad dreams."

Veronica laughed. "Remember how we stayed up after Ginny and Val fell asleep, and we tried to read what was in Ginny's notebook but she had it tied to her wrist with a string?"

"I remember. And then we sat on the roof and watched the sun come up."

"Let's do that again," Veronica said eagerly.

"Maybe we will." Reed sipped her coffee with a thoughtful smile. "There's so much we need to catch up on. Are you seeing anyone, Vee?"

Veronica thought then of Jason Dietrich, Little Vee's old boyfriend from Chester. He used to arrive late to high school every day just so he could make a grand entrance on his Harley. As Ginny so helpfully reminded her not too long ago, Veronica had been drooling over him for months when Reed decided to ask Jason out. It had all seemed rather sudden to Veronica, especially since Reed had made it a rule never to ask a boy out herself.

But how could Reed resist Jason's sensitive blue eyes and his crush-worthy bod? Veronica couldn't. Not that she would have done anything about it; Jason was really more a Reed type of guy.

Veronica wondered if she should bring up the little matter of Jason moping around school after Reed left town, of how pitifully sad he had been. She looked at her friend, arms crossed against the early morning chill, her button nose red and shiny, and decided against it.

What's past was past, she thought.

"Me? No. I would have told you. Are you seeing anyone?"

"I was," Reed said. "For about four months."

"Why didn't you email me?" Veronica was a little surprised and more than a little hurt.

"It was no big deal," Reed shrugged and looked into her coffee cup.

"What happened?"

"He was a wannabe film producer, about our age. Went right into the business after high school. Family connections, you know?" Reed sighed. "He was a really great guy. And so cute. But he was always busy. Every night he had to meet someone for dinner or drinks. I hardly saw him alone."

She looked away, off toward Hollywood Boulevard.

"Funny thing is, he was just supposed to be a contact. Someone who could hook me up with auditions or make a recommendation to a casting director."

"Did he?"

"No. But I fell in love with him anyway. I will *never* make that mistake again." Reed's lips curled upward in a rueful smile. "It's pretty hard to meet someone that's any good here, Vee. Someone who doesn't want to use you or someone you don't want to use. It's all about the business."

"Is that lesson number three?" Veronica asked gently.

"Yeah, I guess it is."

Veronica saw in Reed's eyes a profound sadness. It made her want to wrap her arms around her and hold her tight, tell her everything was going to be okay: Big Vee was here now. But there was a coldness in those eyes too, a detachment Veronica had never seen before.

"You'll find someone, sweetie. Someone *great*. I know you will."

"Thanks." Reed brightened. "What should we do today?"

Veronica peered into her cup of black coffee and grimaced. "We have *got* to take you grocery shopping."

chapter 11

n July 16, thanks to her helpful Vees, Veronica opened Reed's mailbox and found the letter her mother had written to her father on July 16, 1989. Her fingers trembled with anticipation as she lifted the flap:

Dearest Moose,

Finally, my high school plays came in handy. I actually had to deliver a monologue for an audition today! I think I did a pretty decent job of it. I brought my brand new head shot along, and the director seemed to like me. There were a ton of girls for the audition—maybe sixty or more. The line stretched all the way out to Hollywood and down Vine.

Oh yes! Veronica thought with a start. She knew where that was! Hollywood Boulevard and Vine Street. She had passed there with

Reed just yesterday! There was a Metro station to the southeast and a giant brown hat—a symbol of the famous Brown Derby restaurant that had long since been demolished—on the same corner.

Nineteen years ago, Diana would have seen the real thing.

My mother's Hollywood, Veronica mused. Would it have been so different from her own?

Veronica closed her eyes and placed herself on the corner of Hollywood and Vine—this time, observing the huge line of hopefuls, each of them waiting for the audition that would mean her big break into show business. Young and pretty, they tapped their feet impatiently, practiced their lines, touched up lipstick and brushed blush across cheeks. They waited. They *wanted.*

And among them was her mother.

After a brilliant audition, Diana would have skipped past that line, would have peered up Vine and found the Capitol Records building, the top of which would have been pulsing "Hollywood" in Morse code to the rest of the world—just as it did today.

Following the pink and grey stars set into the sidewalk, their famous names written in gold block letters, Diana would have passed Grauman's Chinese Theater, the Roosevelt Hotel, and the El Capitan and Egyptian Theaters.

Her heels would click-clack on the cement as she passed the pawn shops and the tourist traps and the lacy lingerie in the Frederick's of Hollywood storefront.

Would she pause for refreshment at one of the diners, Veronica wondered. *Grab a slice and a Coke at a corner pizza parlor? Or would she anticipate future success and splurge on a Caesar salad and shrimp cocktail at Musso & Frank's?*

The image in Veronica's mind was so real, so vivid, she felt she could reach out and grasp her mother's hand.

Oh, the history! The glamour! And to share it all—to see the same sights, to breathe the same air her mother had—filled Veronica with pride and hope and yearning.

I'm here! Veronica wanted to shout. *I'm following your dreams!*

And she would be successful. After all, she had a legacy and a destiny to fulfill. She would find the permanent place among the tinsel that had obviously eluded her mother. She would prove to her father, to her Vees, to herself that she could do it.

She would find success. She simply had to.

Veronica opened her eyes and found herself back in Little Vee's tiny apartment—the creased green sheets of the letter in her hand.

"I'm here, Mom," she spoke quietly. "I'm here."

Head shots were those ubiquitous photographs that all serious actors possessed: black and white, 8" x 10" semi-glossies, usually with a white border on the front and a resume on the back. According to Reed, the resume listed the actor's recent experience, acting teachers, workshops, movement classes, vice coach and special expertise like kayaking and Portuguese accents. It also listed the actor's height, weight, hair color, eye color and shoe size.

Imagine, Veronica scoffed, being evaluated for a job based on a wide or narrow foot?

"The highest compliment an actor can receive is to be told she looks exactly like her head shot," Reed told Veronica later that morning. "I'm going to take you to the best guy in town!"

Veronica thought of her bank account. *C'était vrai*, there was money. But she didn't have *beaucoup* bucks, and she needed her savings to last until she landed her first role. She was quickly learning things like food and rent and gas cost a lot more here in the big city than they did back in Arizona.

"Um, those head shots, are they expensive?" she asked timidly.

"Every real actor needs them," Reed asserted. "It's like you don't exist without them." She fixed Veronica with a serious gaze. "Expense should not be an issue. This is your career."

Veronica felt a flutter of excitement in her chest: her career. Yes, it was. "Okay," she agreed. "You're the boss."

Reed held up one of her own photographs, a striking image of Little Vee staring directly at the camera in a daring, confrontational way—her gaze challenging her audience. Veronica was impressed and awed by her friend's command of the medium. She hoped— god, she hoped!—that she would have a head shot even half as authentic.

"Love it, Vee," Veronica said. "You're gorgeous."

Reed studied the photo intently, as if she were a scientist with a microbial sample. "Not bad, I guess. It's worked for me so far. But don't worry. He can make anybody look good."

Veronica stood, then, her hands clutching the wrinkly balls of her cotton underwear which she had just hand-washed in the tiny bathroom sink, she asked, "Do you have a dryer in the building? I just want to fluff these up before I put them away."

"Don't waste your money on that," Reed said, rising from the couch. "You can hang them there," she said. "Over the shower rod."

Little Vee's own panties were already hanging there, minuscule wisps of sheer fabric fashioned into tiny thongs. Veronica blushed. "I couldn't," she stammered. "I mean, mine are . . ."

"Yours are what?" Reed asked. She grabbed a pair of Veronica's underpants and draped them over the rod. "Don't be silly. There you go."

Veronica stared at the two sets of underwear hanging there, at her own Jockey for Her briefs in pink cotton next to Reed's so-small-they-couldn't-fit-a-label-on-them thongs. The contrast was striking. Almost painful.

Veronica smiled weakly. "Thank you."

"Reed, is that you?" A husky voice called from the other side of the photo studio, an empty white space with a single barstool in the center surrounded by a trio of lights mounted on stands.

A man in his fifties, with a slight paunch above skin-tight Levi's and heeled cowboy boots, greeted the girls as they entered. "Reed, my dearest!"

Reed kissed the photographer on both cheeks and accepted a long hug in return. "Andre, this is my friend Veronica." She took Veronica's hand and led her through the studio, whispering in Veronica's ear. "Isn't he fabulous?"

"Bonjour, my dear," Andre said.

"Bonjour, monsieur! Comment ça va?" Veronica asked, pleased she could actually use an entire French phrase for once.

Andre tilted his head to one side. "Eh?" Then he walked back over to his camera where he lit a thin brown cigarette and sipped an espresso.

"He's not French?" Veronica whispered to Reed.

"He's from Cleveland, I think." Reed smiled and placed her hands on Veronica's upper arms, rubbing them slightly. "Now don't be nervous. Andre knows just what to do."

Veronica glanced over at Andre who was fiddling with his camera. Smoke curled around his hands. That couldn't be good for the pixels. "Reed, does everyone smoke in L.A.?"

Reed wrinkled her button nose. "God, no. It's a very health-conscious city. No one smokes in L.A."

"Over here, please," Andre called.

Veronica took a few tentative steps over to the stool in the center of the room.

Andre crossed his arms and sized up the situation. "First, you will stand." He looked through the lens of the camera and back up to Veronica. He moved the tripod back a few inches. Again, he looked through the lens; again, he moved the tripod back a few inches. Another look through the lens, another step back.

"Is something wrong?" Veronica asked nervously.

"No, no. Everything's fine." He walked over to Reed and conferred with her quietly. The two of them peered at her and began whispering to each other.

Veronica folded her arms protectively around herself. In all her years on the stage she had never felt so curiously on display.

"If you'll excuse me a moment, I need to change lenses," Andre said. He adjusted the camera and placed his eye against the viewfinder. "Ah, much better. Now, my dear, I want you to place your chin against your chest and look up."

She remembered the photos from the reception room and tried to imitate them. Andre frowned and shook his head. "Try this," he said as he swiveled his right shoulder forward and his left back. "Now you do it."

Veronica attempted to twist as he demonstrated but couldn't manage to separate one shoulder from the other. They both wanted to move forward at the same time.

"Aren't you familiar with this from your movement classes?" Andre asked, flustered by Veronica's lack of physical prowess.

"She's not taking movement class," Reed answered for her.

"Yoga?"

"Nope, nothing."

"But I will be," Veronica piped up. "Very soon. I'm sure I'll be doing all those things."

Andre rubbed the back of his head. "My dear, why don't you sit on the stool?"

Veronica took a seat, crossing one leg over the other and lowering her hands to her lap.

"Very nice. Now, look up at me. No, don't smile! Not so big," Andre admonished. "Try again."

Veronica didn't smile. But she thought about smiling and her lips curled like the Mona Lisa.

"There we go." As Andre snapped away, he murmured, "Very good. Yes, that's lovely."

Veronica thought about her journey to this point, about her mother's journey. About the brand new head shots Diana had written about nineteen years ago.

This was Veronica's first step to her great career as an actor. People would take notice and applaud her as they had in Arizona. She felt a surge of confidence fill her lungs.

Just the first step.

"That's it," Andre said. "Beautiful."

And then, out of the corner of her eye, she saw Reed frown. "What is it, Vee?"

"Your hair," Reed said. "It looks sort of funny."

"How do you mean? Is it sticking up somewhere?" Veronica began smoothing her hair down with her hands. "Is that better?"

Reed cocked her head to one side, a thoughtful expression on her face. "No, no. It's nothing. I'm sure it's fine."

chapter 12

"The next step on your road to fame is to enroll in my movement class," Reed said as the two girls lazed by the pool at Reed's apartment complex.

"Movement class . . . is that like the mirror exercises Jim Neece used to make us do?" Veronica asked, adjusting her one-piece suit.

Reed laughed. "Oh my god. Remember those? Those were hilarious."

Veronica chuckled as she mentally revisited a particularly *awkward* exercise when Biff was her partner. Somehow they had ended up in a pile on the floor—Veronica atop Biff and his two left feet.

"This is completely different." Reed rubbed sunscreen on her face and then across her midsection. Veronica loved the bikini Little Vee was wearing. She thought she recognized it from a Barbie doll she owned as a child.

"The class I take, the intermediate level, is all about set work,"

Reed went on. "We learn how to move within the space with props and set dressing. It's to help you feel more confident in front of a camera or on a stage."

"You mean like in the theater?" Veronica asked brightly.

"No, no," Reed said. "Out here, a stage means a big warehouse kind of thingy at a studio. A *sound*stage."

"Ah."

"You'll see," Reed intoned. "It's totally hard." She lowered the straps of her bikini top. "Oh, I've got an audition this afternoon, so we can go to Larry's evening class."

"Another audition?" *So many auditions for Little Vee, so many acting jobs,* Veronica thought. She really should be taking notes. "What's it for?"

Reed frowned. "A commercial, I think? I don't remember. I have to ask Marilyn."

"Marilyn, your agent."

"Mmmm."

"Do you think she'd consider taking me on?" Veronica asked hopefully. "Not that I have the kind of experience you have but maybe—"

"Maybe," Reed said. "Let's see what your pictures look like."

"Oh, sure. Thanks, sweetie," Veronica said. "So I'll, just, uh, I'll hang out here until you get back."

"You could try the In-n-Out on Sunset," Reed suggested.

"The burger place? Yeah, I could do that."

"I hear they've got amazing fries."

"Oh?"

"Not that I know personally. I don't eat that junk anymore."

Veronica waded into the pool. She flipped on her back and floated face-up, letting the cool water lap at her fingertips and feeling the warm sun on her cheeks. As she bobbed up and down, she could hear the rush of water in her ears, deadening all sound.

Her mind wandered away from the pool, away from L.A., back to Chester and Daddy and May May. They were making plans for the wedding now, plans for their future. A future without her.

And did it matter? Veronica had her own plans, her own future. Why, in just a couple of months, long before December 20—the date of the dreaded nuptials—she was certain to be in the midst of acting jobs galore. She would be able to return to Chester as a pro— a real working actor. She'd show them just how much they'd held her back all these years. She just needed to put Reed's plans into action.

But plans cost money.

Reed had been right. Those head shots were *not* cheap. And now the classes . . . movement, acting, yoga . . . at this rate, she'd drain her funds in a few weeks!

"Vee! [*Gurgle, gurgle*] sunscreen, Vee!" she could hear Reed scold her as she floated just below the surface. "[*Gurgle, gurgle*] get wrinkles!"

Veronica held her nose and sank below the surface.

At this point, she thought, wrinkles were the *plus petite* of her worries.

For her inaugural visit to Larry's movement class, Reed drove them both in her BMW. Veronica's Ford needed a good wash and wax after sitting on the street under shedding palm trees.

Reed was dressed in a maroon velour track suit that looked almost exactly like one Paulie Walnuts had worn in an old episode of *The Sopranos*, but on Little Vee, it looked hip, not quite so gangster.

Veronica herself had only a pair of terry shorts and a Gap T-shirt, an outfit she preferred to sleep in, not bounce around in in front of a million strangers.

"Don't be nervous, Vee," Reed said.

"I'm not," Veronica countered. "Actually, I'm excited. Movement classes! I can't believe it's actually happening!"

"Well, if you have any problems, just watch me. Larry's given me some extra help now and then. I think he has a crush on me."

Veronica didn't doubt it. Who wouldn't have a crush on Little Vee?

The studio was a small linoleum-tiled room in the Hancock Park-adjacent area known as Larchmont Village. Everything in L.A., Veronica learned, was "adjacent" to something better: Apartments and communities and office buildings were "Beverly Hills adjacent," "West Hollywood adjacent," "Santa Monica adjacent." It was like nothing could just be itself. It could only be something in relation to something better.

Clumps of wannabe actors were scattered around the room, chatting and posing. They certainly looked casual to Veronica, but upon closer inspection, none of them *really* seemed to be paying attention to their conversational partners. Instead, they all had their ears pricked up, their eyes peeled. Like they were contestants in a reality show, waiting to be discovered.

"All right people, let's go." Larry, clearly fortysomething but trying to look 29, clapped his hands and did a little jog in place. "Feet parallel, hands by your sides. And roll the head to the right and two and three and four, and to the left and six and seven and eight . . ."

"Follow me," Reed told Veronica.

Reed rolled her shoulder. Veronica rolled her shoulder.

Reed swung her arms. Veronica swung her arms.

Reed did deep knee bends. Veronica did *a* deep knee bend.

"Today we're going to work on set blocking," Larry said as he continued to lead the warm-up. *He looks more like a former athlete than an acting teacher,* Veronica thought. Well-built and strong, wearing snug sweatpants and a Crunch tee, he didn't resemble Jim Neece at all.

Veronica turned to Reed and started to whisper, "Hey! Do you remember when Jim . . ."

But Reed wasn't listening. Instead, she was gazing at a guy a few chairs away. He was nothing much to stare at, if you asked Veronica. A little on the plain side, with soft malleable features and a flop of brown hair. She poked Reed's thigh.

"Huh?"

"Who's your boyfriend?" Veronica asked.

"Robby Donovan," Reed whispered. "He's Michael Donovan's son. That guy from the cop shows?"

Veronica grinned. "Do you like him?"

"Me?" Reed scowled. "Hell no. But if *he* likes *me*, I might be able to score a walk-on on his dad's show."

Veronica nodded. That had been lesson number one. It's all about who you know.

"And that's the basics," Larry was finishing up at the front of the class. "Okay, let's start. Here's your scene." He handed out "sides," which were small Xeroxes of scenes from a script. Then he pulled a table and two chairs into the center of the space.

Veronica eagerly accepted the handout and scanned the lines quickly. Ah, dialogue! Wonderful! She got bored with plays that had a lot of stage direction. She was an *actor*. She wanted to emote through words, through her voice, not by posing in the background.

Larry tapped the back of a chair. "You'll start here and make your way to there." He pointed to a stool about ten feet away. "The whole time, you should be reading your lines."

"That's it?" Veronica whispered to Reed. "Why would you need a class for that?"

She straightened up, confident. She could do this in her sleep—and occasionally had on some anxious nights during CCT's run of *Cleopatra*.

Reed hadn't exaggerated in her emails. She *was* leaps ahead of the rest of the people in the group.

"Who's first?" Larry asked the class.

No one said a word. Veronica was astonished by the students' lack of response. "You people are actors," she wanted to say. "You should be jumping up and down at a chance to recite lines in front of an audience."

Apparently, Veronica was not telepathic, since everyone remained in their seats.

"I'll do it," she said, thrusting her hand in the air.

"New girl," Larry observed. "Come on up."

As Veronica rose from her chair, she noticed Reed's hand slightly raised. Had Little Vee been offering her a high-five? She didn't mean to leave her hanging. She smiled at her friend, slapped her hand and clambered over her to the stage where Larry held out a chair.

"Okay. Volunteers?" Larry scanned the room. "Robby, read with New Girl."

Robby the TV actor's son ambled onto the stage and took a chair opposite Veronica.

Easy-peasy, Veronica thought. There were all of ten lines of dialogue in the scene. She would stand on . . . line four and then begin walking on . . . line seven, arriving at the stool by line ten. Perf.

Larry pulled out a roll of white paper tape and measured out several long strips. "Here are your lights," he said, placing four big X's to Veronica's right and left. "Here are C-stands with flags." Veronica had no idea what those were, but Larry blocked them off by pasting more X's in front of the lights. It was a bit of an obstacle course, but still, no problem.

Then he pulled off two very long strips and placed them in parallel lines leading toward the audience. "Here are your dolly tracks."

"My what?" Veronica asked.

"The camera dolly," Robby explained kindly. "It's how they move the camera around smoothly."

"So watch out for that," Larry said with a smile. "And don't step on the lights or the stands."

It makes the scene a little *more complicated,* Veronica thought, *but no worries. Easy-peasy, lemon-squeezy.*

"Also watch out for the camera itself and your first AC," Larry said, pulling a boy and girl from the class and setting them on the "tracks."

"The AC pulls focus," Robby further elaborated.

Veronica swallowed. "Of course," she bluffed.

"And don't walk into video village and the script supervisor," Larry said, adding another pair of students to the side of the "camera." "And I'll be the director." He stood next to the X representing the "video monitor." "Okay. Ready, New Girl?"

"Um . . ." Veronica felt suddenly claustrophobic, surrounded by lights and stands and mechanical people. She found Reed in the audience and tried to make eye contact, but Little Vee seemed intent on her cell phone.

"And . . . action."

Veronica glanced down at the page and then up at Robby.

"What are we going to do about Dad?" she asked him. "He's been so forgetful."

"What do you mean?" Robby said, staring at the paper in front of him.

"He missed his medicine the other day and nearly had a seizure."

"Oh, come on, Sis. You're exaggerating."

Veronica would have to stand now if she wanted to time her walk right, but there was that boy—er, that *camera*—standing not two feet away. She rose awkwardly from the chair and began to move forward on her line.

"We called 9-1-1 and they came right away," she said. "Thank god."

As she walked closer to the stool, the boy and girl, (camera and AC) started walking toward her, spurred on by a push from Larry. Veronica glanced over at him.

"The camera's moving in for a close-up," Larry said. "Try to ignore it."

Ignore it? She was so near to the "camera" that she could smell the onion and tuna fish on his breath.

"What's your solution?" Robby asked from behind her.

"We need to put him in a home," Veronica said, inches from the camera. "Here! I have the papers!" She swung around toward Robby, using her script as a prop, and hit the camera in the nose.

"Ow!" the boy yelped. He held his nose and began to sway comically. The class giggled.

"Not so big," Larry cautioned too late. "You almost knocked the camera over."

"Oh, I'm sorry!" Veronica was horrified. *Quel dommage!*

"That's okay, keep going."

Veronica aimed herself at the stool and took a couple of steps forward.

"Uh, uh, uh!" Larry said, wagging his fingers. "You just stepped on the dolly tracks."

Veronica hopped back self-consciously. "Sorry!"

"And now you're standing on a light."

The class tittered as Veronica ducked reflexively. *Okay, this is harder than I thought,* she admitted. There was no place left to move. "Can I start over?" she pleaded.

Larry dismissed Veronica with a quick smile. "Good try, New Girl." His gaze swept the room. "Who's next?"

Later, Reed tried to comfort Veronica as she drove them home.

"I told you it was hard," she clucked. "But don't worry. Next time it will be better."

Veronica leaned her head against the window and a shiny residue appeared where her skin smushed against the glass. "There won't be a next time," she moaned. "I can never go back there. I totally embarrassed myself."

"Sure you can, Vee. You have to go back. You have to keep trying."

"I hit that kid in the face!" Veronica exclaimed. "His nose will probably swell."

Reed laughed. "That was kind of funny."

"Thanks for the support."

"You can't worry about other people," Reed said. She put on her signal and sat in the left turn lane at Gower and Hollywood Boulevard. "It's their own fault if they get in your way."

When the light turned red, Reed zoomed through the intersection on the tail of the car ahead of her. "Driving lesson number one: In

L.A., two cars always go left after the light turns red. And when the guy ahead of you doesn't go, you have to honk at him so he knows he's wrong."

Veronica nodded absently, paying more attention to the thoughts swirling in her brain than the traffic patterns on the street.

Not so big, she heard in her head. *Not so big!* Why had her arm done that anyway? Why had it flung itself so randomly, seemingly on its own?

Because that's what we do on stage, Veronica's brain answered. *That's what we were trained to do for many years, so the people in the cheap seats can see what we're doing.*

She set her lips in a grim line. *Well that's not the way we're doing things now*, she argued with herself. *We're trying to be a movie actor now.*

"Here we are!" Reed announced as she shifted the car into park and grabbed her purse.

Veronica picked her head up from the window. "Where?"

"Mayfair," Reed said. "We're gonna get you a little pick-me-up."

"Me?" Veronica roused herself and followed Reed out of the car.

Mayfair, she learned, was an upscale grocery store on Franklin Avenue in Hollywood.

"The Church of Scientology's Celebrity Centre is right down there," Reed said, pointing back toward the street. "They let normal people in for brunch on Sundays."

"Were you there? What's it like?" Veronica asked, hoping for some inside scoop on the secretive organization. "Did you see Tom and Katie?"

"I haven't been," Reed said. "Bianca says it's for weak-minded people." She stepped across the grocery store's threshold and scanned the bakery area first. "Snag one of those baskets, would you, please?"

Veronica took a plastic basket from a stack by the door. "What are we buying?" This was one area she was comfortable in, the purchasing of food items. She was fairly certain she wouldn't smack anyone in the nose with a bag of Fritos.

"Can't decide," Reed said, moving slowly yet purposefully through the produce section. She stopped to squeeze a cantaloupe while simultaneously glancing around the fruits and vegetables. "We could blend some fruit smoothies."

"With ice cream?" Veronica asked hopefully, but Reed laughed.

"That kind of defeats the fruit part," Reed replied with a grin. "But this is to cheer *you* up, so let's get what you want." She waved a hand at the produce. "Pick something out and we'll make it happen."

Veronica picked up a peach and rolled it in her palm. Not quite ripe. She picked up another. "Remember our freshman year when we skipped school to go shopping at the mall, and we got nabbed in the food court by our home ec teacher?"

Reed paused and tilted her head to one side in thought. "Yeah. What was her name again?"

"Morales," Veronica answered promptly. "Mrs. Morales. She used to drive a minivan covered in bumper stickers. They all had to do with vegetarianism."

Reed bagged a head of Romaine lettuce. "How do you remember all of this?"

"I don't know," Veronica said. "I just . . . I liked her, I guess. She taught me to cook." She found a peach that was slightly soft to the touch and put that in a bag. A blend of peaches and strawberries with a pint of Ben & Jerry's vanilla would be a perfect treat. Maybe a hint of chocolate? Maybe.

"Hey," Reed whispered. "Salad bar."

"I really don't want—"

"At the salad bar."

Veronica followed Reed's gaze toward the back of a guy at the salad bar. He was reaching across the containers of veggies—under the sneeze guard! Veronica wrinkled her nose with disgust. Didn't he see that plastic shield his head was bumping into? Didn't he understand that he was contaminating all of the croutons by brushing his mangy T-shirt over them? Didn't he realize his hair falling into the bowl of—

Didn't *she* see that she was staring at a major television star?

"Vee! That's the guy from that show!" Veronica clutched at Reed's arm.

Reed poked her in the ribs. "Go talk to him."

"Me? Are you insane? I can't talk to him!" Veronica busied herself with the peaches.

"Come on, Vee," Reed tugged on her arm. "You have to maximize your opportunities. Remember? Plus, you have to have *some* fun. This is Hollywood! Go talk to a celebrity."

"But what would I say?" Veronica rolled another fruit around in her hand.

"Just imagine we're at Charlie's back home," Reed suggested. "And he's one of the Carls, drunk and spitting peanut shells onto the floor."

"Neither of the Carls ever looked like that," Veronica protested.

Reed poked her in the ribs. "Go on. Before he leaves the salad bar." She took Veronica's bag of peaches and gave her a little push.

But what will I say? The walk to the salad bar didn't take nearly long enough for Veronica to think of something clever. Her feet got her there in about three seconds.

Up close, the TV star did not look like a Carl or any other average human. Even under ugly fluorescent lights, he had sparkle. His skin was perfectly smooth with just the hint of a five o'clock shadow, and his hair, although it looked from a distance like it had been cut with garden shears, was actually quite stylish. And that mangy T-shirt probably cost a hundred bucks.

"Um . . ." Veronica said, hoping that would be witty enough to get a conversation going.

The star turned to her and smiled. His teeth were immensely white. He looked like he had just stepped out of a dentist's chair or a toothpaste commercial.

"I . . . um, I . . . love tomatoes, don't you?" Veronica said.

The star nodded and continued filling his plastic box.

Veronica took that as a sign to continue. "Have you ever had the Minnie Pearls?"

"The what?" he asked, the corners of his eyes crinkling into a smile.

"The Minnie Pearls," Veronica said, blushing as she said it. "They're a particular kind of tomato." She could tell he was intrigued; who wouldn't be when it came to these sweet little things? "They're, you know, tiny. *Très petite.*"

"Tiny?" he asked. He held his thumb and forefinger about an inch apart.

"Yes, tiny," she replied, repeating the gesture with a giggle. She looked around the salad bar. "There they are. You should try some. They're delicious."

"Which are they?" The actor's eyes were on her as she pointed to the Minnie Pearls.

"Those . . . right . . . there." Veronica reached under the sneeze guard to get the tomatoes and her arm brushed his.

Veronica gasped. Electricity shot through her. Her arm had touched a TV star's!

He used the tongs to grab a few of the tasty tomatoes. "Thanks for the tip," he said.

Veronica blushed. "No problem."

"So, where are you fr—"

And then Reed was by her side. "Let me help you, Vee," she said cheerfully. She looked up at the actor and smiled, cute as a button. Then she surveyed his tray. "Oh, you really should have picked more greens."

He smiled back. "I don't like greens."

Reed feigned shock. "Oh, but you should. They'll help you live forever!" She picked up a plastic box and sidled up next to the television star. "Here let me help you."

Veronica continued to stare, watching in awe as Little Vee made her move. If the past was any indication, the actor would soon fall under Reed's spell. Yet she wondered, if Reed hadn't come over, would *she*—

Veronica shook her head. No, that was silly.

She turned and wandered over to the bakery section. Part of her was thrilled to have met such a handsome and popular celebrity. The other part of her decided, *Screw the fruit smoothie.* Suddenly she needed a huge slice of chocolate cake.

chapter 14

t was 7:30 in the morning when Veronica's cell phone rang. She rolled over the inflatable bed and tried to snatch it before it woke Reed up. They had been up late the night before, strategizing Veronica's next career move, and Reed had wanted to sleep late.

Veronica didn't recognize the number. "Hello?"

"Hello, this is May Sanchez. May I speak with Veronica, please?"

"May May?" Veronica shook her head. Impeccable phone manners, that woman had. "You're calling my cell. Who else would answer?"

"Oh Veronica, it's May Sanchez."

"Yes, I know." She rolled her eyes. "Is everything alright?"

"Oh, everything's fine. How are you?"

"I'm fine." Veronica struggled to rise from the floor. She glanced over at Reed, fast asleep, and decided to take the phone out into the hall. The sun had not yet warmed the concrete steps, and a chill shot up from her toes through her legs as she went downstairs.

"Are you still staying with Vivian?"

"It's just Reed now."

"*Perdon?*"

"Never mind. I'll send you an email about it." She sat down on the bottom step, crossed her arms over her chest and pulled her T-shirt tighter. "Yes, I'm still with Vivian."

"Is it a nice place?"

Veronica looked around the apartment complex. The walls were overgrown with vines, weeds poked up through cracks in the side-walk, and there were candy wrappers and empty soda cups in the bushes. "It's very nice, May."

"Have you found acting work yet?"

"Well, there's so much to be done first. Head shots, classes. It's not that easy."

"But you're so *good*," May May said.

Veronica smiled reluctantly. Why did May May have to be so *nice*? "It's okay. I've been pretty busy."

"*Que bueno.*" Veronica heard a light, sweet sigh from May. "You know, I had to make my own way too. When I came to the States, I had no parents, no friends, no nuns. But I've learned some things. I could perhaps guide you . . ."

Veronica allowed May May's voice to trail off to an awkward end. Did she really think Veronica would need her help so quickly? How helpless did she and Daddy assume she was?

"Well . . ." May said. There was a further pause, as if she were about to add something or ask another question.

Veronica decided to speed things up. "Was there anything else?"

"No, no, nothing," May May said. "It's been almost two weeks. I . . . I missed you."

"Oh," Veronica said.

"The ladies at the library are throwing me a shower next month," May said, the words tumbling out in a rush. Then her voice grew timid. "Do you think you can come?"

Veronica closed her eyes. *Next* month? Oh no, that wasn't nearly enough time. She needed to return to Chester on her own terms and when she could prove she wasn't a flailing idiot.

"I don't think so, May. Sorry."

"That's fine," May said quickly. "You can see them all at the wedding then."

"I'm sorry, May."

Veronica heard soft breathing on the line. "Do you need any money, sweetheart?"

"I'm fine," Veronica said.

"It can be just between you and me," May May added.

"I'm *fine*."

"Can I tell your father you said hello?"

"Um . . . well . . ." Veronica and her father hadn't spoken—not since she told him she was leaving for L.A. to follow in her mother's footsteps. "Tell him anything you want."

"Okay, sweetheart. *Adios, mi hija.*"

Veronica swallowed. She studied French in school, not Spanish, but she had picked up enough of the language from Val over the years to understand what May had said. *Goodbye, my daughter.*

Veronica thought of Diana's letters upstairs in Reed's apartment, each one filled with hope and passion and a longing for something that Veronica shared—something that was in their blood.

No. May Sanchez is not my mother, she thought. *Diana was.*

"Goodbye, May."

Veronica stared at the phone before she clicked it off.

She found the next letter from Diana in the early morning mail. Included with the letter was a postcard from Ginny: a photograph of wind-swept sand dunes and the caption, *World's Largest Beach, Yuma, Arizona.* "Having a great time, wish you were here!" Ginny wrote.

High-larious, Veronica thought, and opened her mother's July 25 letter.

> *Dearest Moose,*
>
> *Of course I remember the carnival we went to last May. How could I forget? The Kiwanis Club held it near the lake right next to Patty's Produce where we got those wonderful melons. I still have the pink teddy bear you won for me at the bottle toss. I keep him right on my bed—I even sprayed it with your cologne!*

Veronica winced. Her father's current cologne was reminiscent of rancid oil; she hoped he smelled a lot better twenty years ago.

> *I promise we'll have lots of fun when you come visit. I'll take you to the fancy-schmancy parts of town where I swear I'll live someday! There's so much to do here!*

Exactly, Veronica thought. *So much to do, so many possibilities!* She smiled to herself and hopped off to the shower to get started on the day.

* * *

Around noontime, Reed placed two glasses of ice on the coffee table, along with several packets of Splenda, and took a seat next to Veronica on the couch. She handed an iced tea to Veronica and opened a bottled water for herself.

"Thank you, sweetie," Veronica said as she took a grateful sip. It was hotter than Hades in Reed's apartment—or apartmentette as Veronica had come to think of it—and she had naught but a small fan to circulate the heavy air. "I have to make you Val's fantastic iced tea. The secret is . . ." she lowered her voice to a conspiratorial whisper. "You don't boil the water." She placed a finger to her lips, "*shhh*."

Reed winked. "Gotcha."

Spread before them were two manila envelopes which held 100 copies each of their 8" x 10" glossies and two stacks of resumes, a pile of envelopes, a stapler, a couple of black Sharpies and loads of stamps.

"When casting directors of the future accept electronic head shots," Reed was saying, "that will be a great day for actors everywhere."

"And for trees," Veronica agreed.

"Okay, so you take your head shot." Reed held up one of her prints—a gorgeous black and white photo of her perched on Andre's stool—by the white edging. "And you take your resume." She slid a sheet off her stack. "And you staple them together." She demonstrated. "One staple in each corner."

"Won't the metal scrape their fingers?" Veronica asked. The last thing she wanted to do was to irritate a casting director by drawing blood. "Wouldn't it be better to glue them?"

"This is the way it's done, Vee. Trust me." She picked up an envelope and slipped it inside. "We use our Sharpies and write out the address on the front. Easy enough?"

Easy-peasy, Veronica thought. She slapped her hands together. "Now where do we get the addresses?"

"Start here." Reed threw a stack of *Backstage* magazines on the table. She showed Veronica the casting notices at the back. "You have to look for the ones that say nonunion or independent or open call. Those are the ones you can submit your head shot to."

"And there's nothing online?" Veronica asked.

"Oh no," Reed insisted. "When it comes to casting, this town is totally old-school."

"Wow. You'd think there'd be auditions all over the Internet."

"Trust me. There aren't."

"Huh. Okay." Veronica pulled one of the *Backstage* magazines off the stack. "I thought you had an agent. Why are you sending out your own head shots?"

"My arrangement with Marilyn is what they call a 'hip pocket.' That means that I haven't signed with her, but if I find a job that I want her to submit me for, she'll act as my agent," Reed explained. "And then if I get the job, she'll take her ten percent."

"I think I'm working the wrong end of things," Veronica said with a grin. She scanned the pages of *Backstage*. "Well, there seem to be a lot of jobs."

"True, but there are also a *lot* of actors." Reed gave her a supportive smile. "Don't worry, Vee. You'll get *something*. It might not be, you know, the starring role you're used to."

"Oh yes, sure," Veronica said quickly. "I totally understand. I have to start somewhere."

"Movie-acting is, like, way different from the stage," Reed said. She offered Veronica a packet of Splenda, but Veronica shook her head. "It's all done in bits and pieces. Sometimes it's not even done in the right order."

"That sounds confusing."

"It can be." Reed stirred her water with a Sharpie. "God, I really want to get in a movie."

"I thought you'd done movies."

"Scenes," Reed corrected her. "Extras work. I want, you know, a *role*. Something that will get me in magazines and noticed by millions of people."

Veronica laughed a little. "I'm sure you will, sweetie." She examined one of Reed's completed head shot/resume packages to compare to her own. *Roles: Jan* — Grease, *Chester Community Theater Fall Production, Chester, AZ. Hermia* — A Midsummer Night's Dream. *Stella* — A Streetcar Named Desire . . .

Veronica remembered that last one quite well. She, cast as Blanche, and Little Vee, as Stella, had brought down the house.

"Do you remember in junior high when we'd wear big hats and sunglasses and pretend to be movie stars?" Reed asked.

"Hmm?" Veronica's eyes continued to scan. *Juliet,* Romeo and Juliet, *CCT Spring Production, Chester, AZ.*

Well that certainly wasn't right. Little Vee was here in L.A. while Veronica was playing Juliet back home. How silly! The information must have accidentally copied over to Reed's resume when Veronica had cut and pasted from Reed's computer.

One of those weird techie glitches, Veronica figured.

"What did you say?" she asked.

"The big hats and glasses?" Reed prompted.

"Oh my god, yes! And we'd prance around my backyard with our skirts rolled up to our thighs and make Ginny be the paparazzi! Man, that was—" Out of the corner of her eye, Veronica caught another line on Reed's resume: *Awarded the Leslie Chapman Distinction in Acting Prize, Chester High School. 2006, 2007, 2008.*

What? But the Chapman award had been given to *Veronica*, not to Reed. Three years in a row, in fact. Veronica was puzzled.

"Val was Miss Chester back then, wasn't she?" Reed reminisced. "God, she was beautiful."

"Um, Vee, sweetie?" Veronica started cautiously. She didn't want to come across as accusatory, in case it *was* some kind of computer error. "Your resume lists the Chapman award."

"Oh yeah." Reed looked away, a sheepish grin on her face. "When I got out here, I didn't have anything unique on my resume so I just, you know . . ." She looked up at Veronica. "Do you mind terribly?"

"Well, I . . ." Veronica pointed to the resume. "My roles in CCT too?"

"Come on. Can't we share, Vee?" Reed pleaded. "They never even look at those things anyway. They just want to see an accumulation of credits."

Reed paused. "It's not like we'll be up for the same roles anyway. And you know, theater is dead in this town. No one will know the difference."

Veronica said nothing. In the silence, the mood in the room became decidedly somber. "You know, it's funny," she finally said. "When we were in high school, I never thought you'd be the one who'd go to L.A."

"How do you mean?" Reed asked.

"You never seemed to want to study lines or do the acting exercises Jim Neece gave us." Veronica shrugged. "I didn't think you even liked it. Not until I—"

The phone rang then, and Veronica thought she caught a look of relief on Reed's face.

Reed glanced at caller ID and said, "Sorry. I have to take this."

She opened the sliding glass door and stepped onto the balcony.

Veronica looked at her head shot next to Reed's. She had chosen not a full body shot but one that was strictly head and shoulders. Her hair looked good in this picture, soft and wavy around her face, and she finally looked like she'd had enough sleep: no puffy bags under her eyes, no dark circles or crow's feet. In this one, her head was tilted down, her eyes looked up under long dark lashes. Andre couldn't have known, of course, but this shot was reminiscent of Veronica's infamous Dip. Alas, if only the shot had been in color, then everyone would see her violet eyes.

Veronica suddenly slapped the pictures down. *Why had Little Vee lied on her resume?* she wondered. *And really,* did *it matter?* As Reed had said, it was unlikely they would be up for the same roles, seeing as how they never were back in Arizona. They were such different actors, different in temperament, different in style.

So why had Little Vee lied? Veronica asked herself again.

It didn't *matter,* she decided. Her resumes and head shots would be out in the world soon enough, and that's what she needed to focus on. She would have auditions and jobs of her own, and once she was successful, this was something she and Vee would laugh about over brunch at the Ivy.

"What's past is past," she said aloud as she searched the casting notices. Look, there was one for her! *Actress, 16-24, for nonunion commercial. Must have driver's license.* She circled the ad with Reed's Sharpie. Yes, indeed, she had a great future to look forward to. Starting right now.

chapter 15

Reed's yoga studio was on Fairfax near Santa Monica, on the second floor above a Big and Tall Men's clothing store. The irony was not lost on Veronica.

Reed had left the apartment just as Veronica was waking up that morning, announcing she had a callback for the commercial she had auditioned for the week before.

"Meet me for yoga," Reed had said before leaving. "It will totally rejuvenate you."

At 8 A.M., Veronica was thinking more along the lines of the rejuvenating effects of a shot of caffeine rather than eastern philosophy, but she agreed nevertheless.

Around noon, she found Reed stretching at the front of the yoga studio. She patted a mat beside her when she saw Veronica.

"Oh my god, I'm gonna hate this, aren't I?" Veronica asked.

"Stop. You'll be fine." Reed's outfit today was a pair of slim black pants that rode low on her waist and flared at the ankles. She wore a black crop top that revealed a firm midriff and taut biceps. Veronica felt her own biceps through her T-shirt. "Taut" was not the word that came to mind.

"I had no idea you were so spiritual, Vee," Veronica marveled. "Is this something you discovered about yourself when you came out to L.A.?"

Reed flapped a hand at her as she slid into a straddle split. "This isn't that sort of yoga." She lowered her voice upon hitting the floor. "Seriously, Vee, the best part about this class is who's in it—all industry people. And since it's *not* industry related, it shows you have depth. People *love* depth." She nodded knowingly.

"Oh yeah, sure," Veronica agreed.

The instructor was an African American man in his thirties with long dreadlocks tied into a ponytail. He was wearing what looked to Veronica like loose-fitting pajamas. "Good afternoon," he said in a sexy, late-night DJ voice. "I'm Jamal. Let's begin."

Veronica followed Reed for the first few poses: the cat pose, the downward facing dog, the plank. *This wasn't so bad,* she thought. In fact, it felt pretty good. She mimicked Reed as she breathed into her back and exhaled loudly when Jamal told them to.

As she moved into the cobra position with her arms straight by her sides and her chin to the ceiling, Veronica had an epiphany of sorts. A physical epiphany. She felt all the tension in her muscles release and her back expand. She felt suddenly taller, more open and calm. A rush of exercise-induced endorphins flooded her brain.

God, this feels good, she thought, and heard herself inadvertently sigh aloud. "Ahhh."

She saw Jamal turn to her out of the corner of her eye and

wondered if it was rude—or worse, tacky—to sigh in yoga class. She couldn't help it! She sighed again, "Ahhh."

"Very nice," she heard in her ear. It was Jamal. He placed his hand against her back and pushed down. "Exhale. All the way. That's it."

His dreads smelled like citrus, she noticed, like orange and lime with a hint of peppermint. She suspected it was his shampoo, but she'd rather believe it was his own sweaty essence.

"Now straighten up and we'll do the forward bend," Jamal said. Veronica expected him to move away from her and onto the next student, but he remained by her side. She felt his hand on the back of her knee, and it should have tickled but didn't.

"Very good," he purred. "Pull up through your navel as you hang over to the floor. That's it. Hands flat on the floor. Now shake your head. Good. Keep it free."

Veronica let her head fall to her kneecaps. She had *no idea* she could touch her head to her knees. *Mon dieu!* She wanted to tap Reed on the shoulder and cry, "Look at me, I'm bending!" But wisely, she kept her mouth shut.

"Roll up to a standing position," Jamal instructed. He was still beside Veronica's mat. "Hands over head. And reach. Go ahead, bigger," he told her.

Ohh, yeah, *that was* it, Veronica thought. *Fantastique!*

By the time they were all lying in the corpse position, flat on their backs, hands by their sides, eyes closed, Veronica was simultaneously energized and relaxed.

"Vee," Reed said into her ear. "Ready to go?"

"Huh?" Veronica sat up and looked around. The other students were rolling their mats and toweling off. "Oh yes, I'm ready."

She wanted to thank Jamal—no, she wanted to follow him home

and worship him for introducing her to this wonderful thing. "Where's Jamal?" she asked Reed.

"With his groupies," Reed answered, gesturing to the back of the room where the teacher was surrounded by attractive, yet sweaty, young women.

Veronica smiled. "He's fabulous."

Reed shrugged. "He's all right. Smells funny, if you ask me."

Veronica followed Reed out of the classroom and down the stairs. "Was there anyone here you wanted to see, Vee?"

"Not today. Besides, this was the beginner class. I don't usually come to this one."

"Oh."

"I usually do the power yoga class."

"Oh," Veronica felt her sense of accomplishment shrink to the size of a pea.

"Come on. Let's go to the Coffee Bean on Sunset. It's *the* coffee place," Reed insisted as she wiped her pert face down with a hand towel.

The old adage, "Men perspire, women glow" was certainly true for Vivian Reed. Her skin glistened and her hair, rather than being matted down from wetness, seemed to actually spring to life, looking like she just ran some product through it. *How was that even possible?* Veronica wanted to know.

She checked her reflection in the mirror before they left the building. Her ponytail had gotten smooshed from yoga-ing on it, and bitty fly-aways were sticking out in a million different directions. Her clothes were actually—ugh!—wet in places. "Um, I look kind of—"

"No worries," Reed interrupted. "No one will even notice."

"Are you sure?" Veronica asked ruefully.

Reed clicked open the car doors. "Absolutely."

Veronica spotted a hot pink ticket tucked under Reed's windshield wiper. She groaned for her friend. "That $11 class just turned into a $61 class," she said.

"Whatever." Reed whisked the ticket out and shoved it in her purse. "Hop in."

The Coffee Bean was teeming with rock star types and wannabe rock star types, this being Sunset Boulevard and all. It even had valet parking, which was a huge clue as to its clientele. People here were not stopping on their way to someplace else. *This* was their destination. They dressed up and made up and caffeined up so they could spend hours sitting on the patio in plastic chairs, greeting neighbors and creating a community of their peers.

Reed and Veronica strode to the counter. Reed ordered an Ice Blended, the chain's signature drink and then looked at Veronica expectantly. Veronica bit her lip and squinted at the menu board. Those prices! Money was getting tight. Very, very tight. She was certain an audition—and a fantastic, high-paying job—would come through momentarily, but until then, she really shouldn't splurge.

"Um, I don't think I—"

"It's on me," Reed cut her off. "I got another industrial job. You know, one of those employee training videos? It's not the movies, but it pays decent. Besides, Big Vee, you need a treat. That was a tough class."

It was, Veronica agreed, grateful for the acknowledgment and the treat, and placed her order—a Caramel Ice Blended with a drizzle of chocolate. They retrieved their drinks from the bar and made their way to the patio.

At a prime corner table, Reed and Veronica found Bianca, a vision in turquoise-studded jeans and a gauzy poet's blouse, smoking a long white cigarette and talking on her cell. She was not drinking a Blended, Veronica noticed, but had a cup of ice with a straw. She chuckled to herself. *Must be lunch* and *dinner,* she thought.

Bianca nodded to the girls and finished her conversation as they arranged themselves at the table. "Yes, yes, I'll be there . . . eight hundred. No, eight." She rolled her eyes. "It was eight yesterday. It will be nine in one minute . . ." She smiled. "See you then."

She clicked shut her phone. "Hello, dears. Have a good yoga class?"

Veronica looked at Reed before answering. "It was a little fast for me."

"She did great," Reed said dismissively. "Jamal was all over her."

Bianca raised a finely manicured eyebrow. "Oh, *really?*"

Veronica blushed. "I wouldn't say *all* over—"

"Meet anyone else?" Bianca asked Veronica, as if it had been a bar instead of a sweat lodge.

"No. I was so busy concentrating on my poses, I could barely look up," she joked.

To Reed, Bianca asked, "Was Lauren there?"

Reed shook her head.

"Lauren?" Veronica wondered. "Who's Lauren?"

"She casts for *The Real World,*" Reed said. "I would *kill* to get on a reality show."

Veronica didn't think "acting" had much to do with "reality," but she was still new at this. She would have to defer to Reed and Bianca.

"At the table in blue," Bianca said, staring at Reed. "Next to the Ashton Kutcher lookalike. No, don't turn yet. He's looking over here." Bianca forced a laugh and then stopped. "Okay, look now. Blue shirt, white jeans. God, white jeans are so queer. Whatever.

That's the producer of JJ Abrams's next movie."

Reed and Veronica discreetly turned their heads. He was an ordinary guy, in ordinary clothes, drinking a—yes, an Ice Blended. But what made him stand out were all the beautiful men and women he was sitting with.

"His name is Trey. Friends call him T. And he *loves* short blondes." Bianca tapped Reed on the hand. "Introduce yourself. Say something witty and then have Marilyn send your head shot. Go."

Reed faced Veronica and licked her lips. "Is my makeup okay?"

Veronica squeezed Reed's knee tenderly. "You're gorgeous."

She watched as Reed casually approached Trey's table, her petite but perfect figure drawing the eyes of the better-looking men in the vicinity, but she never let her gaze wander from the producer's face. Within seconds, she was seated at his table.

Veronica shook her head with an awed smile. "How does she do it?" she asked Bianca, not expecting a response.

But the diva had one. "She works very hard at it." She lit a fresh cigarette. "You can do the same. If you're willing to work."

"Me?" Veronica laughed. "I don't think so. Reed has that, you know, that *je ne sais quoi.*"

Bianca pushed her sunglasses up the bridge of her nose with her cigarette hand, leaving a trail of smoke in their reflection. Veronica felt like the woman was studying her behind the oversized designer shades, and she fidgeted, uncomfortable under the scrutiny.

"Sixty pounds."

"Excuse me?"

"You're five-eight? Five-nine?"

"Uh, five eight and a half."

"Lose sixty pounds and you can have what Reed has." Bianca

waved her cigarette at Veronica. "You're pretty, maybe prettier than her, though it's hard to tell with all that hair of yours." She shrugged. "It's just the weight."

Veronica snorted and crossed her arms over her chest. "That's it, huh? I'm supposed to just lose sixty pounds? And how do I do that?"

Bianca held her cigarette up like an icon. "Smoking. Diet. Lipo. Stomach stapling. It'll be gone in no time."

"But . . ."

"But what?"

Veronica was dumbfounded. She glanced around her, at the Size Ones and Zeroes at the café's tables. They were all dressed in the same hip uniform of low-slung jeans, tight tops and high-heeled slingbacks. Highlighted and product-spiked hair was pulled back, tied up, or cut short to reveal hoop earrings dangling from their ears. Collarbones jutted sharply from their necks; ribs protruded from their chests. They all looked designed . . . identical.

"You want what she has, don't you?" Veronica heard Bianca ask.

Don't you? Veronica thought. At that moment, she remembered her mother's words. *I just know I'll be someone special in L.A.*

"Yes," she answered. "I do."

chapter 16

Veronica opened her email three days later to find a letter from Ginny with the subject line all in caps: *DOUBLE STANDARD!!!*

She grinned as she clicked on the email, readying herself for one of her Vee's amazing rants—and she was not disappointed:

Name one fat actress—Kirstie Alley doesn't count because she was only temporarily fat. Go ahead, do it. I bet you'll say something like, "That woman in Gilbert Grape*" or "That actress on* Drew Carey*," but you don't know their names, do you?*

Veronica considered the challenge. Roseanne was one name that came to mind, or Rosie, or Oprah. She went back to the letter.

Now go ahead and name fat actors. I can give you about ten off the top of my head: John Goodman, Jack Black, Horatio Sanz, Kevin James . . . and those are the live ones. What about the dead ones? John Candy, John Belushi, Chris Farley, Marlon Brando, Orson Welles. And those are huge names! Not so for women. Everyone talks about ageism in Hollywood and how men can be a hundred years old and still get Jessica Biel as a love interest.

But what about fat-ism? Everywhere you look, big fat guys get hot chicks in movies and on TV, but have you ever seen a fat girl get a normal guy? NO!

Vee, you have to do your part to combat this. Don't listen to that stupid model. Stay strong! Stay you. I'm counting on you! We're all counting on you!

Veronica smiled. "I'll do my best," she told her computer and then opened her mail.

The next letter from Diana was dated August 1, 1989. It began much the same as the others.

Dearest Moose,

I'm sorry I haven't been in touch, but things here have gotten really busy. To answer your first question: No, I didn't get that role. The choreographer was really nice, but the casting director didn't like me. She said they were looking for younger dancers. Honestly! I won't turn 20 until next year! How much younger did she want?

To answer your second question: No, I can't come home for a visit yet. Maybe in the fall but I can't promise anything right now. Who knows what will be going on then? I have to be available to go on any auditions I get and to start work when they need me to.

I got your check. Thank you. But please don't think you have to send money. I'm going to be very successful, you'll see. I have another audition lined up for tomorrow morning for a television commercial. Once again, keep your fingers crossed for me!

Yours always, Diana

Veronica smiled. So her mother had struggled with money as well! It was all a part of the experience, she supposed.

She just had to keep her chin up. Things would change for her soon—she could feel it.

The intermediate acting class Reed attended was held in a tiny black box theater on Melrose, tucked between two Chinese restaurants. The students sat in folding chairs in front of the small stage.

"Let's sit down front near the teacher," Reed said. "I think she likes me."

Finally, Veronica would have an opportunity to test her acting skills. She had been pursuing all the activities Reed was certain would help her meet people and get acting jobs, and she had been sending out her head shots to every listing in *Backstage*. But no actual *acting* had been taking place, and Veronica was beginning to wonder if she was as good as she thought she was. This class would be the turning point for her; it would tell her whether she was wasting her time or not.

"Did everyone sign in?" asked a female voice from the stage floor. The woman looked about forty-five or so with wavy brown hair that looked like she cut it herself while blindfolded. She wore black leggings with a long loose shirt over them and little blue ballet flats.

"That's Midora," Reed told Veronica. "She's the best. Everyone wants to take her class."

"Let's begin," Midora said and closed her eyes. "God grant me the serenity to accept the things I cannot change . . ."

"It's the AA prayer," Reed whispered.

"These people are alcoholics?" Veronica whispered back.

". . . the courage to change the things I can . . ."

"Midora met the original group at an AA meeting and it kind of blossomed." Reed peeled open one eye. "Those meetings are awesome. They can totally jumpstart your career."

"But you have to be an addict," Veronica said, wondering how Reed came to know this group. "Alcohol or drugs, right?"

" . . . and the wisdom to know the difference."

"Oh, you can be addicted to just about anything these days," Reed said.

Midora consulted her notebook. "Let's pick up where we left off last week. Does everyone have their props for the repetition exercise? Summer and Yvette, will you start?"

Two Britney Spears-alikes hopped up from the audience and took seats in folding chairs onstage. One girl began crocheting while the other put on lipstick.

"You have a red blouse," said the crocheter.

"You have a red blouse," said the lipstick girl.

"You have a <u>red</u> blouse."

"You have a <u>red</u> blouse."

"You have a red <u>blouse</u>."

"You have a red <u>blouse</u>."

Veronica's brain swam and she thought she would soon go insane. "Um, Reed, honey . . ."

"It's a repetition exercise."

"I followed that much."

"The idea is to repeat what your partner is saying, allowing the emotion to come through, rather than the words, which are meaningless."

"Okay, I'm gonna stop you here," Midora said. "Very good, girls. Now, who can tell me what was missing from that? Reed?"

"They didn't incorporate their props," Reed said confidently.

"Very good. Who's next?" Midora looked at Veronica. "How about Reed's friend who was talking throughout the last exercise?"

"Me?" Veronica pointed to herself. "No, thank you. I'm just observing today."

"Nonsense. Life is to be lived, not observed. Come up here."

"Um, all right."

Reed started to follow but Midora called her back. "Let's have someone else work with your friend. That way you can watch and tell her what she did wrong later."

Such an unpleasant woman, Veronica thought. *No wonder she was stuck teaching alcoholics.*

Veronica's partner was Daka, an African American woman whose prop was a basket of laundry she was sorting and folding. *Acting certainly brought out the domesticity in people,* Veronica thought. She rummaged through her purse: lipstick, gum, map, emery board.

Despite her many years of acting exercises with Jim Neece, Veronica was nervous about this one. It was the whole *observational* thing of it. This girl, practically skeletal in appearance, could look at Veronica and say, well, she could say anything about her. Veronica waited for the girl to form her first sentence.

"Your hair is long," Daka said.

Veronica exhaled, relieved her partner was completely self-absorbed. "Your hair is . . . long." She stopped and turned to the teacher. "Do I have to say that? I mean, her hair is so obviously short."

"Words are meaningless," Midora said breezily. "It's the emotion behind the words. You can modify the statement, but the idea is to repeat what the other person is saying—"

"Hence the phrase, repetition exercise," Veronica said with a smile. "Got it."

"Your hair is long," Daka said again, folding a pair of socks.

"Your hair is not long," Veronica said. She drew the emery board across her nails.

"Your hair is not long."

"*I'm* filing my nails."

"*I'm* filing my nails."

The girl expended not one ounce of emotion. Flat delivery, rote repetition, absolutely no observational skills whatsoever. Veronica put the emery board back in her purse and took out her map of Hollywood.

Daka lifted her head. "You're reading a map."

Veronica nodded. "I'm reading a map." She traced a finger along Hollywood Boulevard, found the approximate location of Reed's apartment.

"You're reading a map of Hollywood," Daka said, intrigued.

Veronica stared at the grid of avenues and intersections. Where had her mother lived when she was here? An apartment off Beachwood, overlooking the city, surrounded by trees and birds and possibilities? Diana had hoped and dreamed here in Hollywood. Did she hope and dream what Veronica did?

Daka smiled and placed her finger on the various landmarks: the Capitol Building and the Hollywood sign and the Griffith Observatory.

126

Their eyes met and found a connection, the commonality that all actors in this town felt.

"Hollywood," Veronica sighed.

"Hollywood," Daka's eyes blinked away tears.

"Hollywood," Veronica said with a hopeful note in her voice.

"Hollywood," they said together.

The next sound Veronica heard was applause. First a single short burst and then more and louder. Even Midora was applauding.

Reed's mouth was open as Veronica returned to her seat. "Wow," she said. "That was good."

"Thanks."

"No one ever applauds in this class," Reed said quietly. "No one."

Yes! Veronica thought, raising an inner fist of triumph. She *was* good! She knew it. Now, she just needed the auditions to come and she would be all set.

chapter 17

Veronica's fingers clicked against the keys of her cell as she texted Val while sitting in traffic. "2nite vegan rest," she typed.

"Whas vegan?" Val wanted to know.

"Veg," Veronica wrote. "No dairy. No eggs. Nada from animals."

There was a long pause before Val replied.

"Whas left?"

Reed waved Veronica over from a round table in the center of the vegan restaurant. Lush greenery decorated a brick wall on one side of the place while black and white drawings covered the other. In the back of the restaurant, a vast kitchen with an open air wood-burning oven created a warm, inviting atmosphere, and the aroma was heady.

Seriously? Veronica thought to herself as she threaded her way among the tables. *No meat at all?*

As soon as she saw Reed with Bianca, Veronica immediately felt out of place. Had they texted each other what they were going to wear? Sent photos of their closets on their iPhones? They were both dressed in pastel-colored spaghetti-strap sundresses and kitten-heel mules while Veronica wore jeans and a T-shirt. Couldn't someone have told her this was a dressy place?

"I mailed your head shots out this afternoon," Reed said by way of greeting. "They'll probably arrive in a couple of days."

"You didn't have to do that," Veronica replied.

"I told you it's no big deal," Reed said. Her face was partially obscured by the menu she was handing Veronica. "The post office is right next to the place I get my pedis."

"Well, thanks again, sweetie," Veronica said. "I appreciate it."

"Now, let's talk appetizers," Reed said with a glorious smile. "What do you like?"

Veronica opened her recycled paper pulp menu and was faced with a long list of incomprehensible dishes. They all had names like "Garden Utopia" and "Buddha's Orgasm."

But *mon dieu*! The prices! Fifteen dollars for carrot sticks? Twenty for mushrooms? *Were these vegetables grown in outer space?* Veronica wondered. *Irrigated with Evian?*

"I'm sure whatever you choose will be delicious," she demurred, hoping she could fill up on bread and avoid ordering an entree.

"Oh, come on, Vee," Reed prodded. "You were always good at ordering in restaurants." She leaned closer to the table and addressed Bianca. "Veronica always knew exactly what went with what dish. She was like a pro orderer."

"Um, thanks, I guess." Veronica thought that was sort of an odd talent to have—and to notice.

"That's fascinating," Bianca remarked blandly. "Shall we?" She raised a single digit and a waiter rushed to her side.

"Yes, miss?" he asked.

The girls placed their order, and then Bianca turned to Reed.

"So, you called Trey?" she asked.

Reed nodded. "He said they weren't casting yet, but Marilyn should send my head shot."

"Did she?"

"I assume so."

Bianca sighed. "You can't count on these people, Reed. You know that. You have to get on them." She looked over at Veronica. "No one ever wants to do their job in this town."

"Is that right?" Veronica asked, intrigued.

"Everyone wants to be something else," Bianca replied. "Something other than what they're being paid to do." She waved her hand in the air as if it held a cigarette. "Agents want to be producers. Actors want to be directors . . ."

"Models want to be actors," Reed whispered to Veronica *sotto voce*.

"It's a huge pain to keep people in their place," Bianca said, totally without irony.

"Well, there's only one thing I want to do," Veronica said. "It's the only thing I've done my entire life. And that's act." She sat back in her chair and crossed her arms over her chest, as if daring the bony blonde to contradict her.

To Veronica's surprise, Bianca nodded her approval. "You have a passion. That's very important in L.A. You'll get eaten alive here without a commitment to your craft."

Veronica felt Reed tense up beside her; perhaps Little Vee was anxious to absorb the model's wisdom. It was the first smart thing Veronica believed she had heard come out of Bianca's mouth. She was about to thank her when the waiter arrived with the appetizer.

While Bianca and Reed stared at the dish and seemed to be

merely contemplating the consumption of food, Veronica took a generous portion, not caring if either girl noticed. *Not bad*, she thought as she sampled a bite of a baby pea pod. *This was actual food.*

"What's that I'm tasting?" she asked the girls. "Lemon or lime or—"

"Ginger," Reed said with a knowing nod. "Ginger is a very popular ingredient in vegan dishes. Restaurants around here cook with it in everything. It's a very sophisticated taste."

"Wow, what a difference a few months make," Veronica commented to Bianca. "Reed was the girl who loved sausage on her pizza."

"Sausage?" Reed's eyebrows lifted. She looked at Bianca. "I never eat sausage. Or pizza. Or any animal products. It's so degrading to us as humans to be eating animals."

Veronica chuckled. "Six months ago, you were scarfing down corn dogs and beer at Ginny's house."

"Beer? No way," Reed scowled. Her little pixie face screwed up in distaste.

"Yes, beer. With Fritos and Slim Jims," Veronica added. "They're your favorites."

"Veronica, honestly—"

Bianca interrupted them with a gentle cough. She took a single bite of a single carrot and rose from the table. "If you'll excuse me," she said and left them.

As soon as she was gone, Reed accosted Veronica. "What are you doing?"

"Excuse me?" Veronica asked. "Eating meat degrades us as humans? Who says things like that?"

"I don't know why you would want to put me down in front of Bianca—"

"I'm putting *you* down?" Veronica rolled her eyes. "You invited me to dinner with a woman who thinks I need to lose the equivalent weight of a second grader. To dinner, Vee. To eat actual food alongside her. Why would you do that?"

"Vee, honestly, I just want her to get to know you. You're my best friend from home and she's my best friend here," Reed insisted. "That's not a bad thing. That's a really good thing."

Veronica agreed with a hesitant nod. *It certainly didn't sound like a bad thing when Reed put it that way,* she thought. *But why did it seem so thoughtless in practice?*

"I'm sorry if it came out wrong," Reed said softly. "Maybe I don't say things in the nicest way." She put her hand over Veronica's. "But you know how I really mean them, don't you?"

Veronica sighed and smiled gently at Reed. "We're being silly. We've been friends for so long. " She took a deep breath and then slowly exhaled. "Let's forget all of this and have a nice dinner."

"Absolutely."

Bianca returned and sent the girls an inquisitive glance. "Everything all right here?"

Veronica noticed the model had touched up her lipstick and puffed up her coif, post-barf. But there was a distinct sour milk and lemon smell emanating from her. *The nasty price of staying skinny,* Veronica supposed.

"Yes, we're fine," Reed said with a smile for Veronica.

It was a simple case of being too close for comfort, Veronica thought—the result of living and hanging out together constantly since she had come to town. Once she was working and could get her own place, everything would sort itself out and the girls could go back to being the best Vees they could be.

"Yes," she agreed. "Totally fine."

chapter 18

The next of Diana's letters was dated August 10, which Veronica read on her own August 10. From it, she was able to glean some practical guidance.

My sweet Moose,

Good news for me! I think I might be able to get a waitress job over at Trader Vic's. It doesn't sound like much, but it's a real hotspot for the movie business people and it's hard to get a job there. Everyone you meet wants to be in the movies, and they all want to get their faces in front of casting directors and agents. I have an in, though, because one of my roommates is a cocktail waitress there, and she thinks they'll be hiring some new people.

I didn't want to have to wait tables, but if it means paying rent and putting food on the table, well, I guess I have to do it. I wish I could be with you, Moose, but right now, this is the place for me. I have to do this, *I need to do this. I'll be a happier person, don't you think?*

I know this is short but I have to go now. The girls and I are going out for drinks at this really popular club. Always looking for the contacts!

Yours, Diana

Veronica's share of the bill at the vegan restaurant had totally tapped her dry, and when she visited the ATM the next day, she was horrified to discover she had very few dollars left in her account.

"There was no meat!" she complained to Reed, who was sitting cross-legged in a yoga pose on the living room floor. "It was just vegetables and soy sauce."

"And ginger," Reed added. Her eyes were closed and her palms were turned upward, resting lightly on her knees.

"Is ginger worth fifty bucks a person?" Veronica grumbled.

The fact was, like her mother and lots of other actors in this town, she needed a job. But unlike her mother and all the other actors in this town, Veronica didn't have any waitress experience. Unless you counted her role last summer as Frankie in *Frankie and Johnny in the Clair de Lune.*

No, she thought, *that didn't really count.*

It had been nearly a month since she left Arizona. Veronica really *really* thought she would have had something by now. If not a job, at least several auditions and a callback or two. She was afraid this did not bode well for her future.

"I'm out of cash," she finally said to Reed. "All the classes and photos and postage have taken most of my savings." She swallowed hard. "I think I need to get a job."

Reed nodded sagely. "You'll go to Buzz."

"What's Buzz?"

"It's *the* coffee shop," Reed said.

"You told me Coffee Bean was *the* coffee shop," Veronica said.

"This is different. It's in West Hollywood and everyone gets a job there when they first come to town."

"Did you?"

Reed nodded.

"You never told me."

"It was just for a few months. Pretty much everyone leaves after a few months." Reed stood and continued stretching. "That's why they're always looking for people."

"Do you think they'll hire me?"

"Oh, sure," Reed said. "They'll hire anyone."

Buzz was one of a dozen gourmet coffee house chains with outlets scattered across Hollywood. According to Reed, the branch on Santa Monica Boulevard was very popular among the industry crowd. Writers with their laptops perched on green plastic chairs and composed their masterpieces with the help of the Super Grande Espresso Blend, while producers made deals with directors and agents over Iced Mocha Lattechinos.

And most of their employees were actors.

Reed introduced Veronica to the branch's manager, Philip Caton, her former boss.

"Hey Phil," Reed said when they walked in. "What's up, guy?"

Philip was behind the counter, counting cash in the register. He smiled when he recognized Reed. "Reed, hey. How've you been?"

"I've been awesome," Reed said. "This is my friend Veronica. She needs a job."

Veronica nearly melted when she saw Philip. He was exactly

what you wanted in a boss—or a boyfriend, or a husband, or even just the guy making your espresso. Tall and handsome, with wavy chestnut hair and eyes the color of Hershey's kisses. He couldn't have been more than twenty, but he had a maturity about him, a been-there-climbed-that sort of quality that Veronica hadn't seen up-close in someone so young.

Confidence, yes, that was it. He looked like a person who knew who he was and where he was going. As he reached out to shake Veronica's hand, as his fingers gripped hers, she felt a tingle of electricity light up her face. She certainly had never felt *that* when she shook Mr. Rosenbloom's hand back in Chester.

Confidence was sexy, she thought.

"Uh, hi," she said.

"So, who's still here?" Reed asked. "Is Louise around?"

"She left right after you did," Philip replied. "I think she got a job at Paramount."

"How about Craig and Gena?"

"Yep. But Gena will probably go by the end of the year." Philip glanced over at Veronica. "Lots of people say the first six months in this town are the most important. If you don't get something going for yourself right away, you'll have the next influx of émigrés to contend with."

"Don't scare her like that," Reed teased.

"What? It's true," Philip said with a laugh. "Just ask Donny. I'm sure you remember Donny."

Reed rolled her eyes. "Hell yeah." She addressed Veronica. "Donny's this weird conspiracy guy. Totally paranoid about everything. Don't be surprised if he thinks you're part of a secret government operation."

"Yes, everyone's out to get Donny," Philip said.

"That's funny," Veronica said. "And weird. Very weird."

"So you need a job, huh?" Philip asked. "Can you make coffee?" His smile was encouraging and warm, and Veronica thought she would probably agree then and there to just about anything he might suggest.

Can you build a nuclear power plant with a paper clip? I sure can!

Can you jump the Grand Canyon on a motorcycle? Name the date!

"Um . . ." Veronica giggled. Every word she had ever learned seemed to have utterly deserted her brain.

"She makes amazing coffee," Reed jumped in and saved her from complete embarrassment. "She can work a French press like you've never seen."

Philip smiled again.

Veronica melted again. Okay, that was it. She was officially in massive like with her new boss.

"Good enough for me." Philip tossed a green apron to Veronica. "Ready to start now?"

"Um . . ." Veronica looked to Reed.

"Yes, she is," Reed answered. "I've got to get to set, so I'll see you at home, okay?"

"Set?" Philip asked. "Are you on a shoot?"

"Just a commercial," Reed said breezily. "It's a nonunion thing."

"Good for you," he said.

"Yes, good for you, Vee," Veronica said. This was the first she had heard of it. Reed never told her she had actually gotten the job, let alone had scheduled the day of work. Maybe Little Vee was afraid she would be jealous, like she was lording her success over Veronica. Given how touchy Veronica had been at the restaurant the other night, she couldn't exactly blame Reed for being cautious.

Veronica gave her a big hug. "Thanks, sweetie. I'll see you later."

Reed left and Veronica wrapped the green apron over her T-shirt.

"Come on back here," Philip said. "I'll show you how we grind the beans."

Veronica made her way around the counter and stood behind him. The scent of coffee beans was overpowering. The caffeine in the air was making her light-headed.

Yes, the caffeine. That was it.

"This is our grinder," Philip was saying as he placed a hand on a huge machine. "On our busiest days, we grind the beans every twenty minutes for the house blend and every hour for the special blends."

"Uh-huh," Veronica replied, trying hard to concentrate on him—no! *Not him, Vee, his hand, watch the hand! Be a professional, please.* His hand, rough and masculine and probably tanned from running outdoors on a beach every day, scooped a cup of dark beans and poured them into the stainless steel cache. He pressed a button and the machine whirred, spitting out finely ground coffee into a plastic container.

"Then we take the grounds and pour them into the coffee machine." Philip deftly retrieved the coffee and upended the grounds into a filter basket. "Water is pumped in here and the whole process is automatic." He crossed his arms over his apron. "Got it?"

"I think so." *Easy-peasy,* she thought. "Is that it?"

Philip nodded. "That's the coffee part. Now you're gonna learn about espresso, so we can turn you into a barista."

"A what?"

"That's what you call a coffee server."

"*Barista.* I like that," she said with a smile.

"You do?"

"Ba*rrrrr*ista," she rolled her r's with her tongue against the roof of her mouth.

"I don't think I've heard anyone say it like that." Philip grinned. "I like your attitude."

Veronica beamed. *How long were these shifts anyway?* she wondered. *Could they be infinite? One long shift that never ended?*

"I have a good feeling about you, Veronica," Philip said. "I think you're gonna be a great addition to this team."

"Oh, really?" Veronica cocked her head to one side. "Well, then, we need to talk about this uniform. Are these natural fibers?"

Philip laughed. "We can negotiate your contract later." He led her to the other end of the counter. "Step right over here to our espresso machine."

Veronica followed a pace behind, swallowing a giggle. *Hee-hee!* His laughter was as intoxicating as applause. *Bring it on*, she thought. She had a good feeling about this job too.

And Philip.

Hee-hee!

Veronica arrived home late that afternoon, exhausted from learning coffee preparation, while Reed was still out. Sitting on her doorstep was a giant brown box addressed to her! Yay! She loved getting packages. Who, honestly, didn't love it? A package meant someone was sending you a gift. And even if it was something you ordered off the Internet, it was still a gift to *you*.

She immediately threw down her purse and kicked off her shoes. In the kitchen she found a knife which she used to slice through the packing tape.

"Ahh!" Veronica cried. "From the Vees!"

It was a care package from Ginny and Val! She pulled aside plastic bubble wrap to find a month's worth of food: Twinkies and Ring-Dings, chips and dips, pepperoni sticks and cheese logs. And in a small cooler were Val's specialties: frozen tacos and burritos, guacamole dip, green and red salsas, and homemade nachos.

"Just what I needed," Veronica said, plucking a nacho from the bag. "Ahhh . . ." She poured a Diet Coke, put the frozen food away in Reed's tiny fridge and placed the nonperishables in the child-size cabinets. She popped a taco in the toaster oven and called Ginny and Val on a conference call.

"Vee!" Ginny shouted. "We miss you!"

There was an echo of laughter and Val cried, "*Chica!* Did you like the package?"

"It's wonderful!" Veronica said. She flopped onto the easy chair and let her legs hang over the arm. "I'm cooking one of your tacos right now."

"I didn't send sour cream, sweetie," Val fretted. "Will you make do with guacamole?"

Veronica reached into the cooler and pulled out the tub of guacamole, then spooned a bite into her mouth. "I'm making do right now."

"How's everything?" Ginny wanted to know. "How's Vivian . . . I mean, Reed? Sorry, I still can't get over that."

"In the olden days," Veronica said, "movie stars used to change their names all the time. Cary Grant's real name was Archibald Leach."

"Don't say Cary Grant," superstitious Val scolded. "He's dead. Use someone who's alive."

"So where is she?" Ginny asked.

"She had a commercial shoot," Veronica said.

"A real acting job? Wow, I'm shocked," Ginny remarked.

"Why, Vee?"

"Because *you're* the actor. *You* should be getting the jobs, not her."

"Vee . . ."

"Sorry, sweetie, that's just how I feel."

"I'll get there," Veronica promised. "I send out head shots every day. Reed helps. I know I'll start getting auditions soon. Hey, I started a job today. At *the* coffee shop in town."

"How was it?" Ginny asked.

"Standing on your feet for hours, pouring coffee, flirting with cute guys. *Loads* of fun."

"Ooh!" Val said. "What cute guys?"

"Just one guy, actually. His name's Philip, the coffee shop manager."

"Vee's got a boyfriend," Ginny sang. "Vee's got a boyfriend."

"Don't be silly. He doesn't like me."

"He hired you, didn't he?" Ginny said.

"Only because Reed got me the job," Veronica reminded them.

"Maybe he thinks you're cute too," Ginny suggested.

"I didn't know there were cute guys at coffee shops," Val said. "Maybe I should get a job at one. I can make coffee. Papi loves my espresso."

"You have to be on your feet all day," Ginny said.

"Ooh! New shoes! I wonder if Marc Jacobs has an orthopedic line."

"Listen, girls," Veronica said, swinging her legs back to the floor. "I have to get my taco from the oven and get ready for tomorrow."

"What's tomorrow?" Ginny asked.

"More work with cute guys!"

"Have fun!" Val said.

"I will! Bye!" Veronica said with a reluctant smile. She clicked off her cell, and the apartment suddenly felt empty. The absence of Vees was startling.

"Come on, Big Vee," she told herself. "You should be used to this by now."

She hustled herself from the chair and went into the kitchen. Without even opening the oven, she could smell the melting cheese and seasoned ground beef. It was just like home.

There was another surprise inside the box, a letter from her mother. Veronica settled back into the easy chair and slid the letter from the envelope.

> *Dearest Moose,*
>
> *The funniest thing happened to me today when I was at work. A man left me a $20 tip for a $10 meal! Can you imagine? I hope he comes back tomorrow!*

Veronica laughed and took a bite of taco. She could use one of those customers herself.

chapter 19

A few days later, after the post-lunch crowd had gotten their caffeine fix for the afternoon, Philip stepped outside with a coffee and a cigarette while Veronica wiped down the counter. *Boy oh boy,* she thought, *for such a health-conscious city, there sure were a lot of people who smoked.* She watched him pace back and forth in front of the building.

A moment later a grimy homeless man approached Philip. Trailing behind him was a mutt with a sad face. Veronica watched as Philip shook the man's weather-beaten hand without flinching and then offered him a cigarette from his pack. Then he handed the man the coffee and a small to-go bag with the Buzz logo. The dog thumped a mangy tail as he sat patiently at Philip's feet. Philip bent down and offered the dog a bit of bread which the dog, like his owner, gratefully accepted.

"Who's that?" Veronica asked her coworker Craig. She was

embarrassed by the fear in her voice, but she hadn't had much experience with homeless people in Chester.

"That's Joe," Craig said. "Good guy. Hit a rough patch."

Veronica groaned. "So Philip's generous too? That's totally unfair."

"What do you mean?"

"I need him to be selfish so I won't like him as much."

Craig laughed. "Well, Frank the owner doesn't like Joe hanging around. So we have to keep it on the QT and protect our cutie."

To look at him, Veronica never would have expected Craig to be gay. Resembling a youngish Russell Crowe from his *Gladiator* days with a tanned and muscular torso, a lean waist and tree-trunk sized legs, Craig worked out at Gold's Gym in Venice, where he insisted he had been hit on by Vin Diesel.

And he had a huge crush on Philip, which meant he and Veronica always had something to talk about when they were alone.

"Don't you love the way he runs his hand through his hair when he's thinking?" Craig would start, his brown eyes mischievous and playful. "It's like he caresses every strand."

"I just like his hair," she would reply with a laugh.

"And his hands."

"And his shoulders."

"And his lips."

"And his butt!"

"Oh yes!" Craig would cry. "I love his butt!" Then he would hold his hands up like he was squeezing two melons in the air. "It's so round and tight, and he doesn't even work out!"

But of course they would say none of this when Philip was around.

Philip waved goodbye to Joe and his dog and entered the coffee shop then. He stepped up to the counter and looked at the menu behind Veronica and Craig.

Craig followed his steadfast gaze to the black chalkboard listing the coffee selections. "Something wrong, Phil?"

"I'm a customer," he announced.

"Oh, what can I get you?" Craig asked.

"For Veronica," Philip added. "I think she needs some practice."

"Well then," Veronica said, cinching her apron tighter. "Welcome to Buzz. How may I help you?"

"A cappuccino, please."

"Medium, large or grande?"

"Large, please."

She pulled a white paper cup from the stack. "Ya know, I never did understand where 'small' went. There's 'medium,' which is the smallest size, and 'large' which is a medium. How come they don't call the medium size 'small'? *S'il vous plaît!* What happened to small?"

Craig laughed but Philip stared at her, his gaze unblinking.

"Not a chatty customer, okay, fine," Veronica mumbled to herself as she measured out the ground espresso with a stainless steel scoop. "Large, large . . . three shots of espresso."

"Miss?" Philip called. "Make it a grande."

"Right," she said. "Grande, grande . . ." She remeasured the grounds and began tamping them into the filter which she then tucked under the lip of the machine. She glanced up at her customer. "Would you like full-fat foam?"

Philip shook his head, suddenly the manager. "It's not the foam that's full-fat. It's the milk *in* the coffee. And I'd like light fat, please."

"Yes, sir, light fat." She giggled. "Light fat. What will these Angelenos think up next?" She poured the one percent milk in the bottom of the paper cup and then stopped. What was she supposed to do next? She looked over at Craig who nodded toward the espresso machine.

Ah, yes! The coffee itself. Veronica pressed a button on the machine and hot water shot out and down through the filter basket, quickly compressing the grounds. She returned to the milk; she held the cup under the spray nozzle and watched as hot milk bubbled up. When the dripping was complete, she quickly poured the milk over the espresso and spooned foam on top.

"It worked!" she cried.

"Ta-da!" Craig said.

Veronica capped the cup and slid it across the counter. With a quick glance back at the menu for confirmation, she punched in the cost of the coffee at the cash register. Immensely proud of herself, she said, "That'll be $5.94, sir."

Philip frowned.

"What? What did I forget? Ummm . . . sugar and Sweet-n-Low are on the counter over there. Uh . . . cinnamon? Did you want a sprinkling of cinnamon? Or cocoa?"

"Maybe I might like something else with my coffee."

"Right, geez, I'm sorry." She thumped the palm of her hand against her forehead. "Would you care for anything else, sir? A muffin, perhaps, or one of our freshly baked scones?"

"The scones aren't freshly baked, Veronica."

"It sounds good, though, doesn't it? A warm cranberry scone with a flaky crust, a pat of melting butter on the side or a scoop of jam. Or maybe you'd like to try one of our coconut macaroons. A layer of dark chocolate on top, soft and squishy in the middle. Oooh, I love macaroons. Just a little something sweet to go with the coffee. Sounds good, huh?"

"That sounds amazing," Craig said. "Can I have one?"

Philip stared at her, entranced by her sensuous descriptions of the baked goods. "Uh," he croaked, "that does sound good. But I'm watching my weight."

"You? You don't need to watch your weight." She laughed.

"Okay, maybe just one."

"Good choice, sir. Would you like me to warm it up?"

"I don't have time, miss. I have to catch my bus."

"Melting chocolate, a soft crust, come on . . . it'll only take a second."

"Now, Veronica," Philip broke character again. "The idea is to get them in and out fast. There's no time for melting chocolate."

"I thought the idea was to get them to spend a lot of money," Veronica said.

Philip gazed up at the ceiling. "You're right, I guess."

"And ten seconds in the microwave, why, I can do that while I'm ringing them up."

He grinned and man, did his eyes sparkle! She popped an over-sized chocolate-covered cookie into the microwave and took a breath. She brought a hand to her face; her cheeks felt flush. The microwave must be radiating her brain.

PING! went the oven timer.

"Here you are, sir. *Bon appetit!*" She kept her head down so Philip wouldn't see her blushing.

Philip nodded and took a sip of the coffee. "Delicious." He stepped around to the back of the counter and stood behind her at the cash register. "Now here's where you learn how to enter the employee discount."

She could smell the chocolate and cocoa beans on his breath. Her fingers fumbled on the cash register keys. "Um, okay."

"First, you punch in the total." He watched her. "Now, when it says method of payment, press 1-1-1. That's the code that means it's for an employee. Okay. Now, hit the paid button and enter my employee code. Here, I'll do that." He reached a hand around her shoulder and entered his number. He was taller than she first thought. And his arms were, ah, more developed. The tendons in his forearm were sinewy, like thick ropes. "And there you are." He retreated to a table with his coffee. "Why don't you grab a cup for yourself and take a break?"

He called back to Craig. "You want to cover the counter for a few minutes?"

Craig saluted sharply. "You got it, boss."

With trembling hands, Veronica poured a cup of the house blend. *Stop it,* she told herself. *He's just a guy.*

Philip glanced up at her standing by the whole bean- and travel-mug display. "Come on, take a load off. You heard Craig. I'm the boss and I say it's okay."

She took a seat opposite him. "Thanks."

"So where are you from?"

"Arizona."

"Anywhere near the giant meteor crater? That thing is so cool."

"Chester's a very small town just north of the Mexican border. A meteor the size of a pebble could obliterate it in a second."

He laughed and she felt a flutter of confidence fill her. She made him laugh! *Hee-hee!* It felt just like being onstage. She loved it—*loved it.*

"And you're here to . . ." he prompted.

"Serve the best darn coffee I can," she said.

"Sure you don't want to be an actor?"

"Oh yeah, that's right. I forgot," Veronica teased.

"You do make an awesome coffee," Philip said, holding his cup up to her. "This is probably the best cappuccino I've had since I started working here. So if that acting thing doesn't work out for you . . ."

"Gee, thanks for the support," she said with a lopsided grin. "And you? Are you waiting for that big break too?"

"Me? Nah. I'm done with that."

"Oh yeah? How come?"

"Philip! Philip! Philip!" Another of the coffee shop's baristas came rushing in from the back, his arms loaded with trash. Veronica tried to remember his name.

"Donny, what the hell?" Philip asked, annoyed.

Ah yes, Donny. He was a sophomore at Santa Monica College, she remembered. What was his major . . . hospital administration? Hostel representation? No, no, it was hostage negotiation. She recalled Donny relating to her his failed attempts to join the CIA, the FBI and the local sheriff's department. He had tattoos up and down his arms that he kept covered, he told her, so the Feds wouldn't know he knew what he knew.

She imagined all sorts of *Prison Break* type clues on Donny's skin, but the tattoos were pretty standard fare: roses and snakes and his mother's name. Donny was totally emo with fair skin and gelled jet-black hair, a dead ringer for Chris Carrabba.

"You've gotta shred this stuff," Donny said in a low voice, showing Philip the papers he found. "It's *information*, Philip."

"It's *trash*, Donny."

Mr. Conspiracy Theorist, Veronica thought. And he looked like such a normal guy.

"Please stay out of the dumpster, Donny." Philip sighed and stood up. "We'll have to continue this some other time," he said to Veronica. He must have seen the look of disappointment on her face because he added with what surely was a wink: "If I tell you everything about myself now, there won't be anything left to say, will there?"

Veronica felt a smile cross her lips. Tomorrow, as Scarlett O'Hara said, is another day.

chapter 20

Veronica and Reed exited the Kinko's on Sunset, clutching copies of their scenes for acting class. Because Midora had suggested classics, Veronica chose her scene from Chekhov's *Three Sisters*, a complex drama about social strata and its meaning in the modern world. She planned to read Masha, the middle sister, and hoped she could find two others in class to play Olga and Irina.

Reed, on the other hand, had chosen a scene from *Steel Magnolias*. She wanted to play Shelby, the girl who dies.

Reed started up the BMW and cruised down Fairfax toward Melrose. As they passed Santa Monica, Veronica waved down the boulevard.

"Bye-bye, Buzz! See you soon!" She leaned back against the headrest and felt the warm leather against her neck. "Do you ever miss the coffee shop?"

Reed shrugged and adjusted her sunglasses. "Not really. I'm way happier doing the acting thing."

"Well, yeah, of course," Veronica agreed. "But the people? You must miss them. They're some crazy characters. Like Donny?"

"Oh my god! Total whack job!" Reed slapped the steering wheel with her palms. "He once told me how the government pays farmers to feed their cows hormones. And this *while* I've got the hamburger in my mouth! I was like, 'Thanks for the newsflash.' I told him the FBI was asking me questions about him and that shut him up fast."

Veronica paused. She didn't want to get into the fact that, in this instance, Donny was right, but what the heck was Reed doing with a hamburger when she was supposed to be a vegan?

"Then there's poor sad Craig," Reed shook her head. "Craig's a failed extra. He'll be stuck at Buzz for the rest of his life. And he isn't exactly straightlaced, if you know what I mean," she added with a wink.

"Did that bother you?"

"Well, not *me*, no . . ."

Reed hooked a left on Melrose and slowed her car as she began searching for a parking spot. "You have change on you, sweetie?"

"Huh? Oh yes, sure." Craig and Donny were certainly of interest to Veronica, but what really got her curious was . . .

"What about Philip?" Veronica asked, with as much innocence as she could muster. She tried to imagine herself playing Alice. *Why, what could that mean, 'Drink Me'?*

"Philip? What about him?"

"I just wondered, you know . . . what's his deal?" *And what's that, 'Eat Me'?*

Reed pursed her plump lips in thought. "He used to be a child actor, but he's sort of over that. He runs the coffee house now, and, I don't know, what more do you want to know?"

Reed screeched to a stop when she saw a woman approach the passenger side door of her Lexus. Veronica could hear the *tick-tick-tick* of the turn signal as Reed waited for the driver to leave.

What Veronica wanted to know was Philip's gf-status—or bf-status, if that was the case—his favorite music, movie and first-date meal, and his pet's name and birthday so she could send him a card. In short, everything about him.

"Just, you know . . . that's good, I guess."

"He's not married or anything," Reed said. "No girlfriend that I know of. But he's a total flirt. Every girl who works at Buzz gets a crush on Philip, and every one gets disappointed."

"Why is that?"

"Because he won't date employees."

Veronica deflated. "Oh."

The Lexus driver was taking forever to leave the spot. Reed gave a little tap on the horn and waved at the woman. The woman ignored Reed.

"Here's another L.A. driving lesson," Reed groused. "Whenever you're waiting for a parking spot, the driver finds a million things better to do than leave. It's like they suddenly have no place to go."

Veronica nodded, distracted.

"Did he flirt with *you?*" Reed asked sharply.

"Philip? Well . . ."

"That's just his way, sweetie. You know how some men can be." Reed pointed a finger at Veronica. "Don't get fooled."

Having never had a real boyfriend, Veronica thought, she had never had a chance to experience the difference between being fooled and being romanced. But she sure would like to.

Finally, the Lexus moved and Reed was able to parallel park her BMW.

As the two girls hurried to class, a thought occurred to Veronica. "Did *you* get fooled?"

"Me? Oh no. I was tempted." Reed smiled mischievously. "Philip *is* cute. But Louise clued me in to the no-date rule. That's really why she left, you know. Got her little heart broken." She nodded smartly at Veronica. "So watch out."

Veronica responded with a solemn, "Thanks." *What a disappointment,* she thought. Philip wasn't even available. He might as well be married.

As soon as the girls entered the theater, Daka and Summer rushed over to Veronica.

"Are we doing Chekhov tonight?" Daka asked.

"Well, I have *Three Sisters,*" Veronica started to say. "But I don't—"

"Oh yes!" Summer squealed. "Let's do *Three Sisters.*"

Veronica grinned and wondered if the two even knew who Chekhov was. Probably not. "Only if I can be Masha," she said. Daka and Summer flanked her as they all walked to the front of the stage.

Veronica turned, expecting to see Reed beside her, but Reed was still in the back, eyes on her cell phone. Veronica felt a tug on her arm.

"Come on, let's sit down front," Daka was saying. "I think Midora likes you."

chapter 21

On the morning of August 25, Veronica read a new letter from her mother.

> *Dearest Moose,*
>
> *I know I wasn't very happy when you called, but you caught me at a bad time. I had just found out I didn't get that role in the TV show. I didn't mean to hang up on you. Honest I didn't. You know how much I care about you. It's just that this really means a lot to me, and sometimes I feel so overwhelmed I don't know what to do.*
>
> *I'll get over it. I'm going out with my roommates for drinks tonight at the Whisky. I can feel great things coming!*

Diana had been so upbeat about her life, Veronica thought, as she returned the letter to its envelope. When, she wondered, had it all changed for her? Veronica wanted desperately to call her father, or to write him, and beg him to tell her what went wrong, but she knew he would find a way to avoid the subject, like he had for a dozen years. She would just have to discover the truth on her own.

Veronica prepared an Americano and handed it to Philip who gave it to an elderly man, one of Buzz's regulars. He raised the cup to Veronica. "Missed you yesterday!"

Veronica smiled. "I had an acting class, Mr. Whitman. Did Philip make your coffee?"

The man made a face. "He made the *worst* coffee I ever tasted."

"You did?" Veronica asked Philip.

Philip shrugged. "I guess I don't have the touch."

"She's good." Mr. Whitman pointed at Veronica. "Don't let her get away."

Philip grabbed Veronica's arms and playfully pinned them behind her back. "I try to keep them, Mr. Whitman, but they always manage to escape."

"Help, help," Veronica mock-pleaded. "I'm meant for more than this java joint!" She felt Philip's cheek warm the back of her hair, and she had to fight the instinct to blush. *Remember what Reed told you*, she said to herself. *Philip was a natural flirt. It doesn't mean anything.*

Mr. Whitman smiled. "I think you can take care of yourself."

Veronica watched as the old gentleman left the café and found a seat outside. She squirmed out of Philip's grasp, and when he released her, the air felt suddenly cooler, the room decidedly larger. She immediately missed his body next to hers.

"Guess I'll have to teach you how to make coffee," Veronica said, adjusting her apron.

"Whitman had the first cappuccino I ever made," Philip said, busying himself with some paperwork beside the register, "and it was a disaster. He's never let me forget it."

"When was this?"

"Couple years ago, right after I started work here."

"What were you doing before?" she asked, knowing the answer.

"I was in the business."

"And which business was this?" Veronica teased. "IRS? Border patrol? Department of Motor Vehicles?" She saw him try to suppress a grin and it spurred her on. "Wait—I've got it. Long-haul trucking!" She mimed talking into a CB radio. "Breaker 1-9, breaker 1-9, I got a smokey on my tail."

"Funny." Philip buried his head in the paperwork he'd laid out on the counter, but oh yeah, that was a smile. He could try, but he couldn't keep a straight face. Veronica smiled to herself, loving every second of it.

She decided to let him off the hook. "I know, I know. You were in the movies."

"TV and movies," Philip said. He pulled aside the curtain behind him and yelled, "Donny! Where's your time card?"

Donny appeared, flush and out of breath, his hair sticking up in ways no mere gel could create. He rubbed the tattoos on his arm as he talked. "Phil, come on, I can't give you that information. The CIA can use it to track my movements."

Philip sighed, ever patient. "And I can't pay you without it. How many times are we gonna go through this?"

Donny and Philip locked gazes as Veronica watched, amused. *Donny is seriously more entertaining than cable*, she thought.

"Fine," Donny said, breaking the stare and grabbing the time card from Philip's pile of papers. He waved it in Philip's face. "Two months from now, if I disappear suddenly, every trace of me and my stuff gone—poof! It'll be on *your* head."

"I'll take that risk," Philip replied, with a sly wink to Veronica.

Donny began to walk away.

"And Donny?"

Donny stopped but did not turn around. "What?"

"Don't just fill in your social as 1, 2, 3, 4, 5, 6, 7, 8, 9, okay?"

Veronica could hear Donny mutter under his breath, but he said audibly, "Fine."

"My god, he's hilarious," she said when he was out of earshot. "And why exactly is he still working here?"

"Because he's hilarious," Philip said, grinning. "The customers love him, and the truth is, without people like Donny, lattes can get *very* boring."

She watched as Philip returned to his work. The store was quiet. The few customers they had were sitting in plastic chairs outside, enjoying the late summer sun. Veronica swung open the basket in the coffee machine and lifted out the filter.

"So, TV?" she prompted. "If I Googled you, what would I find?"

"Three series on Nick and a bunch of cable movies," Philip said flatly.

"Oh." She dumped the filter into the trash with a quick flick of the wrist. It landed upside down, the wet grounds splattering the sides of the bin.

"I have no contacts anymore, no agent, no manager and no advice," he said firmly. "I can't look at your resume or give your pictures to anyone. If you do give me your head shot, it will go directly into my cat's litterbox."

Geez, Veronica thought, *that was a little . . . intense.*

A customer approached and asked for a cappuccino with no foam. Veronica prepared it expertly and was rewarded with a dollar in the tip jar.

The store was quiet again.

"You have a cat?" Veronica said. "I would have figured you more as a dog guy."

"And why is that?"

"Well . . . people who have cats always start with one, but then they add another and another and soon their whole house is filled with cats." She stopped and took a sniff of Philip's T-shirt. "And you don't smell like a guy who has a whole house of cats."

He was working hard to ignore her, she could tell, staring at the papers in front of him, but she knew he was listening. His ears pricked up, waiting for her to continue.

"Now a dog guy is different," she went on. "He likes to go jogging and throw Frisbees and play catch. He's way more outgoing than a cat guy."

"He sounds pretty athletic," Philip noted.

"He is," Veronica agreed.

"And what does *he* smell like? Sweat? Gatorade?"

Veronica tilted her head to one side. "He smells like . . ." *Coffee and chocolate*, she wanted to say, but then caught sight of someone outside. "He smells like Homeless Joe."

Philip looked up and followed her gaze to the street where Joe and his dog were waiting patiently. "Oh, hey. Excuse me for a second."

He grabbed some pastries and napkins and was headed out the door when Veronica handed him a large cup of coffee with a to-go lid. "Thanks," Philip said with an appreciative smile.

Another customer wanted a blueberry muffin and a decaf, and

Veronica readily obliged, keeping one eye on Philip and Joe. Philip was lighting a cigarette for Joe and patting the scruff on his dog's neck. *Wow,* she marveled, *he didn't flinch at all, just got right in there.*

"All right, Phil, I'm done," Donny announced, brandishing his time card and pencil like weapons. "Phil?"

Veronica nodded toward the front door. "He's outside."

Donny stepped closer to Veronica and lowered his voice. "He's gonna get in trouble for that some day." He leaned into Veronica. "But I won't tell."

Veronica stared down at Donny—he was at least three inches shorter than she was—and wondered again how he managed to stay employed. He *was* eccentric, that was true.

She glanced from Donny to Philip and Joe, and grinned. All in all, there were worse places to work.

Toward the end of her shift, when Veronica was about to collapse face-first into the display case, an attractive couple stepped up to the counter arm in arm, giggling into each other's necks like a pair of May-December newlyweds.

"Can I help you?" she asked, pasting on a smile. This would probably be the last coffee she would pour for the day, and then she could go home, kick off her shoes and . . . ahhh. It definitely helped to think about that.

The man's gaze flitted past her. He peered beyond the register.

"Philip?" the man called. "Are you there?"

"I think he's busy with something, but I can help you."

"That's all right, sweetheart," the man said in a patronizing tone. He continued to look around her, past her, through her. "I'll wait."

Finally, Philip emerged from behind the curtain, wiping his hands on a bar towel. "Well, hi there, Frank, I didn't know you were back in town. Have you met Veronica? Veronica, this is Frank. He owns Buzz."

"Hello!" Veronica held out her hand. "I really love working here. Everyone is so friendly."

Frank nodded at her hand and turned back to Philip. "Could we . . ." He motioned to the back curtain.

"Sure, sure." Philip smiled at Frank's gal pal, and Veronica felt a stab of jealousy. "I didn't catch your name. I'm Philip."

"*Je m'appelle* Marguerite," the woman purred, taking just the tips of Philip's fingers in her hand and squeezing. The attractive brunette had long silky hair that had been flat-ironed and plaited into a braid down her back; it shone under the fluorescent lights of the coffeehouse.

"*Ah, oui, vous êtes Française?*" Philip said.

"*Tu parles Français! Très bonne!*" Marguerite replied happily.

"*Moi, aussi!*" Veronica said. "*Je le parle aussi!*"

Philip grinned but the French woman ignored her. Veronica felt an urge to stuff the woman's braid in her mouth, but, being a lady, she refrained.

"I know your shift's about over, but would you mind staying for a couple of minutes?" Philip said to Veronica as he passed her. "This won't take long."

"Sure, sure, take your time."

A moment later, Veronica heard Philip's and Frank's voices from behind the thin curtain. "Talk to me," she heard Frank say. "What's the deal with the fat girl?"

Veronica sucked in a breath. The fat girl? Was Frank talking about *her?*

"Frank, that's not—"

"Isn't she?"

"Isn't she what?"

"Isn't she fat?" Frank pushed.

Please don't answer that, Veronica whispered to herself, *please, please, please* . . .

"She's doing a great job and everyone likes her," Philip said.

Not much to look at but she's got a great personality, Veronica heard in her head.

"This is West Hollywood," Frank's voice was insistent. "You put the pretty boys and the babes behind the counter, not the fat broads."

Veronica could feel her lower lip tremble and her eyes sting.

In front of her, directly in front of her, Marguerite giggled derisively. Veronica didn't need to speak French to know when she was being laughed at. She quietly shuffled over to the display case where she could better hear the conversation behind the curtain.

"I like things the way they are, Frank."

"Look, Philip, if you've got a thing for fat chicks—"

"I don't have a *thing* for fat chicks."

Veronica closed her eyes involuntarily in an almost-wince.

And Marguerite laughed.

"Do me a favor, huh, Phil? Put her in the back and let her load the milk and beans."

"No, Frank. Veronica is good and funny and sweet. The customers love her and I like working with her."

"Now, Philip, I don't want to pull the owner card."

"And I don't want to call your *wife*."

Behind the curtain, Frank clucked his tongue, upset at the betrayal but undoubtedly impressed by the choice of material. "Okay, Philip, okay. You can keep your fat chick, but if I hear one word, she's gone. And if you screw up, just once, I will know. Are we clear?"

"Fine."

"Just so we know the definition of screw-up, that includes feeding *my* food to Homeless Joe and his ratty dog. Got it?"

Oh no, Veronica panicked. Would Joe lose his meals because of *her*?

The curtain peeled back and Frank strode out. He brushed past Veronica and hooked a pasty white arm around his anemic girlfriend.

Veronica waited a moment to see if Philip was coming out. She could hear his breath, heavy behind the curtain. If he came out in the next five seconds, she told herself, she would apologize for getting him in trouble, she would apologize for taking food away from Joe, she would apologize for . . . for being fat.

She waited another five seconds but he still didn't appear. She removed her apron, hung it carefully on a hook, then picked up her purse and slung it over her shoulder; it wasn't until the back door had shut behind her and she was safely out of view of the coffeehouse that she allowed a single tear to run down her cheek.

Suddenly, she wished she were in Arizona with her beloved Vees. They, of all people in this world, would know exactly how she felt. They had heard it before, had seen whispers and giggles and pointing fingers at the town pool. They had emerged stronger for it, they told themselves. Better for it. Together they had encouraged and supported each other and insisted that there was nothing each Vee could not do, if only she set her mind to it.

Another tear fell. Without her friends, she felt so unbelievably lonesome.

"Veronica?" she heard. "Were you going to leave without saying good night?"

She turned and saw Philip lighting a cigarette. He kicked one foot up against the wall of the café and leaned against it while he smoked.

"Well, no," she said. "Good night."

"Wait a second, wait," he said. And the next thing she knew he was coming toward her, then standing next to her and peering into her face.

"Hey," he said softly. "Are you okay?"

"Yeah, sure, I'm fine," she replied, looking away and hoping to find a spot where the earth would swallow her up.

"Did you . . . ? Oh geez, I'm sorry. Frank is a total jerk for saying that crap." Philip tossed his cigarette onto the ground.

Since the earth was so obviously not going to oblige her, she would have to hustle her own two feet and get out of this place before a flood of tears washed all semblance of professional composure away. "Um," she said, "I have to leave now."

"Don't go yet." Philip grabbed her hand and led her to the side of the building which couldn't be seen from inside the coffee shop. "Listen, I think you're great."

"Okay." Veronica winced. *That was exactly the sort of thing you said to a fat girl,* she thought.

"I do," he insisted. "I think you're beautiful."

"Okay." *And that was the sort of thing you said to a fat girl who was crying.*

"I want you in the front every day. I don't care what Frank said."

"Okay." She didn't believe him.

"You don't believe me, do you?"

"Well . . ." Another tear welled in her eye, threatening to spill.

Philip dug a hand into the front pocket of his jeans and pulled out a Buzz napkin. As he placed it in Veronica's hand, their fingers touched. She felt gooseflesh rise up on her arms and down the back of her neck, an intoxicating sensation. What was more thrilling, however, was the fact that Philip did not immediately pull his hand from hers.

"You'll come back, right? You're not quitting on me."

She shook her head. Of course she wouldn't. Philip was mere inches from her, and she felt an urge to run her hands through his hair, to caress the stubble on his cheek.

"Good," he said. "I don't want to get stuck serving Mr. Whitman his Americano again."

Veronica couldn't help but smile. "You won't."

"I'll see you tomorrow. Good night, Veronica."

"Good night."

He waited for her to get into her car and start it up before he returned to the coffee shop.

Just a flirt, she told herself. *Philip was just one of those guys.*

Yeah, one of those great *guys,* she thought as she pulled her car out of the lot.

Veronica recalled the warmth, the spark, she felt when their fingers connected.

Reed had warned her about Philip, she admitted, but her warning, it seemed, had come way too late.

chapter 22

The room was dark when Veronica awoke. She was startled at first, wondering where she was. She searched for a sliver of light that would illuminate some tiny corner of her room: Where was her vanity, her poster from CCT's *A Midsummer Night's Dream*, her dresser full of photographs? And then she felt stiffness in her calves and the tingle of pins and needles in her toes as her legs awoke last.

Oh yes, that was it. She had fallen asleep on the couch with her feet up on the coffee table, waiting for Reed to come home. Veronica glanced about the living room, scanning for signs of her roommate, but found nothing. She checked her cell for messages: none. The clock on it said 10:15. She stood and stretched for a full minute until she had woken fully.

Where was Reed? she wondered.

Her stomach growled. She padded into the kitchen, hoping for a morsel of leftover Chinese food from two nights ago, or an old slice of Domino's, or even a crumble of cake, but there was nothing in the fridge besides Reed's soy yogurt cups.

Yuck.

She thought about making coffee to quell her hunger, but the mere idea of a caffeinated drink caused the image of nasty Frank to crawl into her frontal lobe.

Double yuck.

Instead, she decided to take her laptop out to the balcony where the wi-fi reception was best and where two yellow bug lights illuminated her screen.

"You've got mail!" the computer greeted her. Among 25 pieces of spam were two actual letters—one from May May and one from Ginny. She opened May's first.

> *Hello Veronica! I hope everything's going well. The ladies gave me a lovely shower yesterday. Sorry you missed it!*
>
> *I'm sending you some pictures of my dress and shoes, to give you an idea for when you pick out your own dress. Now remember, this is my treat to you for being my maid of honor. I want you to pick out any dress you like. Do you like the shoes? They reminded me of a pair we bought for you when you were going to the semi-formal in ninth grade. Do you remember?*

Yes, Veronica remembered. They were the first heels she had ever worn, and they had been the result of a hard-fought battle between May and Daddy. May May had insisted that a girl be allowed to wear heels to a dance. Gosh, it was the only time Veronica had seen May put her foot down. It was for *her*. And for *shoes*.

And here is a picture of the cake. Your father made me take it.
Guess what's inside?

Chocolate, Veronica thought with a smile. She didn't have to guess; she knew.

These other photos were in the camera, and I thought you might
like to have them. Perhaps you can print one or two out for your apart-
ment. They're from the opening of the new library wing last February.

Veronica scrolled down to the bottom of the email and downloaded the pictures. She remembered that event. Daddy and May May were both so proud—the head librarian and his trusty assistant. They had big plans for the new wing: a multimedia center, a refurbished computer lab, and a reading room where book clubs and classes could hold meetings. It was a new age, Daddy had proclaimed as he cut the ribbon over the door leading to the wing. They were finally bringing Chester's library into the 21st century.

May had forwarded several photos of Veronica with Daddy: posed with the oversized scissors before the ceremony, pretending to read to each other in the meeting room, holding their fingers to their lips, *shhh*, in the stacks. *May May had a good eye,* Veronica thought.

And she had sent one of May with Daddy. Veronica had snapped this one when they were not posed but casually chatting with some members of the town council in the driveway outside the library.

Veronica remembered then when she was nine and had been trying to rollerblade down that very driveway. After tripping and falling and seeing a river of blood pour from her knee, she had howled to the heavens until May came rushing out. Without a moment's hesitation, May May had bundled her into her tiny car and rushed her off to the emergency room.

> *Life holds so many surprises,* May wrote. *I could never have predicted I would be here with your father. I should be a nun in a convent, but here I am, about to become a wife and mother. It's a brand new chapter in my life.*

Veronica suddenly felt guilty for not having attended May's shower. Would it have been such a burden to have traveled home for a weekend? May May wasn't a bad person, she thought, and she certainly deserved better than Veronica could give.

But then they would have asked questions—May and Daddy and all of the library ladies. They would have pestered her about auditions and jobs and when they would see her on *CSI: Miami.* They wouldn't understand that life in L.A. was vastly different from life in Chester. They wouldn't understand how hard it was here.

Veronica sighed, closed the email and then looked at Ginny's. The last time she had written Ginny was to tell her about Philip and to wonder if it would be terribly gauche to ask him out. She hadn't yet told either of the Vees what Reed had said. And how could she possibly tell them about the Frank incident tonight? They would insist she return home. With a heavy heart, Veronica thought she'd never kept secrets from her friends before. She clicked open the email.

> *Vee! Send a picture of your Boss Man from your camera phone! B. hair, b. eyes??? What about his smile? His laugh? His kissable lips? Description is not your strength, sweetie.*

A sad whisper of a smile crossed Veronica's face. If she had read this earlier, she might have laughed and blushed and immediately thought about Philip's kissable lips.

Vee, I'm worried about your career. You're not there to pour coffee. You're in L.A. to be an actor. What's all this other crap you're doing? Yoga class? Movement class? Stalking people in supermarkets? That's not gonna get you jobs. Are you and Reed at least having fun?

Veronica glanced back over her shoulder, at the black hole of an apartment behind her. She shook her head at the computer.

You've been in the theater practically your whole life. Why aren't you doing that? You've got to be you, Vee. Don't ever forget that.

Theater? Theater was dead in L.A., as Reed had told her. Besides, that was the past, Veronica thought. That belonged to Chester, where she wasn't needed anymore. Something would happen soon. There was that industrial she had applied for, and the UCLA student film, and the soap. Something would happen. It *had* to. She had to make this work. She had to really put herself out there, like her mother had.

Veronica hit reply to Ginny's email. *Thanks for the support, Vee. Reed's been great, teaching me everything she knows.*

She heard the echo of her mother's last letter in her head: *I can feel great things coming.*

Veronica modified it for Ginny: *I can sense good things coming my way.*

She hit send and closed her laptop. Now she was really hungry. She returned to the kitchen, determined to find *something* upon which to nosh. It just wasn't possible that there was no food here.

She checked the cupboard below the sink—Lysol.

She checked the freezer—ice cubes.

There was no bread in the bread drawer. No cake on the cake plate.

Her hand reached for the top cupboard and then stopped. Little Vee couldn't possibly climb this high without a step stool. Anything up here would have been left by a previous—taller—tenant.

She stood on her tippy-toes and stuck her hand all the way to the back. Her fingers found something covered in plastic, something long and slender, something . . .

. . . made of beef jerky.

Veronica pulled her hand back and was startled to find a Slim Jim in it.

"Oh my . . ." she said. She turned the beef jerky over in her hands, certain it must be ancient. But it was dried meat—how could she tell if it was bad? With a grimace, she peeled back the yellow and red plastic wrap, readied herself for a deep whiff and then took the plunge. It was chewy and slightly smoky, with a texture not unlike that of a dried sponge. In other words, exactly like a Slim Jim.

Now what the heck were Slim Jims doing in the back of Little Vee's cupboard, on a shelf she couldn't possibly reach? Veronica wondered. Were they Reed's?

No, no, that couldn't be, she told herself. Reed was a vegan now and anti-soda pop, and her favorite new spice, like the rest of the sophisticated palates of Los Angeles, was ginger. Furthermore, nothing inorganic was allowed to cross her plump lips.

And yet, here was evidence to the contrary.

Veronica smiled at the secret cache. She had been feeling bad about herself, had hoped Reed would come home to help her out of her misery, but as it turned out, she didn't actually need Reed, the person.

Reed the secret snacker would do just fine.

chapter 23

Because of her various classes and their conflicting sched-
ules, it wasn't until a week after Labor Day that Veronica
worked with Philip again. Knowing he would be there, she
dressed for the occasion, in her best denim skirt and a V-
neck, pink T-shirt that nicely offset the green of her apron and
showed off a bit of cleavage if she stood just right.

Craig whistled as she walked in. "Very nice."

A few customers turned their heads and Veronica blushed.
"Stop."

"Did you dress up for me?" Craig asked, as he nestled his head
against her neck. "You know just how to make me feel special."

"Enough of the love fest," Veronica shrugged him off. She lowered her voice. "Is he here yet?"

"Uh-uh. Just me and Donny and the whack-job is leaving in a
few minutes for class."

Buzz was quiet on this afternoon. Then again, it was raining, and rain in L.A. kept just about everyone indoors. Like a million Wicked Witches of the West, Angelenos were afraid they would melt under any form of precipitation. Traffic across the city crawled from stop light to stop light; bus travelers huddled against storefronts; and by all accounts, no one owned an umbrella. Or a rain slicker. Or a hat. Or a pair of waterproof boots.

A small shower, out here, was just short of cataclysmic.

While Veronica poured coffee and chatted up the regulars, she kept one eye peeled for Philip. Then, around the middle of the afternoon, she saw Homeless Joe and his faithful dog appear at the front door. Customers cut a wide swath to avoid him as they entered or exited the café, which made the poor guy look even more pitiful, if that were possible.

Veronica's heart twisted. Why wasn't Philip here? How would Joe get his coffee if he didn't show? She stared at the man, at his dog, and suddenly, she felt as if a shade had been lifted from her gaze. Veronica saw him with new eyes—with Philip's eyes—and he didn't look any different from anyone else in the coffee shop. Just . . . dirtier.

And a little dirt wasn't any thing to be afraid of, was it?

Veronica packed a tuna sandwich and two cranberry muffins into a paper bag and poured a large house blend. She walked straight to the front door, directly to Joe, and handed him the food.

"Hi," she said as their eyes met.

"Thank you, miss." Joe's voice was gentle, yet not at all meek. Like Craig had told her, he was just a man down on his luck.

Veronica patted Joe's dog on the head. "You're welcome," she said. "Stay out of the rain." And then she returned to the café.

Philip was standing at the counter, watching her walk in.

Veronica blinked. Had he slipped past her? Come through the back door? Either way, he had a curious look on his face.

"What?" Veronica asked. She cast a glance over her shoulder, saw nothing. She touched her hands to her cheeks. "Is there something on my face? What is it?"

Philip shook his head with a smile. "Thanks for taking care of that. With Joe."

"Oh. It was no big deal," she told him. Yet he continued to gaze.

Veronica felt self-conscious. Was it the skirt? The pink top? Or the newfound cleavage? She felt a blush rise in her cheeks.

"Here," Philip set a drink on the counter, "try this. I think I want to add it to the menu."

Veronica took a seat and a sip. Mmm . . . it tasted like a cup of melted Milk Duds, chocolate-y and caramel-y with a mere hint of coffee. "This is amazing. We have to have these every single day."

Philip laughed and she could tell he was pleased by her reaction. "Not too sweet?"

"It's perfect," she insisted. "I would drink this all day long—if I didn't think I'd gain twelve hundred pounds."

"That's a compliment?"

"It is from a girl in the heart of L.A.," Veronica replied. She titled her head, considered. "You know, we should figure out a way to make a drink with negative calories. We'd make a killing in this town!"

"Ugh." Philip rolled his eyes. "Girls think way too much about that crap."

"And boys don't?"

He shrugged. "We don't care." As if to illustrate his point, he slugged back a mouthful of his own Milk Dud latte. When he took the cup away, a thin circle of chocolate rimmed his lips.

Veronica giggled and pointed to his face. "You have some . . . right there."

Philip crossed his eyes as he tried to look down at his own mouth. "I do?" He licked his lips but a tiny bit of chocolate was left behind.

"No, not . . . right there." She stuck her tongue out of the corner of her mouth and tried to mirror Philip.

Now it was his turn to chuckle. "I hope I don't look like *that* when I do it," he said.

"What?" She fluffed her hair and batted her eyes dramatically. "You mean gorgeous and extremely talented? You wish."

Philip roared with laughter, and a pair of customers at the window turned to look at the two of them. But Veronica didn't care who looked.

Is he flirting with me? she wondered. Is that really all it was?

No, she knew flirting; she had seen firsthand how Philip flirted with girls like Marguerite. *This* wasn't *that*.

Was it—was it possible? Were they *connecting*?

Oh god, if he could read her mind, what he must think of her! He smiled. Oh, he had a beautiful smile. She would do anything to see that smile again. Not anything . . . yeah, okay, anything.

She smiled back and felt the warm glow of mutual attraction surround her like a fog.

Outside, the rain trickled down the awnings and dripped onto the plastic chairs, but she was indoors and she was with Philip and all was right with her world.

When Veronica returned home that night, a little wet but still buoyant from her shift with Philip, she was greeted with an even more thrilling piece of news.

Reed thrust a piece of paper at Veronica before she had a

chance to kick off her shoes. On it was written an address, a phone number and a time, 11:30 A.M.

"What's this?" Veronica asked.

Reed grinned. "You got a call for that soap!"

"What?"

"*General Hospital*, remember?"

Of course Veronica remembered. It was one of the few listed in *Backstage* that didn't require an agent submission.

"I wonder why they didn't call my cell."

Reed shrugged. "I have no idea. But isn't this great? Aren't you excited?"

"Oh my god, of course I am!"

"Yay, Vee! I'm so proud of you."

They hugged tightly and did a little happy dance together. Then Veronica collapsed onto the sofa and stretched her legs in front of her. She was exhausted from long hours of work and worry.

"Oh god, I feel so much better," Veronica said, relieved. "I thought I was . . . well, failing."

Reed patted her shoulder. "Don't say that, Vee. It just takes time to settle in here."

"It does, doesn't it?"

Finally, Veronica thought. She had a job and an audition and she was settling in.

She was right about what she told Ginny: Good things really were coming her way.

chapter 24

Veronica waited in a room not unlike a reception area in a dentist's office. While she sat she pondered the array of magazines on the coffee table before her. She shuffled through a week's worth of *Variety* and *Hollywood Reporter* and found several glossies. The September cover of *Elle* featured Lindsay Lohan in a stunning leopard print bra while October's *Maxim* spotlighted Paris Hilton wearing what appeared to be a set of oak leaves. *Quel choix.*

My first Hollywood audition, she thought with a start. She could feel beads of perspiration form at the back of her neck. She wiped the palms of her hands against her khakis and glanced around the tiny room. She thought about striking up a conversation with her fellow actors, but the Size Zeroes on the vinyl-covered couch and chairs hadn't even bothered to cast their Lasik-perfect eyes at her when she walked in.

God, she was nervous. It had been so long since she had had to audition for something. Back in Chester, when a new play was announced, she simply picked which role she wanted, told Jim Neece and, *voila*, she was cast.

In a fit of self-confidence, she had sent her father an email the night before, telling him all about the *General Hospital* audition and how excited she was to be on television. As was typical, she mentioned nothing of their fight, nothing of his stubborn attitude. Just: *Hey, Daddy! Watch for me on daytime TV!*

And as was typical for Moose May, *he* mentioned nothing of their fight, and nothing of her horrible attitude, in a return email this morning: *Congratulations, sweetheart! I'll set the VCR!*

So things at home were back to normal, she realized. Status quo and all that.

God, she hoped this thing went well. It *had* to go well.

She heard a musical trill and flipped open her cell to find a photo messaged to her. It was Val's feet in a pair of gold-colored platform pumps with leather bows on the vamp. Next to the shoes, Veronica could see Val's hand modeling a matching gold bracelet. The text read: "2 much 4 wedng?"

Veronica typed back. "4 yours? No."

The back room of the casting director's office was set up like a stage, with an open space and a row of folding chairs on one end, and a table where the director and her minions sat on the other. An assistant in a micro-mini directed the hopefuls to the chairs. "Please take a seat, ladies, and when your name is called, stand up and tell us a bit about yourself."

A small, polite cough was heard in the ensuing silence, and the assistant hastened to add: "And this is Gerry Marsh, the casting director."

Gerry was a woman around fifty with the pinched mouth of a lifelong smoker. Her grey hair was wrapped in short tight curls and a pair of half-glasses were slung around her neck by a chain, resting lightly on a wide bosom. She snapped a wad of gum and didn't smile.

An assistant beside her shuffled through a stack of head shots and passed one to her.

"Lana Jeffreys."

Lana, a buxom blonde with a Nicole Richie waistline and legs the width of Pixie Stix, rose smoothly from her chair. "Hi," she said, her voice perky. "I've been on the cover of *Glamour* and I was in my high school play when I was fifteen . . ."

Veronica tuned out and looked down the row of young women. They all were some shade of blonde, naturally or unnaturally, with taut skin and mile-high cheekbones. Each one was squirming in her seat, adjusting a sweater set here, brushing a lock of hair back there. From her perspective at the far end of the line, Veronica could see a bobbing sea of perfect booblies, each set identical twin globes, accentuated by clingy knit tops.

Veronica glanced down at her own pair, nestled in a Playtex 18 Hour Soft-Mold, their natural weight pressing against her rib cage. She could feel the thick band of elastic at the base of the bra strapping her in, folding over itself. She forced herself to remain upright through the next three girls, but by the fourth, she was slumped forward again, her back sore from the strain.

"Veronica May—"

Her head shot up.

"Here I am!" She jumped up and her right leg collapsed. "Damn," she whispered loudly.

"Is something wrong, Miss May?"

"No, no, my foot fell asleep while I was waiting," she said, doing a little shimmy with her leg. The girls tittered.

"We'll just have to speed things up for you," one of the assistants said in a low, let-them-eat-cake voice.

Veronica cleared her throat and lifted her chin, leveled her gaze and began the speech she had practiced fifty times in front of the mirror the night before.

"My name is Veronica May, and I've come from Chester, Arizona to be an actor. For over ten years, I've had roles in our local community theater productions, ranging from *Long Day's Journey into Night* to this year's *Romeo and Juliet*, in which I played Juliet, of course." She pulled out a stack of newspaper clippings from her handbag and held them out toward the judgment table. "Here are my rave reviews." A hush fell over the girls when they saw an assistant rush forward and carry the clippings back to Gerry.

"I've prepared a monologue from *Macbeth* or *A Midsummer Night's Dream*." She waited a moment but heard no response. "Do you have a preference? Dramatic? Comic?"

Gerry looked up from Veronica's articles and spoke for the first time, her gum cracking between words. "Miss May," her voice rumbled. "I'm casting extras for *General Hospital*. It is a soap opera, not Shakespeare. I'm looking for young women who can play nurses wandering the corridors and barflies sitting in a club. I'm looking for babes in short skirts, not drama queens. You may go."

Veronica stood there a moment, unblinking. "But . . . that's it? I don't understand. You don't even know what I can do. If you didn't want me to read something, why did you call me?"

Gerry glanced at an assistant who held up Reed's head shot. "We thought this was you."

"*What?*" Veronica gaped at the photo. How could this have happened? Her mind raced as she tried to remember. There was an ad in *Backstage*, she had written out the address and thrown in her head shot. When had the mix-up occurred? And how?

"Now this is what we're looking for," Gerry announced, gesturing with Reed's photo. She stabbed a yellowed fingertip at the half-smiling black and white face. "Perfect lips, perfect eyes, perfect tits."

The girls in the room laughed, their slender hands covering collagen-injected lips, pink tongues running over capped teeth.

This was all too much for Veronica.

"Mine may not be perfect," she fumed, cupping her hands under her booblies, "but at least they're real."

She snatched her reviews from Gerry's hands and strode out the door.

chapter 25

A long soak in the bath was just about the most decadent luxury on the planet, Veronica thought as she ducked under the surface of the water. Transparent bubbles skimmed the length of her body so that all that was exposed were her suntanned toesies and her Scrunchie-topped noggin. She tried not to move, lest her booblies bobbed into the air. When your booblies got cold, *bien sûr*, no amount of hot water could keep you warm.

Veronica was actually thankful Reed was out this evening. She didn't need a life-size version of the girl around to remind her of her horrible day.

She had received another of her mother's letters in the mail and had waited all afternoon to read it. Normally she would bring a copy of *Entertainment Weekly* into the bath, due to its superior ability to repel water but tonight, she needed a boost from home. This one was dated September 10. More double-columned steno paper, same salutation. Veronica skimmed through the long-time-no-write and got to the good part.

> *The party at the studio was a big success. I was part of a trio that danced as hula girls. We wore grass skirts and bras that looked like coconuts and flowers in our hair.*
>
> *After the show, we met a producer who took us out to a really fun nightclub right down the street from the studio. Everyone was there. Producers, directors, stars—I even saw Ted Danson! Do you remember his show? I used to love it!*

Veronica giggled. Ted Danson . . . like *he* was a star.

> *We met a very handsome young actor (don't be jealous!) who has a new movie coming out next year. It's another sequel to that adventure movie you told me you liked. One of the girls tried to get to know him better by sticking her coconuts in his face, but that seemed so blatant (is that the right word?). He was really intense but sweet, and I could just tell he's going to be a huge star someday. Remember this name: River Phoenix. Big, big star!*

An action movie? That must have been *Indiana Jones and the Last Crusade*, Veronica realized. She and her father had watched that movie together countless times.

> *Well, Moose, this letter is getting long, and I'm starting to yawn. That almost rhymed! I miss you lots.*
> *Yours forever, Diana*

Veronica folded the letter and carefully placed it back in its enve-lope. She stared at it in awe for a moment. If only she could go back in time and sit with Diana at that table of stars-in-the-making. She laughed, imagining her mother in a grass skirt and coconuts cover-ing her booblies, trying to be cool around River Phoenix and gawk-ing at TV stars.

But her mind's eye was cloudy. She couldn't imagine Diana in the hula girl outfit. Why, she couldn't picture her at all. She couldn't even remember the color of her hair. Had she been a tall woman? Or petite?

Stay calm, Vee, she told herself. *Just close your eyes and relax. You can remember. Just begin at the beginning, in Chester, Arizona.*

Her mind brought her back to her father's house, back to the front door: *Take a breath. . . . Now, walk in through the door, that's it, and down the hallway, past Daddy's den on the left, the bathroom on the right, and straight through to Daddy's bedroom. Now, go to the dresser, no, not the one below the antique mirror but the dark maple four drawer near the window. . . . Now, open the second drawer, Daddy's sock drawer and reach in the back. . . . Grab on and pull it out and there, it's right in front of you.*

Now look, Vee, look hard and see the photo in your hand. It's Diana, wear-ing a one-piece bathing suit and sitting on a concrete seawall by the shore. She is posed with her hands on the ledge behind her and her chin lifted up to the sun. She stares not at the camera but rather off into the distance, her gaze somewhere to the right of whomever is taking the picture.

What does she look like?

Her neck is long, and feathered layers of hair frame her heart-shaped face. A wind must be blowing because the white blouse she has wrapped around her is falling off her shoulders.

Her eyes are violet, like yours, Vee, and her hair is thick and brown and a little wiry, although she softens it every month with a hot oil conditioner and occasionally uses a henna rinse to add some red. She fills out the tank suit, not abundantly but enough to cause young men to whistle from passing cars.

Her arms are long and slender, and her legs are toned and shapely. She wears high heels because she always wears high heels, because a lady wears high heels, because she looks fantastic in high heels.

She is beautiful.

She is breathtaking.

She is young and confident and naive and full of optimism and dreams of the future.

Her smile is neither to the camera nor to the person behind the camera but to herself.

She doesn't know that she will die just a couple of years later than the intense River Phoenix, that she will drink too much and too often and lose the peach glow of her skin, that she will leave a young child and husband to mourn their loss, that she will disappoint everyone who knew her, that she will disappoint herself.

For now, she is just beautiful.

"Veronica May, put that down right now!"

She remembered her father's baritone ringing in her ears. In her mind's eye, she whipped around to see him filling the doorframe, his face red, flecks of foam forming at the corners of his mouth. Well, maybe he wasn't actually frothing, but he sure looked angry enough to spit. "Where did you get that?" His eyes narrowed to wafer-thin slits as he stared down at her.

"I—I—I found it," eight-year-old Veronica replied softly. The photo trembled in her hands.

"You know you're not supposed to come in here." Her father snatched away Diana's picture and hastened to return it to its rightful place in the back of his sock drawer. "This is my room and these are my things. Do I go into your room and touch your things?"

"No."

"No, I don't. I ask first, don't I?"

"Yes."

"And that's what I expect of you. It's called common courtesy."

"Yes, Daddy."

"And what does it mean?"

"It means to . . . be nice?"

"It means to do unto others what you would have them do unto you."

"That's the golden rule!" she said proudly and started to leave the bedroom.

"Stop there."

She froze in place.

"Sit down, please."

She hesitated before climbing onto the king-sized four-poster with the chenille spread. Daddy never let her sit on his bed. He always said she messed it up and tracked dirt in on the rugs.

Her father quietly closed the drawer and stood there with his back to her. "Now . . . would you like to tell me why you're in here?"

"I wanted to see her picture."

"Why did you want to see her picture?" Her father still did not turn around.

"Because I couldn't remember what she looked like."

Daddy sighed and then took a seat on the bed beside her. He was old again, old enough to have an eighteen-year-old daughter, old enough to have been a widower for a long, long time. "Please don't tell me that, Veronica. It's only been a year. Of course you can remember what she looks like."

"No, Daddy, it's been eleven years," she told him. "I can't remember and you put all her pictures away in the forbidden box and wouldn't let me keep any in my room."

"It's not right for a little girl to cry all the time. I know it's hard, but we have to move on."

"You didn't give me any time, Daddy. You made me forget her and I barely knew her. Now I don't even know what she looks like."

Her father put an arm around her shoulder and held her still. "In time, everything will get better. For both of us. And we won't cry—"

"But I want to. I want to cry. And I want to hold her picture in my hand and see what she looks like and remember her when she was beautiful and young."

"Ronnie—"

"And I want to see the resemblance between us. I need to see that, Daddy. I need to see her violet eyes and know they're mine too."

"No, Veronica, you don't. There is no resemblance between you and your mother. You are nothing like her."

"Maybe I am everything like her!"

"No crying" was an unspoken rule of the bath, Veronica reminded herself. *It was absolutely, positively the most sure-fire way to ruin a good soak.*

chapter 26

"So your head shot was attached to her resume?" Craig asked a few days later, during the morning rush.

"Get 'em caffeinated and get 'em out" was the mantra for the morning shift. It seemed to Veronica like every person in West Hollywood came through Buzz between the hours of six and nine, and they all had very peculiar instructions for their drinks: no foam, more foam, two shots of vanilla, half-caf, soy milk, extra hot, and faster, faster, faster!

Veronica shook her head. "Other way around," she explained as she handed Donny a double cappuccino and grabbed a cup Craig had marked with an "A" for Americano and a "½" for half caffeine.

"Well, I don't see how that could happen unless someone wanted it to happen," Craig remarked.

"You sound like *him*," Veronica stage-whispered, nodding at Donny. "There's no big conspiracy, Craig. It had to be a mistake."

Craig disagreed. "You don't just randomly staple your photo to another person's resume. It just doesn't happen." He addressed a customer at the counter. "Good morning, Mrs. Hart. Two caps this morning or just one?"

The woman, dressed in a pale green summer suit with a pair of *trop cher* sunglasses on her head, held up two fingers. "Two, please. And Veronica?"

"Yes, Mrs. Hart?" Veronica poked her head around the espresso machine.

"Could you add a shot of hazelnut—"

"After the foam?"

Mrs. Hart smiled. "Yes. Thank you, Veronica."

That was good for an extra buck in the tip jar, Veronica thought with a smile. Donny had once asked her how she was able to remember everyone's names and their likes and dislikes.

"I guess it's sort of like memorizing lines," she had replied. "I make associations and the rest comes easy."

"This is what I do," Donny had said, pulling up his sleeve and showing her his arm. Among his tattoos were names of the café's regular customers and their favorite drinks. Donny had penned them in with black ink.

"What do you do when you shower?" she had asked.

Donny narrowed his eyes then. "What do you mean?"

Veronica let the matter drop.

"All I'm saying," Craig went on, "is that you wouldn't be the first person to be stabbed in the back by a friend."

"Stabbed in the back? By Little Vee?" Veronica pressed the steam valve on the espresso machine while she simultaneously packed a second basket with ground coffee. "I've known Reed for years. She would never do something like that to me. She knows how much it would hurt me."

"Yes, she does," Craig agreed.

Veronica frothed up some milk and poured it on top of the espresso. Then she dropped a shot of hazelnut syrup through the foam. She handed it directly to Mrs. Hart who had slipped her sunglasses onto her nose.

"Have a good day, dear," Mrs. Hart said. "And stay away from that bitch."

Veronica's mouth dropped open in surprise. "I beg your . . ."

Donny and Craig giggled softly to themselves.

"You know what I think you should do?" Craig asked. "Move in with me."

"I have my own place," Donny said.

Craig swatted at Donny with his Sharpie. "Not you, moron. Veronica." He turned to face her. "Sweetie, I'm house-sitting for a friend of mine until the end of the year. Four blocks from here, off Crescent Heights. Three bedrooms, two and a half baths. Lots and lots of closets. Back patio surrounded by jasmine and hydrangea. You'll love it. And the sooner you get away from *her*, the better."

"You've got Reed all wrong," Veronica insisted, tamping down another espresso filter. "She's been helping me the whole time I've been here."

"Helping how?"

"Like introducing me to the great acting class I take—"

"And how many jobs has that resulted in?" Craig asked.

"Well, none yet," Veronica admitted. "But she also got me into a movement class that—"

"Number of jobs?"

"None so far . . . but there's Jamal's yoga class." She held up a hand before Craig could respond. "No jobs, I know, but I don't care about that. I love yoga for its own sake."

Donny handed her two grande cups with "decaf" written on the side. He glanced down at his arm. "That's for Josh and his panther Blair."

"Panther?" Craig asked. He grabbed Donny's arm and stared at it. "That's *partner*, not panther."

"She got me this job," Veronica pointed out. "Doesn't that make her good for something?"

"Not good for us." Donny's gaze shifted to the door. "We thought we got rid of her months ago."

Veronica looked up to see Reed stroll through the door, wearing a tight baby tee over a pair of skinny jeans and wedge sandals. She made a drinking gesture to Veronica and then pointed to the tables outside.

"She's your friend," Donny said. "You can wait on her."

Reed plopped herself onto a plastic chair in front of the café and placed her cell phone on the table, looking for all the world like she owned the place.

Veronica waited until the line had settled down to a manageable level for the two boys and then brought a coffee out to Reed. "Morning, sweetie. What are you doing here?"

"Just thought I'd grace you with my presence," Reed replied and then laughed. "Kidding. I'm on my way to an audition."

"Oh yeah? Which one?" Veronica slid onto the chair across the table from Reed. It was refreshing to be outside, away from the bustle of the shop, and to feel the energy of the city.

Reed took a sip from her cup. "Mmm . . . you do make the best coffee, Vee. You should seriously think about opening your own shop . . ."

"Which audition is this?" Veronica asked again.

"Oh . . . um, it's for *General Hospital*," Reed said offhandedly.

Veronica gasped involuntarily. *General Hospital.* The part *she* had wanted.

"It was so out of the blue," Reed commented. "And how weird, huh? First calling you and then me? I wonder if they knew we were living in the same apartment."

"Weird, yes." Veronica pulled her sunglasses out of her apron and slipped them on so Reed wouldn't see the anxiety in her eyes. She tried to focus on the fresh air, on the passersby, on the cars stuck in traffic traveling west on Santa Monica Boulevard. *Inhale, exhale, inhale, exhale. That was better.*

"Is Philip here yet?"

"Philip?" Veronica's head snapped around. Reed was searching the café through the plate glass window. "No, he isn't. Won't be in until later. *Much* later."

"Oh," Reed sounded disappointed.

"Did you need him for something?"

"I've just been in a slump," Reed said. "And he was always good at getting me out of them. He gives *such* good advice. Have you ever talked to him about career stuff?"

Veronica shook her head.

"You really should ask him sometime," Reed said assuredly. "He has a ton of contacts."

Veronica remembered Philip's comment that he had *no* contacts anymore and could not help anyone. The unspoken rejoinder was "so don't ask."

She wondered what made Reed different. Why was Philip willing to help *her?* Did they have a special relationship? Something that had perhaps begun when Reed worked at Buzz? Would they continue it now that Reed was not an employee?

"Maybe I will," Veronica said vaguely. She spotted a group of six men, sweaty and dressed in shorts and team shirts, entering the café. Craig and Donny would need some help getting them cold drinks. "I have to get back inside. I'll see you at the apartment before acting class?"

"No worries," Reed said. "I'll come hang out after my audition and we can go together."

She followed Veronica inside. Veronica found herself wishing that Reed would just go. Preferably before Philip came within a five-block radius.

"Did you have any head shots for me to mail today?" Reed asked.

Veronica halted in her tracks. She felt instantly bad for wishing Reed would leave.

Reed was my friend, she scolded herself. She *was* trying to help her, no matter what Craig and Donnie said. Veronica should never have doubted it.

"Um, yeah, that'd be great." She reached into her bag and handed Little Vee five stamped and addressed manila envelopes. "Thanks."

"No problem." Reed took her coffee and started to leave. Then she turned back to Veronica. "Wish me luck?"

Veronica hesitated a fraction of a second. "Luck!" she called.

chapter 27

"No one ever seems to notice the hard work I put into arranging these displays," Veronica complained as she placed a pound of Kona Blend on top of a huge pyramid of coffee bags in the center of the store. She stepped back to admire her work.

Craig, his back to Veronica at the coffee maker, shrugged massive construction-worker shoulders that were clad in an "I (Heart) WeHo" T-shirt under his green apron. "People totally suck."

"This place is so empty tonight," she noted as she began to reorganize the bags of coffee yet again.

"Tonight's the premiere of *Desperate Housewives,*" Craig said. "So from nine to ten on Sundays, Buzz will totally clear out. It's happened every year so far." He held up crossed fingers. "Love that show."

"I can't believe the entire city of West Hollywood is watching a television show."

"*Please*," Craig said in a manner which suggested Veronica was still a hick from Arizona. "My friend hosts a game—which I am missing right now, thank you very much, Philip!"

From the back Philip poked his head around the curtain. "Excuse me?"

"My game, Phil. I'm missing my game."

Philip stared blankly at Craig and Veronica and disappeared.

Craig turned back to Veronica. "It's called 'Down the Hatch.' It's a drinking game, kind of like 'Hi, Bob.'"

"Hi what?"

"You play 'Hi, Bob' when you watch old episodes of the *Bob Newhart Show.* Anytime someone enters a room and says, 'Hi, Bob,' which they do like a zillion times a show, you drink." Craig tipped an imaginary glass to his lips.

"So how do you play your game?"

Craig hopped onto the counter, his muscular hands gesturing rapidly. "Each episode, Teri Hatcher is getting skinnier and skinnier, right? Which, may I add, applies to you as well."

"Me?" Veronica cast a glance at her reflection in the window. "I look—"

"Thinner, yes, you do. You have totally lost weight since I met you."

She craned her neck, trying to look at her backside and nearly fell off the stepladder. Could yoga have done that?

"Hello? Pay attention to me, please."

"Sorry. You were saying about Teri Hatcher?" She snuck another peek at her legs. They did appear more muscular—but thinner? "Thin" was never a word anyone ever associated with Veronica May—a word *she* had never included in a self-description. *I'm five-nine, brunette, violet eyes, thin* . . . She chuckled to herself. *Um, no.*

"Each scene she's in, you have to watch for signs of impending Lara Flynn Boyle Syndrome. If you see ribs, that's one drink. Jutting shoulder bones, two drinks. And if her thighs don't touch, that's a whopping three drinks." He smiled. "Lately, we've been getting pretty toasted. I hope she doesn't die," he added, an apparent afterthought.

"Well, *I* should be home practicing my scene for acting class tomorrow," Veronica said. She didn't have the guts to call Philip out the way Craig did; besides, she liked working nights with the boys. People weren't as cranky about their coffee in the evening, although to be honest, their dessert drinks took much longer to make.

Craig gestured to the empty café. "You can practice here if you want."

"Oh god no. No, no, no."

"Why not? It's just me and Philip."

Veronica nodded emphatically. "Exactly. Two actors. Two *working* actors."

"Not me," Philip called from the back, and Veronica blushed. That thin curtain wasn't exactly made of lead, was it? "I am only a lowly coffee shop manager."

"Oh, I don't know," she murmured. "Maybe I could."

"What's the scene?" Craig asked.

"*Romeo and Juliet* balcony scene."

"*Boring,*" Philip called.

"Who asked you?" Veronica replied with a laugh. "Besides, I didn't pick it. It's an assignment. We're doing scenes from the classics."

"I *adore* Shakespeare," Craig said. "Let me help you."

"You?"

"I've been doing background and extra stuff forever. I can't remember the last time I did a play." He clasped his hands and put on a pout. "Please?"

"Well . . ."

"I played Romeo once, you know." He bent down on one knee and lifted his face to Veronica. "With love's light wings did I o'er perch these walls. For stony limits cannot hold love out, and what love can do that dares love attempt. Therefore thy kinsmen are no let to me."

Veronica hesitated and then said blankly, "If they do see thee, they will murder thee."

"If I were teaching your class, I'd fail you!" Craig put his hands on his hips. "Put some real feeling into it. Try it again."

Veronica sighed, looking at Craig below her. At least *Desperate Housewives* wasn't over yet, and the place was still devoid of customers. She cleared her throat and assumed a Juliet-like pose on the ladder. "By whose direction found'st thou out this place?"

"By love, who first did prompt me to inquire. He lent me . . . he lent me . . ."

"Counsel," Philip supplied from behind the curtain.

"Counsel, thank you, and I lent him eyes. I am no pilot. Yet wert thou as far as that vast shore wash'd with . . . wash'd with . . ."

"The farthest sea." Philip brushed aside the curtain and slowly walked into the café.

"I would adventure for such merchandise," Craig finished.

"Thou know'st the mask of night is on my face," Veronica projected. "Else would a maiden blush bepaint my cheek for that which thou has heard me speak tonight." Her gaze slowly alit upon Philip standing at the counter. "Dost thou love me? O gentle Romeo, if thou dost love, pronounce it faithfully."

The rest of the night fell away as Philip gazed back at Veronica with a fervent desire in his eyes. She didn't care if it was real or not, if he was acting or not. Her voice softened. "Trust me, gentleman, I'll prove more true than those that have more cunning to be strange." Her hand trembled on the edge of the shelf as she awaited Philip's response.

Philip's voice grew strong as he came around the corner and knelt beside Craig. "Lady, by yonder blessed moon I swear that tips with silver all these fruit-tree tops—"

"Well, do not swear. Although I joy in thee, I have no joy of this contract tonight. It is too rash, too unadvised, too sudden. Good night, good night! As sweet repose and rest come to thy heart as that within my breast." She lifted her hand toward him.

His hand reached toward hers. "O, wilt thou leave me so unsatisfied?" he asked. The air between them was thick, the tension unmistakable and Craig was gone, faded into the background like the extra that he was. Veronica felt a force pulling her toward Philip, an almost magnetic attraction to him. It was a force beyond her, beyond him, beyond *them*. Like in a Shakespearean play, could their love be pre-ordained, fated to occur regardless of what transpired around them?

Craig broke the silence with a burst of applause. "That was *marvelous!*"

Or were they simply two coworkers play-acting in a coffeehouse?

Veronica abruptly dropped her Juliet pose and climbed down from the ladder. "Well, it's about ten, isn't it? Those Marcia Cross fans will be coming in soon for their evening lattes."

Craig's cell rang, a tinkle of notes that sounded uncannily like "YMCA." *Craig was nothing if not an ironic gay man,* Veronica thought. "Hi! Did you win?" he asked.

Philip wandered over to the center island and plucked a bag of

Guatemalan Decaf off the display. "Nice arrangement," he commented.

"Oh, thanks," Veronica replied. She found another bag of coffee to replace the one Philip just took.

"That was, uh, that was pretty good," he said, not looking at her. Veronica noticed his face was flush. *Is mine?* she wondered. She turned from him quickly and fanned under her chin with a rag.

"I saw what they were doing in Starbucks," she said. "And I thought—"

"No, no," Philip laughed. "I meant, the scene was good."

"I did a little theater back home," she said.

"A little?" He was behind her then, at the counter. "Why are you wasting time with commercials and soap opera crap when you could be doing real acting?"

She glanced over her shoulder at him. "You think I'm that good?"

"Hell yes. I think you're a natural," he said. "Almost as good as me."

"Almost?" Veronica grinned. "I guess I better keep working at it."

"Yeah, you better."

Their eyes met and Veronica felt an instant, renewed connection to Philip. It was as if she were back up on the ladder, playing Juliet. Her breath caught in her throat; she knew in that moment that—warning or no warning—she was in love with him.

Behind her, the café door opened. A customer would be asking them for something soon. And then another would probably enter directly after, and the moment, this wonderful *connected* moment, would be over for the second time this evening. But she didn't want it to end, and she could sense a hesitance in him too, a reluctance to leave her and return to work. Was it possible he felt the same way as she did?

"Excuse me," Philip said in a quiet voice, "I have to get this."

"Oh yeah, sure," she replied. She watched him walk away, watched him laugh and joke with the customer at the counter, watched his fingers draw out a name on a cup . . .

. . . and wished those fingers were intertwined with hers.

She was in love with Philip, she thought, and an inner smile lit up her whole body.

She stood a moment, then blinked. *Oh no*, she thought. She was in love with Philip.

chapter 28

The waitress at the Melrose Ice Cream Cafe pulled a pencil out of her black apron and tapped it on her pad as she waited impatiently for Veronica, Craig and Donny to order. *She looks kind of familiar,* Veronica thought. She was probably an actor. Was everyone in this town someone else?

"Can I go first? I know what I want," Craig said, thrusting his unopened menu at the sullen waitress. "I'll have the Super Sludge Sundae with one scoop of pistachio chip and one scoop of butter pecan."

"I'll have the Super Sludge as well," Veronica said, "but I'd like a scoop of chocolate chocolate chip and a scoop of vanilla fudge."

The waitress hovered over Donny. "You want somethin'?"

Donny used the menu to cover the tattoos on his arms protectively. "I'm thinking."

The waitress sighed, irritated. Behind and around them,

Veronica could hear the clamor of other customers. "Don't mind him," Veronica said. "He has a hard time making decisions."

"That's not true," Craig said. "He's just crazy." He grabbed at Donny's menu. "Come on, dude. Pick something."

Donny shot Craig a look. "I will take . . . two scoops of unadulterated vanilla."

"Un-what?" the waitress asked.

"God, Donny," Craig said.

"He'll have plain vanilla, please," Veronica explained.

"Ya want fudge or whipped cream or jimmies?" the waitress queried.

"Nothing of a non-ice cream nature," Donny intoned ominously.

"No, thank you," Veronica interpreted for him.

After the waitress left, Craig shook his massive head at Donny. "Leave the crazy at home, would you please?"

Donny winced and Veronica quickly intervened. "He can't help it, Craig. That's the way he is."

"That's right," Donny said, more confident now that Veronica appeared to be on his side. "You'll thank me one of these days."

"*Mon dieu*, this is just like being with the Vees," Veronica said, a little wistful. "My friends back in Arizona," she clarified for their puzzled faces. "They argue a lot over little things. I miss them."

"We'll be your Vees for now," Craig said. He stretched his arms over his head. "Ahh, it's so good to get out of that coffee shop."

"And away from those people," Veronica agreed. "Nothing is ever good enough for them. Coffee's too strong, too weak."

"Too hot, too cold," Craig added.

"No offense, but I can't wait to get out of there permanently," Veronica said. "I've been sending out tons of resumes and pictures, and I've only gotten one call. I don't understand it." She was honestly bewildered by the lack of response. "Back home I had no trouble at all getting roles."

"Sweetie," Craig sighed, "L.A. is all about style and personality."

"I have style," Veronica said. "Don't I?"

"I love your style." Craig cocked his head to one side and gave her a pitying smile. "But you might want to perk it up a bit."

"You know who gets lots of roles?" Donny asked.

"Cate Blanchett?" suggested Veronica.

"Kate Winslet?" suggested Craig.

"Kate Beckinsale?"

"Kate Hudson?"

"Kate Holmes?"

"Someone named Kate?"

Craig and Veronica giggled, but Donny pointed a knowing finger at them. "Blondes."

"Blond . . . women?" Craig asked.

Veronica leaned closer to Craig and whispered, "Another conspiracy theory."

"No, no, no," Donny said emphatically. "Listen to me. Look at all the actors out there. Who gets the parts? Blondes. Not brunettes or redheads. There's like, a million blonde actresses. Drew Barrymore, Scarlett Johannssen, Cameron Diaz, Uma Thurman, Gwyneth Paltrow, sometimes Lindsay Lohan." He paused and looked at them. "Do I need to go on?"

"Um . . . yes," Veronica said. "A little farther, please."

"You," Donny nodded at Veronica, "should be blond."

Veronica fingered the ends of her hair.

"He might have a point," Craig said, as he gave her a thorough once-over. "You would look fantastic as a blonde. Not platinum or anything, but we could definitely lighten up the top, put in some subtle layers around the face, and you should get a new cut anyway."

"I kind of like my hair," Veronica said, brushing said hair behind her ears and off her shoulders. She shook her head as if to prove to the men that brown hair could do the same things blond hair could.

"I think she should have hair like Jessica Simpson," Donny said.

Craig shook his head. "Too trashy. Veronica's a serious actress. She needs serious hair."

"Like Meryl Streep?" Donny asked.

"Too old, but you're on the right track." Craig crossed his arms over his chest and stared at Veronica. "Let's stay in the Cate Blanchett range of blond. Very natural looking but commanding. She was an Oscar nominee."

"Charlize Theron!" Donny nearly shouted. "She *won* an Oscar."

"Yes*ssss*," Craig drawled. "A classic blonde."

"Um, if I could just point out one thing," Veronica said, her finger raised like a schoolgirl. "Charlize Theron won her Oscar playing a brunette." She sat back, feeling triumphant.

The boys looked at each other and shrugged.

"True, but she probably got the role when she was a blonde," Craig said.

"Here ya go," the waitress announced as she arrived with their desserts. She placed a massive plate of ice cream in front of Craig.

Craig sat up in his seat. "Ooh, thank you!"

Donny received his ice cream warily, spinning the cup around and around and examining it from every angle.

"Decadence is making a comeback," Craig said as he dug into his sundae with vigor. "Mark my words, people are gonna eat real food again very soon."

Veronica laughed, then picked up her spoon and took a delicate bite of her own sundae. She savored the cool creaminess of whole milk sweetened with sugar and chocolate chunks.

"This reminds me of the time the Vees and I tried to eat Ben and Jerry's for dinner. We were, like, eleven, and my father came home and threatened to make us eat frozen green beans—until we gave him some." Veronica giggled at the memory.

"I like these Vees," Craig said, tickled by the story. He bobbled his spoon at Veronica. "I wish you'd brought them with you. They sound like lots of fun."

"You know," Veronica said, punctuating the air with her own spoon, "Reed is a Vee. I mean she *was* a Vee."

Craig rolled his eyes and exchanged a glance with Donny, whose focus was laser-like on his plain cup of ice cream. "Uh-huh."

Veronica sighed. Why didn't anyone believe her? "You've got her all wrong. She was a great friend in high school. We used to do everything together."

"People change," Craig said quietly.

"She's not a very nice person," Donny remarked. "She was always making fun of me."

"And me," Craig added. "Thank god Philip fired her."

Veronica looked up from her sundae. "No, no. She left because she was getting a lot of acting jobs. She told me."

"Oh, really? What else did she say?" Craig asked.

"I *know* she was talking about me," Donny insisted. "I just know it." He clenched his spoon in his fist. "*Damn* it."

"Well . . ." Veronica thought back to her conversation with Reed in the car. Reed had also told her that everybody who worked at Buzz had a crush on Philip, but the boys probably knew that already.

(204)

"She's such a frickin' liar!" Donny said loudly. "Whatever she said, don't believe her."

Craig cleared his throat but for once did not contradict Donny. "Philip fired Reed because she wasn't very good. She was always late. She never called when she needed a sub. And she made the worst coffee imaginable."

"People complained all the time," Donny said. "Even Frank wanted to fire her, and he *always* likes the pretty girls."

Veronica bristled at the mention of Frank. "She said she was getting lots of work as an actor," she said, still desperate to salvage her friend's reputation.

"And what have you seen her in?" Craig asked.

"Well . . ."

"Trust me, we all have to keep second jobs," Craig assured her. "I work probably ten days a month—and those are union days—but I still have to keep my job at Buzz. Just in case."

"Really? Ten days a month? You . . . ?"

Craig narrowed his eyes. "Why? What did she say?"

"Oh, nothing." Veronica wasn't about to tell him Reed called him a failed extra. Or that she had fed Donny's paranoia. But there was one point she'd like a little clarification on, while they were at it and all. "She did say one other thing. She said Philip liked her. Kind of." She winced as she asked, "Did he? Like her?"

Craig stared into his sundae and shrugged. "He may have had a little crush on her. But I don't think it was anything serious."

"And he doesn't date employees?" she asked.

"Not since I've been there," Craig said but added, "Maybe he just hasn't found the right person."

And then the entire conversation became utterly moot as the

door to the parlor swung open and Veronica saw Reed stroll through.

She started to call Reed over but then noticed something odd. Philip was following her. *What a coincidence,* Veronica thought, *both of them arriving at the same time.* Reed must have gotten the message Veronica left on her cell about meeting the boys here. And Philip, well, he must have had a craving for a cone. . . .

And then the two of them were shown to a table on the far side of the place, where they each took a seat together. Next to each other. At the same table.

Metal clanged against tile, and Veronica was not at all surprised to see that it was her spoon which had fallen to the floor.

"I'll get you another," the black-clad waitress said in passing.

Veronica felt flush and weak and nauseated like she had suddenly contracted the flu. She had only felt like this once before—the day Ginny told her about Reed asking Jason to Homecoming.

Veronica had disbelieved her friend at first—had thought that what she was hearing couldn't possibly be true—but after the reality sank in, she had felt faint and queasy.

Until she met Philip, she had come the closest to falling in love with Jason Dietrich. Reed had known that and still made a move. Veronica thought that part of her life had ended when high school did, but apparently, old habits died hard. Reed was still taking what she wanted, including Veronica's credits, her auditions—and now, once again, her guy.

"Veronica? Are you okay?" she heard Craig ask.

At the table on the other side of the room, Reed sandwiched Philip's hand between her two small ones. Philip, Veronica noticed, did not pull his away.

Veronica inhaled sharply. Even if Philip didn't date employees, Reed was no longer an employee.

You should have known, Veronica scolded herself. *You should have known that this was the way events would unfold. You should have seen this coming.* She turned away from the couple, back to her own dates for the evening.

"Craig, would I have my own room in your house?" she asked in a small voice.

"Sweetie, you can have your own bathroom."

She nodded and whispered, "I'll take it."

chapter 29

There was just one catch to the new digs.

"His name's Max," Craig said. "You'll love him."

Max was the largest, most slobbering Golden Retriever Veronica had ever met. His cranium was larger than hers—larger than Craig's! And he needed to be walked three times a day. Instead of rent, Veronica would assume Max duty, taking him out in the morning, at lunchtime and then again before bed. Craig insisted she didn't have to throw a Frisbee or toss a tennis ball, but if she could pet him once in a while, Max's owner would be forever grateful.

Veronica had moved in on a night when Reed was out with Bianca. She had left a message for Little Vee on the back of a Slim Jim wrapper. It wasn't the classiest of maneuvers, but hey, it got her point across.

The house, as Craig had described, was on a quiet street off Crescent Heights, a few blocks from Buzz, in a manicured neighborhood of hydrangea bushes, magnolia trees and date palms. Veronica loved that she could walk to work, walk to yoga, walk to Gelson's grocery store. If she had to walk the dog, at least she would have someplace to go.

She quickly found her favorite spot in the house which was actually outside of it: a large flagstone patio in the backyard surrounded by tall hedges which dampened street noise and the neighbor's music. She could sit at the glass-topped table with a Coke and a bag of chips and not be bothered by anyone or anything except Max, who seemed content to curl into a fat ball of fur atop her feet and accept the occasional Ruffle.

And it was the perfect location from which to send her head shots.

"Look at this one," she read to Max from her computer. "Industrial needs woman, 18-24." She grabbed an envelope and scratched out the address. "Check! Next."

Craig had been quick to correct Veronica about the Internet. "What century is this? You absolutely *have* to use the Web," he told her. "Why on *earth* would she have told you not to check online? Oh, wait. Don't answer that. I think I already know." Then he sent her a list of his favorite websites to view casting notices and nonunion auditions.

It was like a whole new world had opened for Veronica. She spent hours in front of the computer, scouring the Web for jobs.

She quickly found another. "Commercial, nonunion only. No SAG/AFTRA. Must be able to walk-n-talk." Veronica looked down at Max. "You know, a few months ago, I would have laughed at that. But believe me, it's not as easy as it sounds." She grabbed another envelope and assumed a mellifluous television voice, as if she were extolling the virtues of a tube of toothpaste. "But now, thanks to yoga, I can walk and talk at the *same time!*" She tilted her head to one side and smiled brilliantly.

Max tilted his head too. And it seemed to Veronica that he tried to smile.

"That's it, boy!" Veronica patted the top of the dog's head. "Maybe we can get you into the business too!" She looked back at her computer. "Why, here's another one. An indie short. Also looking for women 18-24. Let's send one to this guy too. In fact, let's send one to everyone. What do you think, Maxie?"

The dog nudged Veronica's elbow.

"What's that for?" she asked him. "You think that's a good idea or no?"

Max nudged her knee this time.

"Okay, I get it. Time for a walk." She stood and gathered her envelopes, slapped some stamps on them and finished her Coke. "Come on, let's go mail these."

She was in the kitchen looking for her cell phone and keys when she heard the doorbell ring in the front hall. "Craig! Can you get that?"

There was silence in the house.

"Craig?"

The doorbell rang again, and Veronica hurried to it with Max on her heels.

"Yes? Oh, hi."

Reed stood on the top step, her hands stuffed in the pockets of a velour hoodie. She wore a pink backpack strapped tightly to her shoulders. Without makeup, Veronica noticed, Little Vee looked young enough to be carded at an R-rated movie. "Can I come in?"

"I was just about to leave—"

"This won't take long," Reed said quickly. "Please?"

Veronica hesitated. If Craig were around, she knew he would

hate to see Reed walk through his house. "Okay, but just for a minute." She opened the door and ushered Reed into the living room. Little Vee unstrapped her backpack and perched on the edge of an expensive sofa. Veronica didn't know how much it cost, but Craig told her the color was called "hydra." Wal-Mart rarely named any of its furniture "hydra."

Veronica sat in one of the matching wingback chairs and waited for Reed to speak first.

"I got the note you left," Reed said. She curled her hoodie up around her ears as if she were trying to hide. She looked up at Veronica with a sad smile, and Veronica could almost read the girl's mind: *Please don't tell anyone I eat junk food.*

A *soupçon* of guilt crossed Veronica's conscience. The Slim Jim note had been petty; she had known that when she was writing it. Still, she said nothing.

An interminable minute of silence followed and then Reed reached into her backpack and brought out a box of See's candies. "This is for you."

Veronica eyed the box but didn't take it. "For me? Why?"

"I felt bad about you moving out so suddenly," Reed said. "Did it have anything to do with me? Did I do something?"

The candy began to wobble in Reed's hand.

"Well . . ."

"You have to tell me, Vee," Reed said anxiously. She placed the box on the coffee table, another expensive item made of wicker and glass. "We've been friends for so long."

Veronica debated whether to tell the truth and wondered if she would sound lame and insecure. "I saw you with Philip Friday night," she said, the words reluctantly escaping her mouth.

Reed's brows twisted in confusion. "Me with Philip? At Buzz?"

"No. On Melrose?" Veronica prompted.

"Oh, that," Reed relaxed and slumped back against the couch. "We were talking about acting. He wanted to give me some advice. I told you he gives *amazing* advice."

Veronica kept her gaze on Reed. "Really?"

"Of course, sweetie."

"Just acting? Nothing more?"

"Nothing. Swear to god."

"And he's not still . . . into you?" God, that was a hard question to get out.

"Even if he were, I'm not into *him*," Reed insisted. Then she raised a finger. "He's off-limits while you're working there, don't forget."

"Oh, I know."

"You don't want to get your heart broken like Louise."

"No, no. I won't."

Reed smiled and reached out to hug Veronica. "I'm so glad we straightened that out. I never want us to be mad at each other."

Max, who had been lying at Veronica's feet, suddenly sat up and began wagging his tail.

"I hear voices out here. What are you watching?" Craig stumbled flat-footed into the living room in a T-shirt and pajama bottoms. "Reed?"

Reed waved genially at Craig, apparently oblivious to his dislike of her. Veronica hastened to stand and hoped Reed would follow her lead, but the girl remained seated on the couch. "Reed dropped by with some chocolate," Veronica said, pointing to the box of See's.

Craig looked from the candy to Reed and back. "Reed brought this?" He picked the box up and gestured with it to Veronica. "Do you mind if I open it?" he asked with a mischievous gleam in his eye. "I love See's."

"Um . . . okay," Veronica said. She wasn't sure what Craig was up to, but anyone wanting to eat chocolate first thing in the morning—unless his name was Moose May and he lived in Chester, Arizona—was suspect.

Craig lifted off the top and peeled back the protective layer of plastic-coated paper. He stuck his nose in and took a deep sniff. "Mmmm . . . which one should I have first?" His fingers hovered over each piece. "Which one, which one . . ." He held the box out to Reed. "Reed, darling, which one is your favorite?"

Reed shrugged her shoulders with a tiny smile. "You know See's. They're all good."

"Seriously, which is the best?" He shoved the box under Reed's chin and rattled it back and forth below her nose. Reed grimaced as if she'd been struck by a wave of nausea; Veronica covered her mouth with her hand to stifle a fit of giggles.

"Go ahead, pick one," Craig insisted.

Reed jerked her head back. "I'm sure they're all fine."

"You're probably right." Craig chose a milk chocolate square. He popped it in his mouth and chewed slowly with his eyes closed. "Oh god, that's good." An expression of pure bliss appeared on his face. He opened his eyes and offered the box again to Reed. "Sure you don't want to try?"

Reed shook her head quickly. "I don't eat junk food."

"You don't?" Craig said, his voice filled with wonder. "That's not what I heard." Then he patted Max on the head and left the girls alone.

Reed picked up her backpack and sighed dramatically. "It's sad how failure destroys a person. Isn't it?"

Veronica thought about responding but decided discretion was indeed the better part of valor. She walked Little Vee to the door.

"Thanks for coming by, sweetie. I'll see you later?"

Reed spotted the envelopes in Veronica's hand. "You want me to drop those at the post office for you? I don't mind." She reached out for them but Veronica dodged her.

"That's okay," she said. "Max and I are going out for our walk now. Right, Maxie?"

The dog happily wagged his tail at the mention of "walk" and charged headfirst into Reed's legs. Reed yelped and Veronica lunged, grabbing Max's collar before he could knock the girl over. "Max! Max!" Veronica looked up at Reed and smiled apologetically. "Sorry about that."

Reed nodded and walked quickly down the front walk with a little wave to Veronica.

Veronica waved back and then, taking one last look at the box of candy on the table, closed the door.

chapter 30

Veronica's next letter from Diana, via the Vees, was dated September 24.

My dear, sweet Moose, Diana's missive began, *I miss you now more than ever. You should never have tempted me with your surprise visit last week! Wasn't the beach wonderful? And weren't the sunsets spectacular? They were even more beautiful with you beside me. Frankly, I couldn't have guessed how romantic you were!*

Good news! They're doing a new musical called Forever Dancing, *and I've got a good shot at one of the lead roles. A reporter from the* Daily News *came to interview us at the audition and he talked to* me. *This is it—I'm going to be famous!*

Please don't give up on me—I'm coming back to you as soon as I can prove myself. It's so important to me that I do this. I know you know that.

Promise me you'll never grow tired of me, that you'll love me for-
ever—as I will love you.

Yours, Diana

P.S. The phone rang as I was licking the stamp—I just got a
walk-on part in The Bold & the Beautiful! Things are definitely going
my way. Isn't life grand? You never know when you'll get your big
break!

Success, at last! Veronica was overjoyed. Maybe if Diana had
found it, she would too.

When Veronica clocked in at Buzz the next morning, Philip was
already there, serving two Size Zeroes who were giggling and fawn-
ing all over their handsome barista. Veronica rolled her eyes. She
had seen these girls before; they usually ordered one latte with skim
and split it while chain smoking outside in the green chairs. Craig
said having the girls around was a Catch-22 for business: They
attracted lots of attention, but no one wanted to stick around and
suck in all that nasty smoke.

Veronica didn't care; she was there to do a job and move on.
That was all.

"You all moved in at Craig's?" Philip asked after the Zeroes
departed. He began emptying the contents of the refrigerator, swap-
ping out old milk for new and replenishing the sandwich supply.

"Yes sir, I am." She cinched her apron tight, then pulled out the
filter basket in the coffee machine and dumped its soggy contents in
the trash bin.

"Should have called me," Philip said. "I could have helped."

Veronica felt herself smile but tamped it down. *Flirt*, she told herself. He was a *flirt*. "Thanks but I just had a few suitcases. No biggie."

"Reed told me about the mix-up at *GH*," Philip said. "That really sucks."

"Yeah, I guess so." She hit the grinder with more force than she had intended. The machine whirred loudly, conveniently drowning out anyone trying to discuss embarrassing mix-ups and ex-roommates.

"—other auditions," he was saying as she cut off the grinder.

"Beg pardon?"

"I said, what other auditions have you had?"

"Well . . ." Veronica looked away and tended to the stack of paper cups beside the register. "Not as many as I had hoped."

A customer suddenly appeared in front of the counter. She was dressed as if she were on her way to the opera, with a purple cape over her shoulders and a pair of long white gloves in her hand. "Do you have non-caffeinated coffee?" she asked before Veronica could welcome her.

"Um, yes, we have decaf. Would you like—"

"And does the non-caffeinated coffee come with sweet flavorings?"

"We have hazelnut and vanilla. Can I get you—"

"And do you grind your own non-caffeinated beans for the coffee?"

"Yes, we do, ma'am. Should I—"

"And do you use the same grinder for your non-caffeinated beans as you do for your caffeinated ones?"

"Excuse me?"

The woman slapped her gloves against the palm of her hand impatiently. "Do you use the same coffee bean grinder for your non-caffeinated beans as you do for your caffeinated ones? Is it the same grinding machine?"

Veronica glanced over at Philip and their eyes met. He nodded gravely. "Yes ma'am, it is. Did you want something?"

The woman lifted her chin and paced in a tight circle, examining first the counter, then the cake display, the tables, the paintings, and finally, Veronica. "You," she said as if making a queenly proclamation, "are a lovely girl."

"Why, thank you."

"But you wear far too much makeup." And with that, she turned on her purple-pumped heel and walked out the door.

Nervous giggles spilled out of Veronica's mouth as soon as the door had closed behind the woman. She looked over at Philip, whose hand was clamped over his own mouth. As their eyes met, they both began laughing. Great gales of guffaws rang out, filling the coffee shop and suffocating the street noise.

"Good lord, did you see her—"

"That cape, those gloves—"

"And her makeup—"

"Telling *me* I wear too much makeup—"

"Are you sure it was a she—"

"Non-caffeinated coffee—"

"What the hell is non-caffeinated coffee—"

"Maybe Donny was right! Someone *is* watching him!"

Philip poured two cups of coffee and handed one to Veronica with a playful grin. "Maybe it *was* Donny!"

"*Mon dieu!* Purple is *so* not his color." Veronica took her coffee to her laptop, which she kept out of sight below the counter, and quickly found a wi-fi signal.

After a moment, she felt Philip's presence behind her. "Can I help you?" she asked.

"Just being nosy."

She allowed him to look over her shoulder.

"I thought you were a stage actor," he said, sounding a little disappointed.

"I am," she replied defensively and moved her body back in front of the screen. "I mean I am *also* a stage actor. Right now I'm trying to pursue movies and television."

Philip leaned against the counter and stared at her. His gaze was intense, boring into her and through her. She felt like he could read everything about her in that one pin-prick of a moment but she couldn't read him. Her years of acting had left her vulnerable and open while his had locked him up tight. At least, it seemed that way to her.

She forced her glance back to her computer. "Not that I need any help. I've got a good feeling about my move to Craig's. I think it's a really positive environment. You know, with the dog and everything . . ." Her voice trailed off to a whisper.

"I was only helping her talk through some options," Philip said in a low voice. "She wanted someone to listen, that's all."

"I don't know what—"

"The ice cream parlor? I saw you on your date with Craig and the Illustrated Man."

"It wasn't a date," she scoffed.

"Neither was mine."

She felt a little relieved by his admission, corroborating Reed's as it did. But the hands, she wanted to ask, the touching of skin to skin? And the past . . . was it really past? No one was addressing *that*.

"You don't need to say anything, Philip," Veronica said. "It's not any of my business." Her finger tapped the mouse pad, scrolling through a bunch of casting notices on Craigslist. She chuckled to herself as she thought about her own Craig and what *his* list might be if he had a website like this.

"I know I don't need to explain," he said. "I want to."

Off-limits, she heard in her head and concentrated on her work. She found an ad for an open audition that day. The production company was looking for young women, ages 18-21, to play extras in a "major motion picture." She could do that, she thought.

"That's a cattle call," Philip noted, again peeking over her shoulder.

"Where everyone shows up and gets a number?" Veronica was intrigued. Maybe an anonymous number could work in her favor. "That sounds cool."

Philip nodded. "You have to do it once in your life. And then you'll never do it again."

A customer rapped on the display case to get their attention. "You open?"

"Yes, sir, what can I get you this morning?" Philip asked, assuming his manager's role.

Veronica closed her laptop when she saw a line begin to form. She stood next to Philip and took the marked paper cups from him, filling them with espressos and lattes and half-caf cappuccinos. "So . . . you think I should do it?" she asked Philip.

"Why not?" He shrugged as he wrote a customer's name on a cup. "You're lucky you found that one when you did."

"What do you mean?"

"It'll probably come down in about half an hour," he said. "I'll bet they've already got a hundred people lined up and waiting."

"Oh no!" Veronica quickly finished the latte she was making and handed it to a customer. "Should I go now? Do you mind?" She was already unwrapping her apron and moving toward the back of the store when Philip called her back.

"Wait! You can't leave me with all these people!" he cried.

"Oh, um . . . I'll call Craig," she said with a wink. "I'm sure he'll be happy to fill in."

And then she ran out the door.

There was a very famous saying about actors, Veronica remembered, from the very famous director Alfred Hitchcock: "I never said all actors are cattle. I said all actors should be *treated* like cattle."

Thanks to reality television shows, everyone in the world knew what an open audition looked like: mile long lines curled around city blocks, some of its sad participants having slept overnight to secure their places. Veronica had stared at those lines and wondered not about the sanity of the people in them but what the heck they did when they needed a bathroom break.

Disappointingly, this cattle call was not so grand. It was held in a studio space in North Hollywood, and there was just one line that extended perhaps half a block out the door. Inside, it was dark and chilly. Veronica signed in and exchanged her head shot for a paper number which she pinned on her shirt. She saw other girls cleverly placing their numbers on flat stomachs just below their cleavage. Veronica thought about doing that but realized her booblies would obscure the numbers so she put it, non-cleverly, over the left side of her chest.

She was surrounded by women between the ages of eighteen and twenty-one, blondes, brunettes and redheads of all races. Veronica watched as each girl sized the others up, determined the approximate competitive advantage and dismissed them—all in one glance, all in a matter of seconds.

"Group one!" a disembodied female voice called. "Over here please, ladies!"

The group was the first number on their tags. Veronica's was a two.

The actors assembled themselves in haphazard lines in the studio space, jostling for spots in pools of light which spilled from the catwalk above.

Two women approached the group as if it were a military inspection, with the younger woman following her leader two paces behind and carrying a clipboard and pen.

Veronica clenched her hands into fists, nervous for the group, watching for clues.

Who would be picked and who would be rejected?

She could see no rhyme or reason to the choices the woman was making. They were tall and short, dark and light, attractive or not.

"Group two! Hurry, please, ladies!"

Veronica's group! She joined the herd heading for the center of the studio.

The casting director moved swiftly through this group, examining every woman's head shot but only taking one out of every ten. *Those are brutal odds,* Veronica thought.

"These things totally suck," a brunette next to Veronica whispered. "But you never know. You could be an extra in some scene, and you're in the shot behind Keira Knightley, and they give you a line to say to her." The girl nodded sagely. "That happens."

"Really?"

"Yep. People tell me all the time how I look like Keira Knightley."

Veronica found herself nodding along. The girl did sort of look like the famous actress with an abundance of slightly crooked teeth and piercing blue eyes, but in the back of her mind, Veronica thought, *Why would anyone want to see Keira talking to herself?*

The casting women were closer, a few feet away from Veronica and then *bam!* They were so close Veronica could smell the director's Opium, a spicy scent that overpowered her younger assistant's Vera Wang body spray. She not only smelled like she was stuck in the 80s, she looked like it too: She had fluffy, feathered hair and wore high-waisted, tight-ankled pants and a jacket with shoulder pads so thick she could double as a crash test dummy in her off-hours.

"Hello, dear, what's your name?" Veronica heard the older woman say to the brunette beside her as she reviewed the girl's head shot and resume.

"Melody." Her voice was musical and sexy.

"Just Melody. No last name?" The casting director asked. "Like Cher?"

Melody cocked her head to one side and wrinkled her nose. "Is she still alive?"

Oh god, Veronica thought, rolling her eyes. *Is that what it took to get attention: brazen self-confidence?* The girl was either terribly sly or terribly cocky, and Veronica wondered which the casting director would choose to see.

"I like her," the older woman told her partner. "She reminds me of Keira."

"Very cute," the younger woman agreed.

"The French restaurant with Orlando and Heath." The casting director handed Melody's picture to her assistant and wagged a finger at the clipboard. "Write that down."

"Perfect choice."

And now it was Veronica's turn. She waited, trying to imagine what she might say about her name. *Veronica May*, she heard in her head. *My name is Veronica May.* Was there anything witty she could say about it? Perhaps the woman would notice Veronica's violet eyes and comment to her assistant, "She reminds me of Elizabeth." And Veronica could smile and Dip her head, as a lock of hair fell seductively across her face.

But the woman did not even pause, nor did her assistant. They walked past Veronica with nary an extra blink. Veronica felt a cool breeze as they moved on to the next woman.

Veronica's heart sank in her chest. What was wrong with *her*? They didn't even give her a chance. They didn't look at her resume, or her head shot, or even her face. *She* could be an extra in a scene with Orlando and Heath as well as anyone else in this studio—better even!

"Um, excuse me?" she heard herself say. "Excuse me?"

The casting director paused but did not turn. "Yes, dear?"

"Don't you want to look at my head shot?" she asked, holding out her photo like an offering.

"No, dear, I don't."

"But . . ." A few women behind Veronica chuckled. "It's just that, well, you saw everyone else's but you didn't see mine."

"Don't need to, dear," the woman said and continued on her way.

The assistant called out, "Group three! Next!"

Veronica slowly walked away as the next group of women filed in and around her.

"As if they would ever pick *her*," she heard a voice whisper loudly.

"Even in the background she'd be huge," a second voice agreed.

"Is that why they named it a cattle call?" The first voice asked, and then the two dissolved into giggles.

"Oh you're so clever," Veronica muttered to herself. She held her head high and tried to walk faster without making it look like she was escaping. And then, out of the corner of her eye, she caught sight of a tiny girl in group three hopping from foot to foot. Veronica's head snapped around to take a closer look, and her body soon followed.

She couldn't believe it: Standing not ten feet away from her, wearing a silky camisole top over a pair of low riders, was Reed. Veronica thought she looked exactly like a mini-Bianca.

What the hell was she doing here, she wanted to know. Reed, who had an "arrangement" with an agent, who went on dozens of auditions, who got jobs just by flirting . . . what was *she* doing at a cattle call?

And what of Little Vee's assertion that she never went online for jobs? Or maybe it was just Veronica who wasn't supposed to do that. She watched and waited and fumed to herself. She would have to say something; she would have to speak her mind. She didn't know what Reed's problem was, why she couldn't be honest with her, but she would soon find out.

The casting director approached Reed. She accepted her head shot, glanced at the back . . .

. . . and then returned it to Reed and moved on.

Reed stopped moving and just stood there, hands inelegantly hanging by her sides, her shoulders drooping. One of her spaghetti straps slipped off; the effect was sloppy rather than sexy. Veronica couldn't see Reed's face, but she knew it would not be her usual cheerful self.

"Group four! Hurry, ladies!"

Veronica hung back in the shadows of a background flat and waited as groups four and three switched places. She watched Reed walk off alone, adjusting her camisole strap and fiddling with her jewelry.

Pauvre Vee, she thought, in spite of herself, in spite of all she had been feeling before. Seeing Reed sad and lonely while the other girls skipped away in groups of twos and threes reminded Veronica of how she felt on that first day in L.A., when Reed told her about the boy she loved who broke her heart. Then and now, she wanted to take Little Vee in her arms and tell her everything was going to be all right.

Veronica stepped out of the shadows and started for Reed, but as their paths were about to cross, Little Vee's cell rang.

"Hi!" Reed cried and her whole demeanor changed. Her face brightened, her energy lifted and she was Reed again, not Veronica's Vee. "It was amazing! Well, of course I did!" She laughed loudly into the phone. "You did not! You didn't! All right, I'm on my way!"

She tucked her purse under her arm and sauntered out of the studio as if she had just landed the lead role in a Steven Spielberg film—as if nothing bad had ever happened to her.

Veronica watched her walk away.

chapter 31

Veronica read Diana's October 10 letter on October 10 while she addressed her envelopes on the back patio at Craig's house.

Dearest Moose,

They love me at the soap! Did you see me last week? I was the maid in Brooke's bedroom, picking up the lingerie on the floor. No lines yet but soon, I just know it. I'm going to be Famous with a capital F and everyone will know who I am. All those people back home who thought I couldn't do anything. Ha! I'm going to be as big as Michelle Pfeiffer someday!

And good news number two: I was cast in that musical! Now you know why I'm going to be huge! I read in Variety that the budget is getting bigger and bigger, and they're trying to get some really major stars. We've got so many rehearsals, so much work to be done, so much cho-

reography to learn before they shoot our scenes, probably in early November. Between that and the soap, I'm so busy! I'm sorry I can't come for a visit.

Love and miss you lots,

Yours, Diana

It took less than two weeks for Veronica's new attitude to make a difference. New house, new roommate, new off-limits love . . . oh well, two out of three were pretty good odds.

So with all of this new positive energy in her life, it wasn't a huge surprise to Veronica when she got a phone call to audition for a commercial.

What did surprise her was that she got two more phone calls for two more auditions!

"Oh my god!" she squealed to Donny on the evening she got the third call. "That's number three! I have three auditions scheduled!"

Donny shrugged and the tattoos on his biceps shrugged too. "Whatever."

"Aren't you happy for me?" Veronica wanted to take the boy by the shoulders and shake him. With his blasé attitude—so unlike her own newfound enthusiasm—Veronica believed Donny would be either the best or the worst hostage negotiator, if he ever finished his courses.

"I have three auditions!" she said again, this time with a stronger emphasis on the three. "Not one, not two. Three!"

"I told you to be a blonde," Donny said. "You coulda had thirty auditions by now."

Veronica wanted to tell the world, but she settled for a quick email to Ginny and a text message to Val. She also sent an email to Daddy, preferring to write her father rather than risk getting May on the phone and having to hear the woman remind her yet again that she needed a dress for the wedding.

And then there was Philip. She casually sauntered through the café to the back where he was smoking a cigarette and picking up trash.

"So, um, Philip?"

He looked up and smiled when he saw her, a smile so honest and sincere it seemed to Veronica like no one had ever smiled at her before. He crushed the cigarette beneath his foot.

"Nasty habit."

Veronica agreed. "My dad smoked unfiltered Camels until I was ten."

"He quit?"

She snapped her fingers. "Just like that."

Philip was impressed. "Wow, cold turkey, huh?"

"Turkey sure helped," she said with a laugh. "So, um, I just wanted to tell you I have some auditions scheduled, so I'll probably have to switch my shifts with Gena or Craig."

"Sure, whatever," he said, as he bent down to pick up the cigarette butt he crushed.

"Did you hear me?" She touched his arm to get his attention again. "I said *some* auditions."

"Some, huh?" Now Philip grinned. "Yeah, I heard you. That's awesome."

"Thanks." She felt a little disappointed by his response. She wasn't sure what she had expected, but it was probably something more than a friendly smile.

"Okay, well, I'm gonna go now. See if I can call Gena." She started for the back door.

"*Merde*," Philip called behind her. She turned to look at him.

"That's what we say in the theater," she said.

"I know," Philip said with a twinkle in his eye. "You can do this, Veronica. I know you can. I believe in you."

I believe in you.

Veronica felt a surge of adrenaline shoot through her, as if she had just swallowed a shot of Buzz's Triple Espresso Blend. She recalled her initial meeting with Philip, when she had shaken his hand and felt his confidence.

Now *she* had it and there was nothing she couldn't do.

The commercial audition was held in the office of a casting director in Beverly Hills. When Veronica saw the address on Wilshire, she was hugely excited—her first trip to the fancy-schmancy section of town! She imagined seeing celebrities in their natural habitat: shopping for diamond bracelets and silk lingerie, getting their hair done by thousand-dollar stylists. But all she saw were tourists taking pictures of themselves in front of signs for Rodeo Drive.

The casting director's office resembled a walk-in health clinic more than anything else.

"Hello, Veronica," the assistant at the desk said, shaking her hand. "I'm Nadine. I'll take your head shot now."

Veronica handed the woman her photo and resume. "Can you tell me what this is for?" While she watched television the night before, she had been picturing herself as the spokeswoman for Coke or Pantene or the new and improved Ford Focus.

What a coup to go home to Daddy and May with something like that! She would turn on the TV and casually announce, "Oh there I am at the wheel of the special edition H3. Did you know it's got a hemi?"

"It's a new diet product called AlwaysSlim," Nadine told her with a big smile, like Veronica should be thrilled there was yet another product on the market for people of size. "It hasn't been approved by the FDA yet, but it's very big in Canada and France." She picked up the phone on her desk and pressed a button. "We have Veronica May here."

Veronica waited while the woman finished the call.

"You can go right through that door."

Unlike at the cattle call or the soap audition, this casting director was seeing people one at a time. It was just Veronica in her office.

"Hi there!" the casting director said cheerily. "I'm Donna." She was a young woman, Veronica thought, basing her decision on an absence of wrinkles and grey hair, yet she looked older, perhaps because she was dressed sort of matronly, in a khaki pant suit and matching scarf.

"No, don't sit down," Donna said. "I want to see you first."

Veronica stood in front of the desk as Donna came around and scrutinized her.

"Would you mind turning around please? Slowly?"

Veronica twirled in a circle.

Donna sighed and gave her a friendly grimace as she leaned back against the edge of her desk. "I'm afraid you're not right for the role," she said.

Veronica's mouth dropped open. "But I haven't said anything yet!"

"You're much larger than we thought," the woman said with an exaggerated un-smiley face. "Thank you for coming." She returned to her chair, dismissing Veronica.

"But . . . this is for a diet product," Veronica protested weakly.

"Yes, but we need people who are TV fat, not really fat." Donna frowned as if she had accidentally swallowed a bug. "Real fat people are much too large."

Veronica left, feeling like someone had slugged her in the stomach. Still, she shrugged it off as best she could, reminding herself that she still had two more auditions.

A few days later, for the industrial, Veronica dressed in a navy blue skirt that came to just below the knees (a most flattering length for her) and a gauzy white blouse with three-quarter sleeves that buttoned to just above her cleavage (a most flattering cut on her).

She was surprised the audition was held in a regular two-story building. For some reason, she pictured it in some lonely warehouse in an office park on the outskirts of Culver City.

As she waited with two other women for the casting director to call her, she was beginning to feel like a pro: walk in, smile, hand over head shot and resume (assume they lost the first one you sent), smile, perch daintily on a chair while pretending to read a magazine, stand gracefully, glide to the door, smile, wave goodbye to your fellow auditioners, and be very, very nice to everyone you meet. And smile.

"Good morning, Veronica," this casting director said. "I'm Wayne. I write, produce, direct and edit everything. Saves me a buttload of money." He scanned her resume. "Have you ever read from a teleprompter?" he asked.

"No." She smiled modestly. "But I think I'm pretty smart."

"I'm sure you are." He was a tall man, broad-shouldered yet thin, with a grey ponytail at the back of his neck. Veronica had to admire the man's sartorial style for its sheer off-beatness: he wore an L.A. Dodgers T-shirt beneath a maroon corduroy jacket and buttonfly Levi's with a pair of old-school Adidas. He caught her staring at his outfit.

"Go Blue!" he said, pumping his fist in the air for emphasis.

Veronica half-smiled and returned the gesture, having no idea what she was doing. "Yay, blue!"

Wayne walked her into a tiny studio behind his office and showed her the teleprompter, essentially a screen with a scrolling script. He pointed out the controls off to the side. It looked just like a computer to Veronica, complete with keyboard and monitor.

"I'll just roll a few lines and we'll see how you do."

Veronica cleared her throat a couple of times and smoothed down her blouse. She glanced down at her chest and frowned. If Reed were here, she would be flaunting her assets in front of a male casting director. Should *she*? She reached down and sort of plumped up her breasts from below her bra line. She thought about opening the top button of her blouse but decided against it; there was a fine line between sexy and horribly, horribly tacky.

"All right, Veronica," Wayne said from behind the teleprompter. "Just follow the script as it flows over the screen but don't stare at it. Watch the camera instead."

Camera! *Mon dieu,* she thought. Here she was, shoving her booblies around and she was in front of a camera! How had she not seen that before? What kind of actor *was* she, anyway?

An extremely nervous one, apparently.

The text scrolled very slowly, line by line. Veronica read the first line to herself.

"Out loud, please," Wayne called to her.

"Oh! I'm sorry." She stood up straighter. "For years, housewives have had to make do with mediocre anti-stick surges . . ."

The text stopped and Wayne's voice called out again. "Not surges. Surfaces."

Veronica giggled. "Oh my gosh! I didn't see that. Could you slow it down please?"

"Just a little but try to keep up, okay?"

She nodded and started over again on that line. "Mediocre anti-stick surfaces. Teflon, Anolon, T-Fal. But now there's a new product. Hold up product. It's called Duralon."

Wayne sighed. "Don't say, 'Hold up product.' Hold up the product." His finger appeared from the dark and pointed in her direction.

Veronica looked frantically around her and found a grey-colored pot on a table behind her. "Oh, of course. Sorry."

"But now there's a new product." Veronica lifted the pot to the camera with a flourish.

"Not so big!" Wayne called. "You nearly took out the lens."

Veronica was reminded of her very first movement class when Larry had gone on about what he called her bigness, her tendency to exaggerate her movements.

"You're not playing to the back row," he had chided her. "The camera brings the back row to *you*."

Come on, Veronica, she said to herself, *you can do this.*

She closed her eyes and tried to think of one of the many infomercials she had watched late at night, either alone or giggling with the Vees. The dulcet tones of Ron Popeil extolling the virtues of his magic knives came to mind and made Veronica smile. She had ordered the set for Father's Day one year, thrilling her father who had immediately set them up all over the kitchen and at his grill. That was one of his favorite gifts that hadn't involved chocolate.

Veronica opened her eyes and took a breath. She calmly held the pot up to the camera as if it were the most natural gesture in her repertoire and smoothly read from the teleprompter. "It's Duralon, and it's the toughest surface known to man." She paused and winked. "And housewife."

"Very nice," Wayne said, with a bit of surprise in his voice. "Much, much better."

As they walked back to Wayne's office, Veronica felt as if a gigantic boulder had lifted from her shoulders. Sure, it was only a cheesy infomercial, but it was acting and she had finally gotten it right.

When Wayne opened the door, Veronica was startled by a sudden burst of noise. Crammed inside the waiting area were at least 40 women, laughing and talking and reciting lines. Veronica's heart sank upon seeing them: beautiful, skinny, model-types. She felt a pat on her back.

"We'll be in touch, okay?" Wayne said.

She wanted to thank him, to impress upon him how much she enjoyed meeting him and learning about Duralon and how she really, really needed an acting job to prove to herself that she didn't completely suck.

"Go Blue!" she said, pumping her fist.

But Wayne was already onto the next girl.

Dejected, Veronica stumbled out of the office and into her car. *One more audition,* she told herself. She had one more audition. This one she simply had to get.

Her third nicest outfit was a pair of tailored black pants and a silky lavender blouse that accentuated her violet eyes. She wore this with strappy black sandals which added an inch to her height. May May had helped her pick out the pants in the Macy's Women's World department back when she was a freshman in high school. Away from all the cute junior clothes cut to fit nonexistent hips and waists, from all the skirts and dresses that Veronica had enviably and unsuccessfully tried to force herself into, she was finally in the land of clothes that fit. She had felt like a grownup for the very first time.

She hoped this outfit would give her the little extra boost she needed. Because when you looked good . . . well, you looked good, *oui?*

The third audition was for an episode of a television show Veronica had never watched— until last night when she and Craig found it on a cable channel neither of them realized they had.

"I guess it's sort of funny," Veronica had remarked during a commercial break.

"Sweetie, this commercial is funnier than that show," Craig said.

It was a typical sitcom about a wacky family in the suburbs and their meddling neighbors with a kitchen set and a living room set and a staircase to nowhere. Veronica tried to laugh when the young son attempted to hide his bad grades from his parents, only to be mortified when they invited his teacher over for dinner, but she was pretty sure she had seen that same recycled plotline in an episode of *Malcolm in the Middle, The Simpsons* and *That 70s Show.*

"So it's not original," she told Craig, trying to find something positive in a bad situation comedy. "Why mess with a classic formula?"

The cable network was located on Gower near Sunset Boulevard. Disappointingly, it looked like just another office building. There were no people wandering around in costumes or carrying flats or props. It could have been an insurance company with its bland façade and ficus plants. The only concession to its place in the show business industry was a bank of televisions behind the reception desk, all showing the cable network's own programming and promos.

Veronica pasted on a magnificent smile and took a seat on a couch in a small waiting area where a cluster of attractive actors were studying sides and thumbing through Blackberrys. She held a highlighter in her hand as she skimmed the script for her lines. She would be reading for the role of Tanya, a beautiful exchange student who stays with the family and on whom the oldest son develops a huge crush. *This plotline probably dated back to the very first sitcom ever produced,* Veronica thought. *Easy-peasy, lemon-squeezy.*

"Veronica?" A production assistant entered the waiting room. "They're ready for you."

Veronica followed the PA to a screening room where two women and a man, all wearing sober suits and white shirts, sat in a row. A video camera was set up on a tripod.

"I'm Veronica May," she said in her most professional actor's voice. "Nice to meet you." No one said anything so she added, "Love the show. Very, very funny."

The executives nodded, apparently preferring to remain anonymous. The door opened then and another woman entered, heading straight for Veronica. She had a short, soft natural haircut and was dressed in a skinny black pencil skirt and wrap top; she was the only one who smiled. "I'm Brenda. I cast for the network. You have sides?"

Veronica held up her pages. "Tanya, the exchange student. Did you want an accent?"

Brenda shook her head and took the sides from Veronica. She gave her another set. "Sorry. They made a mistake. You're reading for Missy, the twins' babysitter."

"Oh, uh, okay." Veronica stalled as she tried to find a character description.

"Are you ready?" Brenda didn't wait for Veronica to respond but instead pressed a button on the camera. A red light blinked on.

"I'll read Stephanie, the mother," Brenda said. She held the script in front of her. "So ding-dong, the doorbell rings."

Veronica found a description of the character at the top of the scene.

The door opens and MISSY, 17, stands there, grinning. She is about 30 pounds overweight, wearing tight low-riders with a hefty muffin top. She has a Snickers wrapper in her hand and a smear of chocolate over her lip like a mustache.

Veronica's eyes froze. The words "muffin top" and "smear" stood out from the page as if they had been written in red ink. *This* was Missy? *This* was the character she was reading for? She rubbed a temple with her fingertips and felt her pulse throb through the skin.

"Are you okay, Veronica?" Brenda asked. "Can we try again?"

Veronica nodded but couldn't speak, couldn't breathe. She forced herself to inhale and felt the air hiccup in her chest. She closed her eyes, exhaled slowly, and tried to conjure Jamal's sooth-ing voice from yoga class. *Let the bad air out, breathe, breathe. Maybe the writers redeemed themselves later in the scene,* she thought, *when they realized how insensitive they were being to poor Missy.*

She opened her eyes and flipped through the next couple of pages. She saw Missy tell the father an inappropriate joke about sex, saw her steal slices of a special birthday cake, and finally, saw her sit on an antique chair and break it.

You can do this, she heard Philip say in her head. *I know you can.*

"So, ding-dong, the doorbell rings," Brenda said again.

Veronica tried to blink away her anger, but that nasty script with its horrible words was still in her hands, gripped by her shaking fin-gers.

I believe in you.

"Veronica? Ding dong? Veronica?"

Chapter 32

"It was too degrading," Veronica shook her head into her cell as she walked to the coffee shop for the evening shift. "I left without reading one line."

"Good for you, *chica*," Val said from Arizona during a three-way call with Ginny. "You stood up for yourself. I'm proud of you."

Veronica felt a lump in her throat. To play the butt of the joke simply because of her size was something she had never stooped to in all her years as an actor. But another actor would. The role of Missy, and others like her, wouldn't go away just because Veronica said no.

"You'll find the thing that's right for you," Ginny insisted. "Didn't you tell me you could sense good things coming?"

"Yeah, something like that," Veronica mumbled. She arrived at Buzz in record time, her disappointment and hurt having propelled her down the sidewalk at the speed of light. "Later, Vees." She clicked off the cell and ducked in the back through the employee entrance.

"Craig!" she called as she grabbed her apron from a hook on the wall and fastened it around her waist. "Craig? We need food for Max! I gave him the last of the gourmet stuff this afternoon, but I didn't have time to go to Petco and—"

"Hey."

"Oh, hey, Philip." Veronica stopped short as she pushed the curtain aside. Philip was behind the counter, wrapping his own apron around his hips and tying it behind his back. "Is Craig late?"

Philip shook his head and kept tying his apron. "Craig and I switched shifts tonight. He wanted to go to some party."

"Is Donny coming in soon?"

"Nope. He has a night class."

"Gena?"

"Uh-uh."

Veronica whipped her head around. "You're kidding."

"It's just you and me tonight."

"Um. That's gonna suck," she said. "It gets pretty busy in here."

Philip handed a customer the key to the bathroom. "Look, it's Wednesday." He waved a hand at the few patrons they had. "Everyone's home watching *Lost.*"

Veronica laughed. "It's not Wednesday."

"Oh." Philip made a face. "Well, then we'll only have to split tips two ways tonight."

"Yeah, okay," she agreed. "That's a bonus." Secretly, she felt a little thrill at the possibility of it being just the two of them on the shift tonight, working side by side. She could picture it now: He passes her a cup to fill, a half-caf cappuccino perhaps, their hands touch, sparks fly, the wind machine kicks up and the music swells, and then it's over and they walk hand in hand into the sunset. It would make all the nastiness of this past week magically go away.

"So how were all your auditions?" he asked.

Veronica's spirits sank, and the image of holding hands in the setting sun dissipated from her mind. "Not exactly what I hoped for."

A customer wanting . . . *something* . . . interrupted her at that moment, and Veronica was thankful for the distraction. She had had three auditions and three miserable failures. How could she tell Philip how horrible she was, how much of a loser she had become since she came out here? She was beginning to think she should have stayed in Arizona.

As Veronica had predicted, the night got extremely busy, and while they did touch hands as they passed cups to each other, the only thing that flew between them was spittle as they shouted orders back and forth. The sun set with absolutely no handholding.

They had a moment to breathe around eight o'clock. Veronica poured herself a cup of decaf and sat at a stool at the counter. Philip wiped the space in front of her and smiled wearily.

"Damn, I would have sworn it was Wednesday," he said.

"Take a load off," Veronica said. "The manager won't mind."

Philip grabbed a can of Hansen's cream soda and sat beside Veronica on a stool. He popped the top and gulped down half of it before taking a breath. "So tell me . . ." He let out a long burp and thumped his chest. ". . . about your auditions."

Why didn't boys say "excuse me," Veronica wondered. *They always seemed to be so enamored of their own bodily functions.*

"You can't let it go, can you?"

"Nope," Philip said. Then he bared his teeth. "I'm like a pit bull that way."

Veronica laughed. "Yeah, all right, I guess I can tell you."

She started with the diet product commercial and ended with the TV show. She left nothing out.

"Bastards." Philip shook his head slowly. "I'm proud of you, Veronica. You have to put your foot down and not let people get away with crap. Because they'll just keep doing it and doing it."

"I know but what can I do? That's how this town works."

Philip wobbled his hand, *comme ci, comme ça.* "Sort of. You have to find your niche and stick to it. You did all that theater in high school, right?"

"Yes, but—"

"I think you should start there. That's what you know, that's what you're good at."

Veronica smiled. "Are you giving me advice? I thought that was against your policy."

Philip hung his head sheepishly. "Sorry. I'll shut up now."

Veronica clasped his hand in hers and squeezed gently. "No, no. I want to hear it." His hand felt so utterly masculine within hers, meaty and muscular and substantive, like if she needed rescuing, this hand would save her. She was reluctant to let it go, but just before she did, she felt him squeeze back.

"I really shouldn't be giving anyone advice," Philip said, his voice low and hollow. "I let the business get to me, and I didn't stay true to what I really loved, which was the acting itself. I was super competitive." He glanced at her and then quickly away and laughed self-consciously. "You wouldn't have liked me back then."

"I think I still would have liked you," Veronica insisted. She leaned on her elbow and stared at him.

"Ultimately, it was all the worrying about other people and the roles they were getting instead of me. That's really why I left the business. It totally aged me. It even gave me grey hair!" He exclaimed, pointing at his head. "Twenty years old and I have grey hair."

"You do not have grey hair."

"You're not looking." He pulled her stool toward him. "Look," he said and bent his head down.

"I don't know what you're talking about." But she looked just the same.

He had a head of straight brown hair, no greys, just brown hair. But then . . . it was not. It was actually a delicate shade of chestnut, not brown, and some of the strands looked golden, as if kissed by the sun. And they were not strictly straight but waved slightly, and she had a flash of a picture inside her head, a picture of Philip with his hair grown long and wavy and—

—and then he bent down farther and she was staring at the crown of his head, at its gentle slope. The hairs on the back of his neck were clipped short, had likely been buzz cut, and she raised her fingers to them and caressed them lightly, first in the direction in which they grew, which made them feel soft and fuzzy, and then in the opposite way, which made them feel prickly and sent a shiver up her arm and—

—and then she felt his hands on her hips, felt them slide across her lower back and pull her closer to him.

His head rose to meet hers.

His eyes lifted to meet hers.

His lips parted . . .

. . . to meet hers.

Their kiss was exquisite, the culmination of months of wanting, months of waiting. Veronica could taste coffee and cream soda on Philip's tongue. His hand pressed the back of her head closer to his so that their cheeks, their noses, and their eyelashes kissed too. They parted slightly, to breathe, and then began kissing again, and Veronica didn't care where they were, if anyone was expecting a macchiato to be made, if anyone was watching. Let them watch, let them be witnesses to what had to be the greatest kiss of all time.

Veronica wished she could rise up out of her body and watch the kiss happening from on high.

"Oh yes, that's exactly right," she would tell herself. "That's the exact way people should kiss. Does everyone see this?"

Veronica felt herself smile, imagining her audience.

"God, that took you long enough," Philip said, grinning.

"Me? What about you? I've been waiting since the day we met," she said and blushed. What an extremely uncool thing to say, regardless of its truth.

A pair of customers entered the coffee shop just then and rapped on the counter to get the couple's attention. They reluctantly pulled apart.

"Damn coffee drinkers," Philip muttered.

"I'll get it," Veronica laughed and hopped up from her stool. She ran behind the counter. "*Bonjour, mes amis!*" she sang. "Welcome to Buzz!"

She had never felt so happy to make a cup of coffee in her life.

chapter 33

The one place where you certainly didn't want to be distracted by something as mundane as a kiss from the boy you loved was yoga class. No matter how many times Jamal reminded her to breathe or how often he moved her limbs into the correct position, Veronica could not retain the knowledge for longer than a second.

The kiss, she thought. *Un baiser parfait.* The wonderful, perfect kiss. Her brain played the scene over and over again like a VCR stuck on rewind. No, no, her entrance was too early. Fast forward a bit. There, right there when he leaned in and wrapped his arms around her back. Yes, that's it. Can we go into slo-mo for a few frames? And could we play back that dialogue, the part where he asks her to go to dinner with him and then she says yes and they talk about restaurants and movies and books and plays and cooking and coffee? Right. Turn the volume up, *s'il vous plaît.*

"Hey Vee," Reed snapped her fingers a few times, plucking Veronica out of her daydream. "Class is over. You need some help getting up?"

Veronica blinked a few times and smiled beatifically. "I'm fine, thanks." Why, she could float herself up off the floor if she wanted to. Float herself all the way down the stairs and out the door and into the atmosphere, if she chose. She had only to will it to make it so.

Behind Reed was Bianca, wearing skintight white yoga pants, her hair wrapped in a topknot and ponytail à la Gwen Stefani. Had Veronica been so preoccupied with Philip that she hadn't seen the blonde Amazon in class? She was actually disappointed she hadn't witnessed the model's attempts to turn herself into a pretzel. That must have been something to watch.

"Oh hi, Bianca," Veronica said. She rolled up her mat and tucked it under her arm as she walked out the door with the two girls.

"You okay, Vee?" Reed asked.

"Hmm . . . ? Oh yes, I'm fine." Veronica giggled and covered her mouth with her hand. "Sorry. I guess I've got a case of the gigglies," she said.

Reed and Bianca exchanged a bemused glance.

Veronica laughed again, then bounced down the stairs ahead of Reed and Bianca to where Reed's BMW was illegally parked in the alley next to the building.

Bianca gave Veronica a long once-over and nodded approvingly. "You've lost weight," she announced as she lit the end of her cigarette with a pink Bic. "Are you doing Atkins?"

Veronica shook her head, grinning from ear to ear. "Nope. It's just me, I guess."

"You're exercising then," Bianca prodded. "Yoga, of course."

"I walk Max." Veronica shrugged. "Does that count as exercise?"

"And the junk food?"

Veronica thought about the last time she had eaten a Twinkie or baked up a batch of brownies. It certainly wasn't within recent memory. She remembered desperately wanting an Entenmann's chocolate fudge cake after her last horrible audition, but instead she went to work and talked to Philip.

Ah, Philip. She giggled again and felt herself blush as she thought about him. "Maybe it's the love diet."

Reed's head picked up then, from where she was playing with her cell phone. "What's this?"

"Philip kissed me," Veronica said and then rolled her eyes. "God, that sounds so lame, doesn't it? But I just realized that whenever I'm around him, I don't feel like eating."

Bianca surprised Veronica with a gentle smile. "He sounds very special."

"Yeah, he is," Veronica whispered. "I really like him." She looked over at Reed who hadn't responded. "What do you think? He's special, isn't he?"

"Oh yeah, totally," Reed said hastily. "He's a great guy." She slipped on a pair of sunglasses and pointed at them. "Don't forget, Vee. You don't want wrinkles."

Bianca patted the top of her head, as if she expected to find her own glasses there. "Where are mine?"

"Car," Reed replied and aimed her remote at the BMW. It chirped twice to let Bianca in.

"So . . ." Reed began when she and Veronica were alone. "When was this kiss?"

"Last night," Veronica sighed. "We're going out Saturday."

"Oh, *Saturday*, that reminds me," Reed said. "I heard about an audition for a movie that's shooting in Venice Beach. Great role. You'd be perfect for it."

"Not you?"

"I am *way* too busy for this one. Here, let me give you the number of the guy." Reed wrote a phone number on an old parking ticket and handed it to Veronica.

"Wow, thanks, Vee," Veronica said. "That's really sweet of you."

Reed shrugged. "No worries. I'm sure you'd do the same for me." She gave Veronica a little air kiss. "I'm so sweaty," she said by way of explanation. "Ciao!"

Then she slid behind the wheel of her car and waved to Veronica as she pulled out of the alley, mere seconds before a cop on a motorcycle came charging through.

Veronica shook her head with a grin. Little Vee was a very lucky girl.

chapter 34

Venice was called Venice because of the canals, *naturelle-ment*. Albeit on a much smaller scale. The area known as Venice Beach was famous for its colorful residents: the snake-charmers and free-range cockatoos, the impromptu drum groups and urban magicians, skateboarders, Rollerbladers and Razor riders.

Conrad Cooke's studio was located about a block east of Venice Beach on Abbotkinney Boulevard, a quaint stretch of antique shops, coffee houses and real estate offices.

He had told Veronica over the phone that this film, a story about lost love, was destined for Sundance and would secure him a studio development deal. The pay was nominal, but the potential for exposure immeasurable.

"So, Conrad," Veronica said as she watched him set up a clunky video camera in the center of his sunlit attic studio. "Have you auditioned many people yet?"

"You're the first." He fiddled with a switch on the tripod, and the entire contraption fell to the floor with a thud.

"Can I help you at all?"

He shook his head, and a golden curl fell out from under his Angels baseball cap. "I borrowed this from a friend. Mine's in the shop." He struggled to right the camera.

Veronica glanced around the dusty studio and saw a well-worn surfboard in one corner, a pile of dirty clothes in another. "Would you mind if I looked at the script while I'm waiting?"

"Help yourself." Conrad gestured with a dark hairy arm to a metal folding table where a stack of black and white head shots and a dog-eared, handwritten script sat next to a bowl of candy corn. "There's beers in the fridge if you want one." A small dorm-sized refrigerator sat next to the folding table.

Veronica casually brushed a hand through her competition and couldn't help but notice all the women were on the heavy side. Some attractive, some homely; half the photos professionally-shot, half blown-up Polaroids. She picked up the script: *Virgins of Brighton Beach.*

Um, okay.

"Ready!" Conrad crossed his arms over his chest and looked her up and down. "You're gonna be Cassie, the virgin who hooks up with Steve at the club. Take a look at page 14."

She flipped to a dog-eared page and glanced at the scene description:

"Cassie, a twenty-year-old virgin, waves to Steve across a crowded dance floor. He waves back."

So far, so good, she thought.

"Cassie: You're cute. You want to dance with me?"

"Steve: Sure. You're cute too."

"I'll read Steve's lines," Conrad said. "Why don't you stand right here?" He came behind Veronica and took her by the elbows, moving her a few feet closer to the camera. She felt a bristle of his sideburn against her shoulder and smelled Doritos and stale beer on his breath. It was a slight invasion of personal space but nothing she couldn't handle.

"Now, look right into the lens and pretend it's Steve," Conrad said. He pointed a finger at her and then switched on the camera.

"You're cute," Veronica said. "You want to dance with me?"

"Sure," Conrad replied from behind the camera. "You're cute too."

Veronica's eyes slid down to the page in front of her. "My name's Cassie. What's yours?"

"Steve."

"Hi, Steve. Do you come here a lot?"

"This is my first time. I just moved here from New York," Conrad said.

"Wow, New York. I've always wanted to go to New York."

"Bounce around a little more, like you're dancing at a club," Conrad directed her.

"Bounce?" She hopped up and down a little but immediately felt self-conscious as her chest and arms and belly shook. "I really don't think—"

"Here, like this." Conrad took her by the arms and did a sort of Fifties-style twist, which in itself was fine, but his thighs rubbed against hers as he moved and his hands kept brushing the sides of her breasts, making her flinch.

She pulled back out of his reach. "I think I got it," she said and began a little step-side, step-side instead, every inch of her body gripped so tightly it couldn't possibly move on its own.

Conrad's face was flushed, and a trickle of sweat rolled out from under his cap and down his sideburn. "Sure, that's fine. Let's keep going."

Veronica held the script at arm's length and tried to read the lines while managing a two-step. Her director, she noticed, remained in front of the camera, less than a foot away. She tried to ignore him. "Do they have a lot of virgins in New York?"

"No, we don't have any virgins in New York."

"Wow. You know, I'm a virgin."

"That's it, keep dancing. Now turn around a little, keep dancing. Good."

"I hate being a virgin. Do you think you could show me how to have sex?"

"Sure. We can do it right now if you want." Conrad paused. "Okay, now this is where you unzip your dress and shake 'em in his face. Okay? Go."

She stopped dancing. "Maybe there's another role I could play?"

"What? You don't like this?" He took the script out of her hands.

"I'm just not terribly comfortable with sex scenes."

Conrad flipped through pages, shaking his head. "I don't really have any scenes where the chicks aren't getting it on with Steve." He put the script aside and moved closer to Veronica. "Maybe you just need a little practice," he said and pulled Veronica toward him by her bottom, squeezing her butt with one hand while he dove his chin into her chest.

"What . . . what are doing?" she shrieked.

Conrad ran his hands down her thighs and breathed heavily into her neck. "Come on, sweetie. I'll give you the lead role."

Veronica pulled her arms in close to her, took a deep breath and then with one quick move, shoved Conrad away from her with all the strength she had. He went tumbling to the ground, landing in a sweaty heap in front of his tripod. She was tempted to land a sharp kick in his groin, but instead, she snatched up her handbag and took the stairs two at a time.

Her hand was on the front door when she heard him call out to her.

"Could I call you? Could we go out sometime?"

She ran all the way to her car.

A porn film, now that was rich, she thought, as adrenaline sped through her body. That just took the cake. She should have known: the hand-written script, the director who couldn't use a video camera, the beers in the dorm fridge.

The nerve of that pervert! She felt like she'd been slimed. Every part of her that he had touched felt contaminated and used, and she needed a long hot shower to wash the disgust off her skin and out of her head.

She was lucky, she thought, that it hadn't been worse. She was lucky she hadn't walked into a more dangerous situation. And she was very lucky she was bigger than Conrad Cooke. Someone like Little Vee might not have fared so well.

She sat in her car, exhausted and spent, and felt the heat of the autumn sun soak into her face and hair and limbs. She closed her eyes and breathed and felt her body slowly stop shaking. All she wanted to do was to act. That was all. She loved it, had always loved it, and was good at it. She thought—she hoped—it would be the one thing about her that made her stand out from other people, the one thing that made her special.

Not her weight.

She was tired of being called in for jobs because she was heavy or turned down for jobs because she was heavy. It was a no-win situation. Couldn't she be loved for who she was, the way she was?

When she arrived at the café, she heard Philip's voice behind the curtain, talking to a customer. Veronica sighed, relieved. She needed to hear his words of kindness, to feel his lips brush hers, and to have him make it all better again. She pushed aside the curtain and saw—

—Reed at the counter, giving Philip a long, lingering kiss on the lips, straining on the very tips of her toes to reach him but looking oh-so-cute doing so.

Veronica gasped and the couple turned. For a second, Philip looked dazed and confused.

"Vee, you're here," Reed said, and Veronica saw the tiniest smile curl Little Vee's lips. In that instant she knew—she *knew*—Reed had set her up.

She'd set her up for the porn audition—and to witness this little scene. Veronica had been played.

Veronica felt the eyes of the café's customers on her, and she dragged Little Vee by the elbow into the back.

"Are you kidding me? This is Jason and Homecoming all over again," she fumed.

"Excuse me, what?" Reed feigned innocence.

"You knew I liked Jason and wanted to ask him out, so you asked him first." Veronica crossed her arms over her chest and stared Reed down.

"So what? He never would have gone out with you anyway. You were too *fat* for him."

Even though she was angry with Little Vee, even though she knew this was most likely the end of their friendship, that still hurt. God, did it hurt.

Veronica swallowed hard before speaking. "You should have given me a chance to try. I saw him first." She sounded like a child. *It's mine, mine, mine!* But she didn't care.

"Well, I saw Philip first," Reed said, equally childish. "And I came out here first. And you shouldn't be here now doing better than me. Like you always do."

"What?"

"All the best roles, all the best reviews, all the awards. You had to win the Chapman every year, didn't you? You couldn't let me win it just once." Reed was starting to get agitated, Veronica noticed. Her pixie face was flushed and she kept chewing at the corners of her lips. "I knew, I just knew you'd win that award our senior year. I knew you'd get the lead role in the class play. I knew . . . why do you think I graduated six months early?"

Veronica was mute, dumbfounded by Little Vee's confession.

"I had to get away from that town and from Arizona and from *you.*" Reed balled her hands into fists at her sides. Veronica could see the girl's eyes fill with tears. "I never wanted you to move here," she whispered fiercely.

"But you told me to come!"

Reed shook her head. "I never thought you would. I never thought you'd leave your Daddy. And now you're here and you're doing better than me. Again!"

"But what about all your auditions? The commercials, the movies?" Veronica asked.

"I never had any," Reed admitted bitterly. "I used to hang out with Bianca or take a yoga class or just drive around town. After almost a year in L.A., I have nothing. But you . . . you're getting calls, and you have a job and all these friends. And Philip." She lifted her chin and blinked long lashes against her hazel eyes. "But now I have him. It's the one thing I know I can do better than you."

"So what am I supposed to do, go home?"

Reed stared at Veronica. "Yes."

Veronica could feel tears in her own eyes. Why hadn't she seen this side of Little Vee before? Or had she just not *wanted* to see it? "Life isn't a competition, Vee."

"Yes, it is," Reed said. "Everything is a competition in L.A." She wiped below her eyes with her fingertips and slowly regained her composure. "I'm sorry, Veronica. I'm not your Little Vee anymore. I'm Reed now." Then she waved to Philip, who was still standing at the counter. "See you later, sweetie," she said and sauntered out of the café, her purse swinging by her side.

As she watched Reed walk out of her life and out of their friendship forever, Veronica thought, *I guess that's my last Hollywood lesson: Never trust the people who say they're your friends.*

She felt herself wrap the green apron around her waist and tie it behind her back, felt her fingers adjust the plastic name tag that said *Veronica*. She saw her feet move her from the curtain to the coffee maker. She heard a customer behind her ask if there were any blueberry scones left.

"Yes, we have blueberry scones, sir. How many do you want?" That was her voice talking to the customer, acting like a professional barista, doing her job. That's why she was here, wasn't it, to do a job? That was the *only* reason she was here tonight.

As she slid back the glass door of the pastry shelf, she sensed Philip approaching her from behind. She held up a hand without even looking at him.

"She's pretty and sexy, I know," Veronica said. "Jason thought the same thing."

"It wasn't like that," Philip protested. "It was all her idea."

"Then why didn't you push her away the minute her lips touched yours?" she asked, her voice calm and even and professional.

"Well, I . . ."

"Can I heat that scone up for you, sir?" Veronica said brightly to the customer at the counter. She smiled as if she didn't have a care in the world, as if it were her lifelong dream to be serving *this very scone*.

Her fingers tapped the keys of the cash register and the drawer popped open. She exchanged the customer's $10 bill for some ones and change and handed it back to him.

"Come again," she said because that's what you were supposed to say when you worked in the service industry. You said 'please' and 'thank you' and 'come again' and 'can I get you some more of that?' and you didn't think about yourself and how all you really wanted was to tear off your apron and go scarf down an entire chocolate marble cheesecake with a side of Hostess cupcakes and a giant glass of cold whole milk. Nothing skim, nothing diet, nothing lo-carb or lo-cal or lo-so. She wanted hi-everything.

"Veronica?"

She turned to Philip and saw an intense curiosity in his brown eyes. His gaze was searching hers, trying to connect, trying to figure out what was going on inside her head.

"Let me explain, please?" he asked. "Please?"

She felt her fingers untie her apron, felt her hands fold the coarse fabric into a small square and place it on the counter.

"I know you like her, Philip, and I'm not going to fight her for you," she said. "If she wants you, she'll win and I'll just get my heart broken. Oh, by the way, I quit."

She strode through the front door, past the customers standing in line, patiently waiting for coffee, wondering perhaps why their beloved barista was walking out the door. Philip was a couple of paces behind her, not as quick on the draw as he should have been to catch up.

"Veronica, wait!" he called. "Please don't go!"

She wanted to stop then when she heard his voice. She wanted to return to the café, to return to his arms, to hear him beg her to stay. But she didn't know if it was her he wanted—or his barista. And she wasn't about to find out.

She left.

chapter 35

Max was the only one she wanted to talk to. Not the Vees, not Craig, certainly not Daddy or May May.

"Did I ever tell you my mother was a star?" Veronica said to Max as they sat out on the patio. She sipped a glass of iced tea, made from Val's famous no-boil recipe, and rested a hand atop the dog's massive head. She could put her whole palm on his crown and still not cover it. She liked that about him. He was a dog of *size*. A dog of *substance*.

"I'm going to read you a letter she wrote my father on this day exactly 19 years ago." She glanced down at Max. "Don't worry. You'll catch up fast."

She unfolded one of the letters and held it up to her eyes in the fading afternoon light.

"Dear Moose." Veronica stopped and addressed the dog. "Moose is my dad."

"Dear Moose," she started again. "The shoot's been pushed. That's what they call it when you postpone things. You say the shoot's been pushed or your call time's been pushed. Now it looks like late November for a start date for us. Thank god, though, because we have a ton of rehearsing to do.

"I got some lines on the soap. Nothing big, but as you know, or don't know, a line means a big difference in what they pay you. Without lines, you're just an extra. With a line, you're what they call a 'day performer.'" Veronica stopped and pointed at Max who was listening attentively. "Make a note of that," she said. "Good to know."

She went back to the letter.

"Did you really mean what you said in your last letter, Moose? Will you really wait for me forever? I can't tell you how much that means to me to have your support. I know you're busy too, and I'm so proud of the work you're doing at the library. They'll make you the head librarian very soon, and we'll be a superstar couple!"

Veronica's eyes stung with happy tears. She tried to picture her parents as a power couple in Chester, Arizona. Would they have gone to movie premieres at the 99-cent theater on Main Street? The openings of the new Wendy's and Dunkin' Donuts outlets? She laughed to herself and choked back a tear that tried to escape.

"What happened?" she asked Max. "Why did she have to die when she had so much going for her?"

Max nudged her hand with his nose, leaving a wet spot on her palm.

"Yeah, I don't know either," Veronica told the dog. She refolded the letter and placed it carefully inside its envelope. In the package, Val and Ginny had also sent a swatch of material and several Polaroids.

This is from May, Ginny wrote. *So you can pick out a dress that will match. Val says you can borrow something from her if you're too busy to shop. And I can loan you a pair of sandals. Your dad's worried it'll rain, but we haven't had rain before Christmas in years.*

Everything okay, Vee? We haven't heard from you in a while. You have to check out your dad's suit in these pictures. Looks like he's waiting for the Great Flood of 2008! May wants him to get a new one for the wedding, but he's being stubborn. You know your dad.

Do I really know him? Veronica wondered. He had kept so much of her mother hidden from her, things she should have known that might have given her insight into what had happened to her. Insight into Veronica herself.

She glanced at the photos of her father. His suit pants were so short, she could see a strip of skin between sock and pant. And were those . . . why, yes they were: white athletic socks. Classic Moose May. No wonder May May wanted him to buy a new suit; in their wedding pictures it would look like she was marrying a homeless man.

Veronica fingered the silky maroon material sample from May. It was soft enough. She held it up to her skin and grimaced: Without a tan, this would be a horrible color on her.

Her cell phone rang then, and she tossed the swatch aside. She didn't recognize the number and was tempted to let it go to voice mail, but she hadn't actually spoken to a real human in a while.

"Hello?"

"Is this Veronica?" a male voice asked.

"Yes."

"This is Harvey from the casting office at the Santa Barbara

Rep." Harvey sounded like he had swallowed a handful of marbles and they had gotten stuck at the back of his throat. "We'd like to bring you in for an audition."

Veronica ran through the most recent ads she had responded to—god, there had been so many—but she couldn't remember a theater company. However, any listing that had the word "casting" in it got a little package from Veronica May, so it was entirely possible she had sent one in and forgotten about it.

"That's wonderful," she said. "Thank you so much."

"How about Thursday at 2?"

"Yes, absolutely."

"Okay, well, grab a pen. Here's the address."

chapter 36

Veronica's audition for the Santa Barbara Rep was held at City College, just off Cabrillo Boulevard, a stretch of road running along the Pacific. She arrived early, grabbed a cup of coffee and stared out at the ocean. There was a grayish haze hanging over the water which obscured the view but did nothing to alter her enjoyment of it.

She wrapped a long cotton sweater around her skirt and silky violet shell and hugged her arms over her chest to ward off the chill. The temperatures were falling now that it was getting closer to Thanksgiving. It was by no means cold, but she could feel a subtle change in the air—and in the industry. There had been far fewer auditions listed in *Backstage* and online, although she continued to send out her head shots day after day.

She hadn't realized how much she missed the theater until she was rehearsing with Max on their walk after she got Harvey's call.

"How about *Streetcar*, Max? What do you think, too dramatic?" Veronica had paused in front of a four-plex with a small plastic slide in the front yard. She bent down and grabbed the dog's head in her hands. "I, I, *I* took the blows in my face and my body! All of those deaths! The long parade to the graveyard! Father, Mother! Margaret, that dreadful way! So big with it, couldn't be put in a coffin! But had to be burned like rubbish! You just came home in time for the funerals, Stella. And funerals are pretty compared to deaths. Funerals are quiet, but deaths—not always."

The dog stared back at her with giant brown eyes, soulful and sensitive. He loved her as she was; moreover, he *appreciated* her as she was.

"Maybe I should just stick to Shakespeare, huh? *Romeo and Juliet?*"

Ah, it had felt good to be big! It felt like breathing again! She filled her lungs with crisp morning air and wasn't afraid to use large gestures, to play to the back row, to *embrace* her bigness.

Yes, she had missed that.

Veronica strolled through the college's main gate, admired the manicured lawns and the stone paths, and eventually found the room where her audition was being held.

"May I help you?" a blue-haired receptionist asked her.

"My name is Veronica May and I have a two o'clock appointment," Veronica answered in the confident, measured tone of a professional actor.

The woman peered down at the papers on her desk, made a check mark with a silver Mont Blanc. "One moment, please." She lifted the phone and pressed a button.

The waiting area was empty, Veronica noticed, as were the halls leading to and away from this wing of the building. She could hear no sounds, no voices coming from any of the rooms. Was it possible they were holding appointment-only auditions? Were they even holding auditions? After receiving the call, she had gone back to her papers in search of the ad she must have responded to, but she never found it.

"You can go in now." The receptionist waved a sun-spotted hand at the door beside her.

Veronica rose as if her head held a pitcher of water. "Why thank you so much," she said smoothly. "I've always depended on the kindness of strangers." She winked at the woman. "That's from *Streetcar*."

She took a deep breath. This was it, she thought, her last chance. The wedding was so close, mere weeks away. If she was going to return home a success, she had to make this one work.

"*Merde*," she whispered and grasped the handle of the door.

Inside the room were a diverse group of about thirty men and women working in trios and quartets. They were running lines and blocking scenes, adjusting their spacing and playing with props, laughing and eager. She could feel the energy among the actors, could hear the passion in their voices: sweet, honest tones, nothing pretentious or fake about them. It reminded her of . . .

. . . home!

Veronica felt a wave of nostalgia sweep over her, warm and comforting. She could do this. This was where she was meant to be. She took a step into the room and allowed the door to close softly behind her. Edging along the back wall of the room, she sneaked over to a table where two older men sat.

"Excuse me," she said to the man nearest her, grey-haired with thick black eyebrows and a cauliflower nose. "I'm here for an audition."

"What's your name?" the man asked. "No, wait, don't tell me." He thumbed through a stack of head shots until he found hers. "Veronica May?"

"Why, yes," she beamed. "Are you the director?"

The man frowned, as if she should know better. "I'm Harvey. I called you." He shook his head. "I honestly can't recall how your picture landed on my desk." He looked over at his friend. "Moe, did you get this young lady's head shot at your office?"

Moe looked her up and down. "Nope."

"Moe does casting in New York and Chicago. I take care of the west coast." Harvey scratched his head with the tip of a number two pencil. "We don't hold open auditions and we don't advertise."

"Don't need to," Moe added with a grunt.

"No matter," Harvey shrugged. "Hey, Rod!"

The director, tall and lean with shaggy prematurely salt-and-pepper hair and thick horn-rimmed glasses, lifted his head toward the voice. "Yes?"

"This young lady's here for an audition."

He extended his hand to Veronica who felt drawn to him like a magnet. "Rod Winters."

"Veronica May."

"Let me get these people to take their seats and we can get started." Rod spoke in a low commanding voice. "Everyone, be seated, please." And the entire room sat at once. Rod turned to her. "Do you mind if they watch your audition? I'd like to see how you work in front of a live audience. That's the beauty of theater, isn't it?" He smiled at her, as if to take her into his confidence, and what could she say?

"Of course, that's fine," she said, trying to keep her voice from shaking like the rest of her was. As comfortable as she was in front of an audience, it felt like light-years since she had done so. She slipped out of her sweater and adjusted her bra straps under her top.

Rod took a seat in a folding chair in the front row and leaned forward, hands on his knees. "So, Veronica, what have you chosen for us today?"

"And it better not be the balcony scene from R and J," someone in the back of the room called.

A chorus of soft yet gentle boos broke out until Rod raised his hand. "Veronica?"

While her mind raced, Veronica stalled with a smile and a knowing laugh, as if to agree with them all that the balcony scene was, indeed, too cliché for this sophisticated bunch. She cleared her throat and lifted her chin. "I'll be doing Maggie from *Cat on a Hot Tin Roof*."

"Excellent choice," Rod confirmed. "Joel, would you read with Veronica, please?"

"Read *with* me—"

But Joel had already risen from his seat and was hobbling toward her.

"Oh wait," he said. "It's the other leg." The group laughed as Joel deftly shifted his weight to the opposite hip. He pulled up a chair beside Veronica and grinned. "Welcome."

"Where shall we pick it up?" Rod wondered aloud. "How about, 'I feel all the time like a cat on a hot tin roof.'"

"You want me to *start* there?" Veronica asked, not wanting to be obstinate but, come on, that was like a total knock-their-socks-off line; you didn't start there, you finished there, most triumphantly.

"Let's go right to the good stuff. I want to see what you're made of." He slid back in his chair and crossed his arms. "Whenever you're ready."

Veronica closed her eyes and tried to compose herself. It helped to put her mind back at the auditorium at Chester High School, with smiles of love and support from a transfixed audience. After a moment, she opened her eyes and thought, *Toto, I don't think we're in Kansas anymore.*

She cast a sideways glance at her scene partner, who was waiting patiently, one leg outstretched, a pained wince on his face. She placed one hand on her hip and swiveled her head toward him fully. "Y'know what I feel like, Brick?" she drawled softly. "I feel all the time like a cat on a hot tin roof!"

Joel looked up at her under heavy lids. "Then jump off the roof, jump off it, cats can jump off roofs and land on their feet uninjured!"

Veronica felt like she'd died and gone to Lee Strasberg heaven. Joel had a voice like gravel coated with orange blossom honey. His eyes, mischievous and fierce, challenged her. She feared her breath would catch in her throat and trip her up just by looking at him, so she turned away and crossed her arms. "Oh yes."

"Do it! 'Fo god's sake, do it . . ."

"Do what?"

"Take a lover!"

She continued to address Joel with her back to him. "I can't see a man but you! Even with my eyes closed, I just see you!" She pivoted on her heel and placed the palms of her hands against the small of her back, and when she finally could raise her eyes to him, she saw not Joel but Philip sitting in the chair, leg stretched lazily before her, his gaze drinking her in. She felt desire and anger and disappointment well up inside her, and she used it, let it infect every inch of her as she posed seductively, largely, beautifully.

"Look, Brick! How high my body stays on me! Nothing has fallen on me, not a fraction," she cried.

"Other men still want me. My face looks strained sometimes, but I've kept my figure as well as you've kept yours, and men admire it. I still turn heads on the street." She ran her hands from the curve of her waist down to her thighs and then glanced up over her shoulder at him. "Why, at Alice's party for her New York cousins, the best lookin' man in the crowd followed me upstairs and tried to force his way in the powder room with me, followed me to the door and tried to force his way in!"

Joel looked at her disdainfully. "Why didn't you let him in, Maggie?"

She Dipped her head to her chin and peered up at him, turning on the full force of her violet eyes. This was everything she had ever wanted, everything she had come to Los Angeles for. All the experiences the Universe had dealt her—death, love, and rejection, rejection, rejection—had come together in this singular moment.

I believe in me, Veronica thought.

"Because," she whispered, "I'm not that common." She paused and then said, "Scene."

There was complete and utter silence in the room until Rod himself began clapping. He was soon joined by the rest of the company.

"Wow. That was wonderful," Joel whispered as he rose from the chair. Veronica could feel her face grow warm and flush at the compliment.

"Thank you."

As the group dispersed, Rod called her over to the table where Moe and Harvey sat. "That was fantastic, Veronica, really amazing. It almost makes me wish we were doing Tennessee Williams this season."

Veronica was thrilled and relieved; she had done it! Finally!

Then Rod's smile slowly faded. "Now, see, here's the problem." He glanced over at the two men and then back to her. "You're not Equity, are you?"

The stage actors' union, Veronica recalled. She shook her head.

"I don't know if we can give you a card. Can we?"

The two men shrugged indifferently.

"I'm sorry, Veronica. But we can't hire you without an Equity card. Come back when you get one. It was really great to meet you," Rod added as he walked her to the door. "You're going to be big someday, I can tell."

Veronica wanted to yell. She wanted to scream. How could she get an Equity card without working on an Equity show? It was a horrible Catch-22. She could feel tears spring to her eyes. But she wouldn't let them fall.

Be a professional, Vee, she told herself. *Pros don't cry.* "Thank you, Rod." She blinked quickly. "Thanks for the opportunity."

"Good luck, Veronica." And then Rod closed the door, and she was faced with Mrs. Blue Hair.

"Everything go all right, dear?" the woman asked kindly.

Veronica could barely nod in return.

"Parting is such sweet sorrow," the woman said with a wink. "I shall say good night 'til it be morrow."

chapter 37

Days passed without a call from the theater.

A week, then two. Still no word.

With a heavy heart, Veronica knew it wouldn't come. She could wish and hope and make little pacts with herself like, "If I hear Santa Barbara mentioned in the next thirty seconds, that's a sign I will get this job," but she knew it wouldn't happen. She was not Equity. She was not what they wanted. It seemed like she wasn't what anybody wanted.

To add insult to injury, Donny's paranoia finally paid off.

On a Sunday morning when Craig and Veronica were having a quiet brunch of orange juice and omelets on the back patio, they heard the doorbell ring insistently. Before they could answer it, Donny came charging around the side of the house, holding fists full of slimy paper.

"I knew it!" he cried.

"What the . . . Donny! Have you been dumpster diving again?" Craig cringed as Donny tracked nasty-smelling wet shoes across the flagstones. "Damn it, get that out of here!"

Donny ignored him and headed straight for Veronica. "Look!" His face was flush with excitement, his vast conspiracy theories having come to fruition at last. His eyes sparkled and shone with pride. "I told you she was bad. Here's the proof." He thrust the trash under Veronica's nose. The stench of sun-dried waste was overpowering, and she had to cover her nose with her hand.

"God, Donny, what are you . . ." And then she saw it: Her own face smiling up at her. No, no, not a smile. Just a hint of one.

"That's mine," Veronica said, astonished. "Where did you get that?" She reached out to take the picture, gingerly, by its edges. It was unmistakably her head shot; her resume was still attached to the back. A manila envelope was in the trash too—she recognized her handwriting. It had been addressed to a casting director for an independent movie. She remembered that listing. The role had been perfect for her. She had been shocked and disappointed that she had never gotten a call.

"I found a ton of them in Reed's trash," Donny said.

"She was supposed to mail these," Veronica told him in a hushed voice. "*Mon dieu!* No wonder I never got any calls!"

Craig narrowed his eyes at Donny. "Why were you in Reed's trash?"

"She hurt Veronica," Donny said defiantly. "So I followed her. Then I saw her cleaning her apartment. She really should shred this stuff."

Veronica smiled warmly. "I know you're crazy, Donny, but you're really sweet."

* * *

And then before she knew it, Thanksgiving had arrived. Funny how quickly time passed when you weren't doing anything but sitting around the house.

Or maybe it wasn't funny at all.

"Who wants the wish bone?" Craig sang out as he finished carving up the twenty pound turkey for leftovers. Veronica and Donny were lounging at the kitchen table, their appetites sated for the next millennium. Max slept at their feet, his furry belly full of treats.

"I'll take it," Donny said, surprising both Veronica and Craig. He had steadfastly refused to do or touch anything that had come into contact with the turkey.

"You know what to do with it, don't you, Donny?" Veronica asked. "You and another person each take a side, and you make a wish as you pull it apart. And then whoever pulls off the largest piece gets his wish."

A smile slowly spread across Donny's face. "Cool."

Veronica and Craig shared an eye roll. *Thank god for Donny,* she thought. He reminded them all how sane they actually were.

"What would you wish for?" Craig asked Veronica. "Lots of money? A fancy car?"

She thought a moment: an acting job? Would merely getting a gig solve all her problems? She shook her head. "I don't know. What about you?"

Craig sighed. "I'd wish you would answer the phone."

"I do," Veronica said, trying not to sound defensive. "So long as it's work-related."

"You're gonna have to talk to him sometime," Craig said gently. "He's been calling and texting my cell, which I should love, but since all he talks about is you, eh, not so much."

"Not interested," Veronica mumbled and leaned her chin on her hands.

There was a moment of gloomy silence in the kitchen which Craig hastened to break.

"Donny, why don't you make yourself useful and set the espresso maker for some cappuccinos?" He turned to Veronica. "Up for a cappuccino, Vee?"

Veronica's head snapped up. "Did you call me Vee?"

Craig smiled. "You looked like you needed it."

She returned his grin. "Yeah, I do." She stood, stretching. "I'm gonna take Max out."

"Don't go too far," Donny said. "I don't have any to-go cups for the cappuccinos."

Veronica stepped out onto the patio and held the door open for Max, who bounded past her and into the yard. She pulled her cell out of her pocket and dialed.

Craig's neighbors butted up against his tiny, well-kept lawn on all sides. Each of them had a pool and a patio and a set of sliding glass doors and at least one had a swing set. Veronica peered up at the grayish sky and listened to the phone ring in her ear.

"Hello?"

"Daddy?"

"Veronica!"

"Happy Thanksgiving, Daddy."

"How are you, sweetheart? Did you have a nice meal? Do they eat turkey out there?" He laughed, an over-laugh, a had-a-bit-too-much-cider laugh.

"Yes, we had turkey. It was good."

"That's good."

She could hear voices chattering somewhere behind her father. "Who's there with you?"

"May May, of course, and a few friends."

It wasn't like her father to have friends at the house—or anywhere, for that matter. Must have been May May's influence.

Her father sighed, and she could almost see him unbuttoning his pants as they strained at his belly. "May spent the entire week researching turkeys. I think she called the Butterball hotline about a dozen times."

"Wow," Veronica said, impressed again by the woman's thoroughness.

"And we had a marvelous onion and pea dish, and fresh rolls and creamed corn and stuffing. And gravy and cranberry sauce and oh! Three pies!" Her father groaned. "Plus cheese and crackers and nachos and guacamole and salsa and stuffed celery . . . so much food."

"Sounds great." Now she could hear music playing, probably in the living room with the new friends. She looked back at Craig's house. Although her friends were inside it, people she liked and trusted, the bungalow suddenly felt cold and impersonal, not like the home she grew up in, which was lived in and loved. And the houses around it, too, appeared lifeless: The swing set lonely and neglected, the pools covered with leaves. A football game was blaring on someone's big-screen TV, but there was no music, no laughter in this colorless neighborhood.

Failure had rendered the whole city lackluster and dull for Veronica.

"Veronica, sweetie? Are you still there?"

"I'm here," she whispered, without meaning to.

"May May and I can't wait to see you, sweetheart. Do you think you can spend some time with us before the wedding or will you be too busy in California?"

"No," she said. "Not too busy."

"Is it warm there, sweetheart? Is it warm like here?"

"No," she said. "Not like there at all."

chapter 38

"Why are you leaving?" Craig and Donny wanted to know.

And, "When are you coming back?"

Then, "*Are* you coming back?"

It's like this, she tried to tell them:

Palm trees were not native to Southern California. They belonged to a tropical climate, like Hawaii or the Caribbean, not the desert of L.A.

Baby palms didn't sprout up in backyards. Mature ones were trucked in on long flatbed trailers and transplanted to their new homes along major boulevards. Like everything in this town, they were *designed*. Giant palms were supposed to appear majestic, to give L.A.'s skyline a unique hyper-real quality, much like the city itself. When you were driving down Sunset Boulevard at night with the top down on your Mustang convertible, you looked up at the fronds swaying in the warm breeze, and you felt like you were part of the design.

Hyper-real.

Surreal.

Unreal.

Palm trees found it difficult to take root, she could have told them. Oh, they tried, they gave it their best shot, but the earth was so dry and the smog so thick that inevitably, their leaves dried up, fell off and crushed unsuspecting Mercedes.

And they were replaced by new ones.

Palm trees just didn't belong in L.A.

The final letter was dated December 10.

Moose, it began abruptly, *my suspicions have been confirmed, and I have only you to blame. Let me set the scene for you, as they say out here. We were shooting a scene from the movie, a huge scene with 100 dancers and big gold sets. They had just called 'cut' and the director was smiling at me and he came up to me to tell me he was moving me into a lead position and I threw up all over his shoes! All the girls thought it was hysterically funny. But I was horrified!!! And why was I so sick? Because I'm pregnant! And it's your fault! Now my life is ruined!*

It's not fair, Moose, it's just not fair! I came out here to do things and to be somebody and now all I'm going to be is somebody's damn mother. This is all your fault.

Veronica stared at the pages in her hand. Fat blotches of ink obscured Diana's signature, and she couldn't remember if they had been there before she read the letter. Broad-sided, that's how she felt, like someone had hit her with a Mack truck.

It hadn't been Daddy's fault that Diana left L.A. and became a damn mother.

It had been Veronica's.

She had failed. And without even knowing it, she had caused her mother's failure.

It was time to go home.

chapter 39

Veronica drove straight to the library in Chester, stopping only for gas and a cup of coffee at the Waffle House. She strode up the back steps, waved to the ladies behind the desk and headed directly for her father's office.

One hand clutched the last letter from Diana.

The other hand knocked politely on the door.

Both hands were shaking.

"Come in."

The door swung open and god, she was eight again, come to beg her father for money for the movies. Daddy's posters of Rita Hayworth and John Wayne were still there, as were his swivel chair and his wide back, but no Camels. Moose May had kicked the habit years ago.

"Veronica?" Her father turned and she half-expected to see his cheeks red, his eyelids puffy, as they were on that day. Instead, there was a look of pure delight on his face. "What a pleasant surprise." He stood and hugged her. "Welcome back. We didn't think you'd be here until next week. Did you have a good drive?"

"Uh, yeah. Daddy—"

"Sit, sweetheart, sit. Can I get you some coffee?" No sooner had she taken a seat than her father was up and buzzing about. "This is such a rare treat, having you here."

She stared up at the movie posters while Daddy fixed the coffee. The letter was burning a hole in her hand as if to remind her why she came for this special visit.

"Daddy . . ."

"Here you go. I'm sorry I don't have anything sweet." He looked around the office as if he could find something to eat on his shelves. "May might have something out at her desk, if you'd like me to check."

"That's okay. I don't need anything."

"So, to what do I owe this pleasure?"

"Well, I—"

"You know, May will be so excited to see you. Should we go get her?" Her father started for the door, but Veronica quickly shook her head.

"No, Daddy. I'll . . . I'll see her later." Her voice softened. "I just wanted a little time alone with you."

Her father put his hands on his knees. "Well, that sounds nice."

Veronica glanced down at her lap. *The letter, Vee, tell him about the letter.* "Everything all set for the wedding?"

"Take a look." Moose gestured to a large rectangular cork board above his desk covered in index cards with notes like, "Call caterer" and "Order flowers" and "Dry clean suit." A giant to-do list of wedding tasks; some of them had been crossed out with red pen while others were still to be completed.

"That's some list," Veronica marveled.

Diana, Vee, tell him you know. Ask him why he never told you. Ask him.

"Daddy," she started. "I need to talk to you."

"About . . . ?" Her father looked at her, expectantly.

"About Diana."

Moose May shook his head. "That was so long ago and it's so much easier—"

"Easier not to, I know. Let's have another slice of cheesecake instead."

"What?"

"Nothing." She pulled the envelope out of her pocket and saw her father's eyes widen slightly. "I found the letters in the attic and I took them. I should have asked you first, I know, but I didn't." She sucked in her lower lip and sank back against the chair. With this revelation, her whole body felt suddenly weak, her knees like puddles of water, and she was glad she was seated.

"I have to know, Daddy." Veronica couldn't look directly at her father, so she stared up at the cork board behind him. "Was it my fault? Did she start drinking because of me?"

Moose May sighed heavily. "I don't know."

"What?" Veronica's head snapped over to him.

"Honestly, I don't know the answer to that question."

"Well, I'll tell ya, that wasn't the right one," Veronica said, her voice burning. "You're my father. You're supposed to say, 'No, sweetheart, of course not.'"

"I can't say that," her father pleaded. "I don't know why she drank. I don't know why she didn't want to live with us—"

"Was it suicide?"

"I don't even know that." Her father turned from her, his wide back heaving, and Veronica was reminded of her childhood, of Daddy when he was a powerful man, bigger and stronger than she was. But now, a decade later, he was just a man. Just an old man.

"She drove off the bridge. She died. End of story."

"Not end of story! Not end of story at all!" Veronica stood and stared down at her father. "She failed and now I've failed and I need to know why."

"Enough, Veronica," he said without looking at her. "We're finished with this conversation."

"No, we're not," she said. "We are—"

"Yes. We are." Moose took a couple of cards down from the cork board and began scribbling on them. He cleared his throat and when he spoke next, it was as if he had never raised his voice to her.

"May and I have split the jobs between us," he said calmly. "But we could use some help." He handed her the cards. "Would you help us?"

Veronica stared at the cards and then, finally, took them. "Fine."

"Thank you, sweetheart." He patted her on the arm. "Let's go see May now. Maybe we can get her to cook something special for your return. Would you like that?"

Well, then, that was it. Her father had made up his mind and nothing more would be said. She nodded. "Something special would be nice."

They left the office together, and Veronica tucked her mother's final letter into the back pocket of her jeans.

Nothing had changed, she thought. She was still eight years old.

chapter 40

f anyone was happy she was back in Arizona, Veronica thought, it should be her Vees. Ginny and Val cooked a lavish buffet lunch for her in Val's kitchen, an entire Food Network lineup of meals.

"Have some more *pollo*," Val insisted, piling a chicken leg and rice and beans on Veronica's plate.

Veronica held her hand over her dish. "Whoa, whoa. I'm stuffed."

"How can you be stuffed? You ate nothing."

Ginny scrutinized Veronica as if she were seeing her for the first time. "You've lost weight," she said in a near-accusatory tone. "Did you?"

"I guess I did." Veronica patted herself down, felt her T-shirt loose against her skin. "There's a little less of me now. Do I look bad?"

"*Coño*, you look beautiful," Val insisted, looking up from where she was putting away leftovers. She waved a caramel-colored chicken wing at Veronica. "We need to take you shopping!"

Veronica waited for Ginny to weigh in. "Vee?"

"You look good," Ginny admitted. "L.A. did right by you."

Veronica smiled. "Thanks."

"Did you ever see any famous movie stars out there?" Val wanted to know. "Anyone from *Ugly Betty*? I love that show."

Veronica shook her head. "I would have told you."

"Maybe you'll see some when you go back," Val suggested.

"I'm not going back," Veronica said with a tentative smile. "I'm staying here."

Val's head snapped toward her. "Where? In *Arizona*?"

"Well, yes . . ."

"Why would you do that?" Ginny asked with a frown that creased her forehead.

"What do you mean, why?" Veronica replied. "Aren't you glad?"

"But you're not supposed to be here anymore," Ginny said harshly.

The warm reception was quickly turning awkward, and Veronica couldn't understand what was wrong with her Vees. They should be happy she was home to stay; life could finally go back to the way it was, before everything changed and got messed up.

Val was the one to soften the blow. "You took the step, *chica*, a big step," she said. "You got out of this little town and you went to L.A. This would be a step backward."

Veronica shook her head. "No, you don't understand. This'll be great." She stared at her friends. "The three of us can hang out all the time like we used to. We can go to Charlie's and have picnics at the lake. I'll do my shows. Things will go back to the way they were."

"How can they?" Ginny asked. "Your dad is getting married. The theater's got new people—"

"New people?" Veronica looked bewildered. "Who are the new people?"

Val glanced over her shoulder at Ginny. "I thought you told her."

Ginny shook her head. "You were going to email her."

"Oh no, *chica*, not me."

"Tell me what?" Veronica cried. "Who are the new people?"

"Jim Neece left CCT. Biff's mother is in charge now," Ginny said quietly. "And his sister is doing . . ." Her voice trailed off to a mumble.

"His sister is doing what, Vee?"

Ginny sighed. "She's doing *Cat on a Hot Tin Roof.*"

"What?" Veronica was aghast. Someone *else* was doing Maggie the Cat? "Let me get this straight. Biff Jackson's mother is the director now?"

"Not the grandmother," Val explained. "She's like fifty million years old. His *mother*."

"And his sister . . ." Veronica searched her memory banks. "Shar-pei?" Her name was really Sharlene, but she had a face like those wrinkly dogs, hence the nickname. "She couldn't find her way out of a dark room with a flashlight. How can she act? She can't act. This is crazy." She looked at the girls. "This is crazy," she said again. "How could this happen?"

Val shrugged. "You went away, Vee."

"Well, it's not like you being here would have prevented it," Ginny said. "It's just that, you know, things change. Life changes."

"Yeah, but . . . CCT, that was my thing." Veronica stared mournfully at a Tupperware filled with leftover lunch that Val placed in front of her. Although it was stuffed with all of her favorites, she couldn't imagine eating a bite of it.

"You couldn't do it forever," Val said. She arranged a tray of cream, sugar cubes and demitasse spoons on the table in preparation for espresso. "You'd have to get married and have babies someday."

"It's time for the next generation to do the CCT thing," Ginny said patiently.

"Next generation?" Veronica scowled. "Shar-pei is one year younger than me."

Ginny sort of nodded. "Yes, well, now it's her turn."

"I think she's going to be good tonight," Val said cheerfully to Ginny.

"I heard she's been taking acting lessons," Ginny agreed.

Veronica was incredulous. "You're going to see her? In *my* show?"

"It's opening night," Val said. "We have tickets."

"And what about me?"

"You can come too."

Veronica cradled her palm under her chin. "I've been replaced," she mumbled into her hand. "Again."

She expected some words of comfort from her Vees but got nothing.

"Um, hello?" she asked. "Didn't you hear me?"

Ginny pulled her notebook out of her pocket and began scanning the pages. "What was that, Vee?" she asked absently.

"I said I've been replaced. Val, did you hear me over there?"

The back of Val's head bobbed. "*Sì, sì.* I heard."

Veronica sat up fully and looked around her. Was she in the wrong home? "So . . ."

"So what?" Val asked.

"Aren't you going to, you know . . ." Veronica made a rolling gesture with her hand, as if to say, get on with it. "You're supposed to be sweet to me and take care of me."

Ginny looked up from her notebook. "Vee, you never even asked us what *we* were doing while you were gone. It's just been me, me, me, and frankly, we've got other things going on."

"You do?"

"You can't be so selfish all the time," Val said. "You want everything to be perfect for you in L.A. You want everything to be perfect for you here. We're getting tired of it."

"That's not true!" Veronica cried. "I was hurt in L.A.—"

"So get over it and move on," Ginny interrupted.

"But . . . you're my best friends!"

"That's why we're telling you this," Val said. She looked directly at Veronica. "Get over yourself."

Veronica gasped and pushed herself up from the table. "Get *over* myself? Get *over* myself? Well, at least I *tried* something new. At least I *left* this stupid town."

"And now you're back," Ginny said simply.

"Okay, that's enough." *What happened to my friends while I was gone?* Veronica wondered wildly. *Who were these other girls in flip-flops and T-shirts pretending to be Vees?* She stomped toward the door and let herself out without saying goodbye.

Selfish! Veronica thought as she left Val's house. These two were telling *her* she was selfish? Val, who spent more time and her father's money on her hair than anyone Veronica had ever met? And Ginny, just sitting there with her stupid notebook, making pronouncements about Veronica, judging her? *That* was selfish. *They* were selfish, not her.

So far, this whole coming home thing had been a waste of time.

chapter 41

With less than a day to go before the wedding, the May household was turning into Matrimonial Central. Daddy had moved the cork board of index cards from his office to his den. The only items left to be done were "Pick up cake" and "Cross knives on mirror." The first was self-explanatory, while the second was a trick to ward off rain, Daddy explained, a superstition left over from May's childhood that would ensure a clear day for the ceremony. Veronica decided to leave that job to Daddy. She would go pick up the cake.

The tension in the house was palpable. Veronica could barely stand to be in the same room as her father and found every excuse to leave. When he walked into the kitchen, she walked out to watch television. When he came into the living room, she suddenly had to check her email upstairs. The unanswered questions about her mother hung over Veronica like a dark cloud.

Worst of all, she had no one to talk to about it.

Veronica honestly couldn't remember the last time she and the Vees were mad at each other. Probably not since high school when Val blew the three of them off to go on a date with one of the Carls. Veronica had been royally po'd at that. You didn't blow off your Vees, and you certainly didn't ditch them for a grope at the movie theater with a guy named Carl.

She fully expected one or both of them to call her or text her or *something* to apologize this time. After all, she had not been at fault. She felt like a wounded animal—and her Vees and her father and Diana and the whole city of L.A. had kicked her to the side of the road.

God, she missed Max. She missed their walks and their talks and his unwavering loyalty. And she missed Jamal's soothing voice and the stretch and serenity she experienced in her yoga classes. She wondered if the Y near the Baskin Robbins offered anything like that.

Veronica picked up the cake at the bakery, careful not to smear the butter cream frosting when she put the box in her trunk. There was a time in her life when she would have sneaked a finger full of the sugary fluff and then blamed the smudge on a particularly tight curve, but she wasn't even tempted now. In fact, the thought of eating a wad of frosting kind of grossed her out. She laughed, thinking how Donny would probably try to shoehorn her repulsion into some conspiracy theory of his. And then Craig would huff and threaten to knock some sense into Donny if he didn't lay off the crazy. And then Philip might tell them both to—

Well, she didn't need to think about Philip, did she?

Most of all, she missed having *hope*. She missed the belief in herself that she had brought with her to Los Angeles, the conviction that she would make it, that it was only a matter of time before she did. That's what she lost in L.A. That's what had been taken from her.

On her way home, her car swung past the high school where the letters on a big white sign spelled out the name of the CCT play, *Cat on a Hot Tin Roof.* The show was in its second week, but Veronica had so far not heard or read anything about it. She had especially not heard anything about Shar-pei Jackson's portrayal of Maggie and how audiences were cheering her delightful interpretation of the role.

No, she had not heard that *at all.*

She left the keys in the ignition—you could do that sort of thing in this town—and slowly walked the steps to the auditorium. Inside, all was quiet. Veronica paused to allow her eyes to adjust to the darkness. The house was not quite full, she noticed, not like when she was here last; there were still some empty patches of seats throughout, but the audience was attentive and polite.

"I feel all the time like a cat on a hot tin roof," Veronica heard. She bit her lip and forced herself to lift her head toward the stage.

"The next generation," Val and Ginny had said. There she was, Veronica's successor, Shar-pei Jackson. *She certainly doesn't look like Maggie should look,* Veronica noted critically. Her wig was too unwieldy, too messy, and she carried herself like she was a mannequin in a department store window. And god, she was too thin! Where were her curves? Where was her sex appeal? When the girl put her hand on her hip, it just sat there, doing nothing, *feeling* nothing. Veronica put her own hand on her hip, felt the flesh of her palm meet the fabric of her pants. Her thumb tucked into a small fold beneath her hip bone, pushing it forward and accentuating her shape. *That* was Maggie's figure, not whatever Shar-pei had going on up there.

And her voice, flat and remote, as if Shar-pei had only just seen the play for the first time this evening and had not yet had an opportunity to add some emotion to her delivery. Veronica would have spent every day of the past two months studying her lines, parsing each word for its nuance.

"Because," Sharlene Jackson said from the center of the stage, "I'm not that common."

Oh well, Veronica thought. *Poor Shar-pei. Maybe the girl could enroll in an acting class over the winter.* Veronica could suggest one or two workshops that might take her.

But the audience roared! They applauded as if they had witnessed the best play ever performed since Thespis in ancient Greece.

Veronica managed to clap politely, but she couldn't muster the same enthusiasm as these people. She glanced around her: Why were they cheering so? Couldn't they see what Veronica saw? Couldn't they hear what she heard?

And then she stopped and wondered, *Had they always been like this? Had they never been able to distinguish fine acting from rote memorization? Had they roared* for me *without discrimination?*

Veronica was horrified! Could that be true? All her dreams and self-esteem built on a series of lies? She ran the reviews of her career through her mind, all the gushing words written by some of these very people.

"A triumph!"

"Stunning!"

"Veronica May dazzles again!"

If she were to read Sharlene Jackson's reviews, would she see some of these same adjectives?

Suddenly unable to breathe, Veronica backed out of the theater and ran to her car. She took in great big gulps of night air, filled her lungs and her heart and her head with it.

She tried to think, was desperate to think, of the things she had accomplished in L.A. She had gotten a job on her own and made some new friends. She had found her way to Santa Barbara and to the beach, and she had made a few people in a few casting sessions notice her.

She had done all right, hadn't she?

Then why are you back here? she heard herself ask in her head.

This was all I had left, she thought as she looked up at the high school. And it too was gone.

She truly had nothing.

chapter 42

When she woke up the next morning, Veronica was surprised to hear the Weather Channel blasting from the television set in the living room. She rubbed sleep out of her eyes and turned down the volume.

"What? What? What?" Her father rushed out of his den, a frantic look on his face, and nearly ran headlong into her as she made her way into the kitchen.

"Is there a problem?" Not that she could focus on any sort of dilemma without her morning jolt of caffeine. "Yeccch!" She peered into the coffee pot. "When was this made?"

"About five hours ago."

"*Mon dieu!* You got up at four in the morning?" She dumped the pot into the sink and set about making a fresh one. It was almost like working at Buzz. But without the meager tips.

Moose May ran back to the radio in his den and then exclaimed,

"The weatherman just upped the chance of rain to 40 percent." He ran a hand through his hair.

Veronica looked out the window. "It looks fine to me. What are you so worried about anyway? You've got a tent on hold. We'll just call and have them deliver it."

But her father was shaking his head slowly back and forth. "It's been beautiful for the past damn month. Why does it have to rain today?"

Veronica replaced the coffee pot with her mug on the machine's burner and watched it drip. "Maybe it won't last."

"But then the grass will be all wet."

She had never seen her father so preoccupied with the weather. "So what?"

"You don't understand. It's got to be perfect."

Veronica snorted involuntarily.

"What was that for?"

"Oh, I didn't mean that. Of course it should be perfect. It's your wedding, after all, why shouldn't it be perfect?"

He stared at her. "Is there something you'd like to say, Veronica? If so, please do."

"Nothing, it's nothing. I'm gonna take a shower now." She brought a hand to her mouth. "Oops! Didn't mean to say shower."

Veronica had just pulled up her pantyhose when the guests started to arrive downstairs. As she greeted each of them, she worried that the smile she had pasted on her face would permanently distort it.

Most of them were friends of May May's from the library or acquaintances of Daddy's from the various committees and boards he had served on. All were delighted to see her, delighted May and Moose were finally tying the knot, delighted to be in their backyard on a crappy, cloudy day.

Val and Ginny arrived in Val's BMW, each of them carrying a gift wrapped in silver and white paper. They were both wearing dresses: Ginny in a flowy teal halter and Val in a clingy peach wrap that showcased her every curve. Veronica could hear them arguing as they made their way up the walk.

"Those shoes are completely inappropriate for this wedding," Ginny said. "You are gonna stub your toe and go flying."

Val shook her head, taking dainty steps in said inappropriate footwear, a pair of spiky strappy heels with a sparkly ankle bracelet. "What if I meet someone? I have to look my best."

Veronica herself was wearing a pair of black pumps with her outfit, a two-piece skirt and top in burnt orange and maroon that she had found in the back of her closet. Seeing the Vees' fancy dresses made her wish she had bought something special for the day, like Daddy and May May had asked her to.

"*Coño!*" Val exclaimed, as her foot caught in one of the cracks on the path and she began to slide. Veronica rushed down the steps and caught her before she fell, just as Ginny rescued the gift.

"Oh, Vee, *gracias*," Val said, turning the save into a hug. "Perfect timing."

"Yes, it was," Veronica said warmly. She took the two girls' hands in hers and walked them up the steps. "I'm so glad you came. I was worried you wouldn't because, you know . . ."

Ginny waved her off. "Vee, please. Water under the bridge."

Val brought a finger to her lips. "Don't say the 'w' word," she whispered.

"Water? Why not?"

Val pointed a finger discreetly at the sky.

"Can I say 'rain'?" Ginny asked with a wink to Veronica. "Or 'thunderstorm'? Or 'precipitation'?"

"No!"

"How about 'drizzle'?" Veronica added playfully. "And 'monsoon'?"

Val turned her pointing finger at the girls. "I'm not listening to either one of you," she said, as she let go of Veronica's hand and wiggled through the door.

Before they went inside, Ginny and Veronica paused to embrace. Veronica closed her eyes, accepting the affectionate apology from her friend. *This was much better than a text message,* she thought.

"Oh, Vee," Veronica said. "I was a horrible friend."

"No, no, that was our lame attempt at tough love," Ginny insisted. "We just want the best for you." She pulled back and held Veronica at arm's length. "You're not going to find what you want here," she said, shaking her head. "I'm sorry, but I think you've outgrown this town. *We've* outgrown this town." She leaned into Veronica and winked. "We want to come with you."

"Where?"

"To L.A.," Ginny said. "When you go back. We want to come."

"You . . . we?"

"Hello?" Ginny gently knocked on the side of Veronica's head. "Is anyone in there?" She grinned. "We, me and Val. We miss you and we want to be with you out in L.A. We want to do big things too."

Veronica was bewildered. Pleased and flattered but bewildered all the same. "I never said I was going back, Vee."

"No?" Ginny cocked her head to one side and studied Veronica. "Well, just in case you change your mind." She smiled and nodded toward the house. "Come on, let's go inside. You have a lot of guests to take care of."

As Veronica followed Ginny through the door, she saw a flash of lightning fill the sky. She peered up at the dark clouds and waited for the inevitable crack of thunder.

Nothing.

She shrugged. Maybe they'd be lucky and make it through the day with no trouble at all.

Veronica deposited the Vees in front of the drinks and appetizers and returned to the kitchen where a million little details awaited her attention. She started with the cake, transferring it from the box to a rectangular foil-covered cookie sheet. Once this was done, she reminded herself, she would have to pull more of the caterer's appetizers from the oven and set them on the warming tray and then get the extra napkins from the top shelf in the linen closet. But first . . .

. . . she heard her father's voice echo in the hallway behind her.

"What did you say your name was?" Moose May asked.

There was a low murmur.

"Nice to meet you, Philip. She's right over here."

Philip? Veronica paused where she was, frozen with the cake half-in, half-out of the box.

And then he was there, shaking her father's hand and wearing a crisp blue suit and a red-striped tie. Philip. *Her* Philip.

And although it hadn't yet started raining, suddenly everything happened underwater. Her father entered the kitchen and pointed to her and then Philip saw her and reached a hand toward her and she was swimming against the tide and she couldn't move, she couldn't get her damn feet to move her from the spot she was rooted to and then a burst of thunder broke the spell and they both looked up at the sky.

"You know, I've driven women away before," Philip said with a wry grin. "But never completely out of the state."

Veronica fixed him with a stare; she would not give him the satisfaction of a smile.

"What are you doing here?" she asked.

Philip cleared his throat and grew serious. "You ran away from me, Veronica. You never gave me a chance to explain."

"So you drove all the way to Arizona to do that?"

"Could we talk for a moment?" Philip asked. He tried to take her by the arm, but she stepped aside so he grabbed futilely at the air.

"Kind of busy here. It is my father's wedding, you know."

"I hope he doesn't mind my showing up."

"What about me? Maybe I mind."

"Do you?" And his eyes glimmered, sweet and charming, and she felt like all her insides would melt. *Oh god, he did that so well,* she thought with a groan. *He always did.*

"How did you know about the wedding?" she asked, tempering her ardor with attitude.

"Craig told me." Philip frowned. "If I were you, I wouldn't trust him with too many secrets. It didn't take much to get this one out of him."

The overhead lights flickered, and then there was a sudden stampede of guests into the kitchen, the hallways and even Moose's den.

"*Qu'est-ce que c'est que ça?*" Veronica asked the house at large and was answered with a tremendous roar of thunder. Outside, sheets of rain poured down, soaking the lawn, flattening the balloons and puddling the plastic chairs.

From behind Veronica came her father's voice: "Oh no . . ." He held the cordless phone in his hand. All the color had left his face.

"It's okay, Daddy," Veronica said. "We'll get the tent up and everyone can go outside. It's fine. What? What is it?"

"The priest phoned," he said, his voice heavy and tired. "A tree fell on his car."

"Did you tell May May?"

"She thinks it's a bad sign." He smiled weakly. "Maybe you could go talk to her for a few minutes?"

"Me? One of her friends must be here . . ."

"Please, sweetheart? Let's keep this in the family, okay?"

"The tent," she started to say, but her father patted her shoulder. "I'm sure your boyfriend will help out. He looks strong."

Beside her, Philip chuckled while Veronica's face flushed. "He's not my boyfriend, Daddy!"

"Please, Veronica. Would you go to May May?"

She relented and started for the first floor bedroom, then stopped and looked back at her father. "Why is it raining anyway? Didn't you do the crossed knives thing?"

Her father held up the index card that read, "Cross knives on mirror."

"It must have fallen off the cork board," he said apologetically.

Veronica shook her head and left her father with Philip. She knocked lightly on Daddy's bedroom door. When she peeked in, she saw May sitting on the bed, her cream-colored satin and lace cocktail dress spread out around her, her hands knotted delicately in her lap.

Just like a porcelain doll, Veronica thought, with her thick hair wound around her head in a loose French braid, sprigs of baby's breath peeking through. No tortoise-shell glasses today.

May looked up and smiled. "Still raining." She let out a deep sigh. "No priest." She dropped her head to her chest and opened her hands. The gold cross she was clutching had left a sharp indent in her palms. "Maybe these are not good signs."

"Oh, May, don't talk like that," Veronica said, taking a seat beside her.

"Your father and I should have married years ago, Lord willing, if it was the right thing to do."

"Of course it's right. He loves you."

"He loves *you*," May said, staring unblinkingly at Veronica. "You mean everything to him. And if marrying me was something that would hurt you . . ."

Veronica looked down at her shoes and said nothing.

"When you were twelve," May said, taking Veronica's hand in hers and pressing the gold cross against it, "we first talked about marriage. You were too young, he said, not even in high school. We talked again when you were sixteen. But he worried about you going to college and being on your own. Finally, I told him, 'This is it, it's now or never,' and he agreed."

May stood and went to Daddy's dresser. She picked up a photo of Veronica and Moose standing at the edge of the driveway, Veronica wearing her graduation gown, Moose a proud smile. May had taken that.

"I never wanted to take your mother's place, Veronica," May whispered. "I only wanted to be in your life, to love you and your father." She returned the photo to the dresser. "My family disowned me long ago, and I felt lucky to find you."

Luck, Veronica thought, *what did luck mean?* A sudden rush of images flooded her brain: her mother's casket at the funeral parlor, rosewood with gold trim, white satin lining, a lace pillow beneath her far-too-young head; her father's rough, calloused hand pulling her away from the daisy-and-carnation bouquet they had placed at Diana's grave; mountains of food—lasagnas, tuna casseroles, cookies, pies—sitting on the door step and the back porch, sympathy gifts from well-wishers. That was her luck.

And then: Daddy and May May in the audience at her first play; Daddy and May May taking photos of her in her junior prom dress; Daddy and May May cheering her on as she accepted her high school diploma. That was her luck too.

When Veronica was fourteen and had mono, May bought her Tampax and *Cosmo Girl* because her father was too embarrassed to buy them himself.

When she was sixteen, May taught her to drive in her tiny car, the one she needed a booster seat to reach the pedals.

And when Veronica was seventeen and had no date for Sadie Hawkins, May brought over a pair of gorgeous handmade skirts and taught her to dance *faldeo* in the kitchen.

That was more than luck; that was being truly *blessed*.

All this time, Veronica had had a mother, and she didn't even realize it. She took the small woman in her arms, careful not to crush the fabric of her dress. "Oh, May, we're *both* lucky to have you in our lives. You were more of a mother to me than my real one. And Daddy, well, Daddy has loved you for most of my life. If those aren't good signs, I don't know what they are." She lifted May's chin with her fingertip. "Don't cry, sweetie, you'll ruin your makeup."

"You know," May said shyly, "one of my names is Valencia. Did you know that?"

"Like the oranges?"

"I'm a Vee too." She hastened to add, "Can I be a Vee?"

The pit of Veronica's stomach suddenly felt hollow and her ribs ached. "Yes, of course." She laughed. "Although the designation doesn't come with as many perks as you'd think."

May reached up and wrapped her tiny arms around Veronica's neck. "*Gracias, mi hija.*"

Thank you, my daughter.

Veronica's eyes filled with tears, and she blinked quickly, lest they spill down her cheeks and ruin her own makeup. "*Si, mami.*"

"You'll be okay until the priest gets here?" she asked and May nodded.

Veronica slipped out to the empty hallway and wondered whether Philip had gotten fed up and left, or if he was still outside with the tent. And wondering about *that* made her wonder why she cared. She felt her cheeks grow warm and flush.

Ergh. She did *not* have time for this nonsense. She was very busy with her father's wedding, with keeping everything and everyone running smoothly. She had the Vees at the bar, May May in the bedroom and a giant chocolate cake on the kitchen counter. Didn't her brain understand all that? She hurried to her bedroom and took a seat at her vanity table where she dabbed translucent powder on her cheeks with a soft-bristled brush.

The delicate hairs felt soothing against her skin; the mere act of brushing calmed her. She stared at her reflection in the mirror, pale from worry and running around and taking care of things, and thought with a laugh, *I look nothing like my head shot.*

She heard a knock on the door behind her. What was it *now*? Who needed something else from her? Veronica turned to see her father at the doorway, his tie askew, his crew cut damp from the rain.

"Is the priest here?" she asked.

Moose May shook his head and stepped into the room. He held a sheet of paper out to Veronica.

"You didn't read the last letter," he said.

"What?"

Veronica took the paper from him reluctantly and felt an instant of revulsion: That damn steno pad page with its godforsaken double-lined columns and black ink scrawl.

"Dearest Moose," she read aloud. "I'm too tired to fight this anymore. It's too hard to get work, too hard to stay working. I don't have the strength to follow my dreams. So yes, I will marry you. I know you'll take care of me, and you'll be a good father and make up for my shortcomings. If it's a girl . . ." Veronica's breath caught in her throat. "If it's a girl, maybe she'll do everything I never could."

There was nothing more. Veronica set the letter down on her vanity and listened to the rain pour out of the gutters.

"I remember the day Diana came into the library," her father began in a quiet, rumbly voice. "She was looking for a copy of *To Kill a Mockingbird*. She had seen the movie and didn't know it was based on a novel by Harper Lee. She asked me for 'that book with Gregory Peck in it.'" He laughed to himself, as if he had forgotten Veronica was in the room.

"I knew she was a restless soul, and I knew she wanted to leave Arizona, but I was so grateful that she loved me as much as she did. For as long as she did." He stared out the window to somewhere far beyond the confines of the May homestead, far beyond Chester and Arizona and this existence. His lips were pressed tightly together, and his voice was a hoarse whisper.

"It wasn't your fault," he said. "Whatever she did, whatever she didn't do, had nothing to do with you. I should have told you about her long ago. I should have told you when you asked, but I just wanted us to move on. I'm sorry."

Veronica felt her father's eyes on her, felt him trying to read her mind.

"You are not your mother, Veronica. You share some of her interests, yes, and you inherited some of her talents. But you are so much more."

Veronica hung her head. "I failed. Just like Diana. I failed."

"What? You haven't failed! You've barely begun, and already you've made friends and gotten a job and you've been on auditions." He smiled warmly and his cheeks grew round as apples. "And you've done it all on your own. I'm so proud of you."

"But you told me . . . you told me my life would still be here when I got back," Veronica protested. "I thought you didn't want me to go."

"Veronica, you will always have a place in my home, no matter where you go or what you do."

Veronica looked down at her lap, feeling foolish. "I thought I was being replaced."

"I could never replace you," her father insisted. "Who else knows how to work that coffee maker?" He leaned forward on the bed and took Veronica's hands in hers. "Give it time. Success will come."

"You really think so?"

"I believe in you," Moose May said, with an almost Zen-like calm. "Follow your own path, not your mother's or Vivian's or any-one else's."

Veronica cocked her head to one side. "Who are you and what are you doing in my father's new suit?" Then she grinned. "Thank you, Daddy."

They wrapped their arms around each other's waist and walked in silence to the door.

"So, tell me about this boyfriend of yours from California," he said as they made their way down the hall, Veronica in the lead.

"Oh, Daddy, he's not my boyfriend." Veronica glanced back over her shoulder and saw her father roll his eyes.

"If you say so."

As they began to part ways, her father looked past her with a sly grin. She turned.

Philip was standing in the front hallway, leaning against the wall, alone and staring at the floor. He looked up when he saw the two of them and smiled self-consciously.

"Don't take too long, sweetheart," Moose May said. "The priest should be here soon." He kissed her on the forehead and left.

"Veronica—"

"Philip, I am all talked out. Truly I am." She took a step, but he jumped into her path, blocking her escape route.

"*I'll* talk. You don't have to say anything. In fact, I don't want you to say anything."

There was a sudden burst of laughter from another room, and Philip nervously pushed her into the closet alcove. "I'm in love with you, Veronica. You're smart and funny and honest and beautiful. You're responsible and practical and silly and fun. And you know theater and literature. You . . . you have substance."

"Substance? Like, I'm *heavy*?" Veronica rocked back on her heels and looked at him.

Philip shook his head impatiently. "I don't care about that. I don't and I never did. I want you the way you are."

"But Reed—"

Philip placed a finger on her lips. "Uh! Quiet!" He dropped his hand but kept it close to her side. She could feel the warmth of it hop the short distance to her leg and shoot straight through to her cheeks.

"Reed knew you were coming to work after that audition and

she chose the exact right moment to kiss me so you would see it," he said. "And you reacted exactly the way she wanted to. You ran away."

Veronica winced at the words. "When it comes to guys, Reed . . . I mean, Vivian always gets what she wants. And if she wants you, then I'm just going to be in the way. And I don't want to get hurt."

"And she wants me?"

"Looks like."

"What if I don't want her?"

"You did."

"True," Philip acknowledged. "That was before I met you." He moved closer to her and put his hand against the wall behind her head. "Why do you underestimate yourself? Why can't you accept that someone would be attracted to you and love you?"

"Well . . . I'm . . . and Reed's . . ." she stammered.

"You have the most amazing violet eyes," he whispered. His fingers played with the ends of her hair. She could feel every strand come to life. "You're you and she's . . . inconsequential."

Inconsequential, Veronica thought. An adjective, meaning unimportant, trivial, *small*.

She smiled. "So you're not dating her now?"

"Would I drive all this way to kiss you if I were?" He leaned forward then and pressed his lips tightly against hers. He tasted moist, soft, a little sweet like a dusting of cocoa powder. She kissed him back and he slid his hands around her waist and drew her closer, perfectly fitting his body to hers.

"Whoa," she said when they stopped to breathe. "This is my father's wedding day."

"Not the proper decorum for a wedding?"

"I wasn't thinking that so much as I've gotta walk down the aisle soon, and I'd rather not have my pantyhose twisted around my thighs."

She held him at arm's length and stared into his eyes. "Look, Philip, sometimes I'm scared to try new things. Sometimes I worry about what people think of me. I think . . . I really think I'm a good actor and I'm coming back to L.A. to try it again."

"You are good, Veronica," Philip said. "You shouldn't need anyone else to tell you."

"Thank you." She bowed her head to his chest. "I'm glad you came."

"So am I." He kissed her lightly on the lips. Then they clasped hands and walked out into the living room.

"Hey, one question?" she asked.

"What's that?"

"Could I have my job back?"

They entered the backyard where the sun appeared to be bursting through the dark clouds, spreading light and warmth over the guests milling about.

The Vees waved to her when she approached with Philip on her arm. Val blew her a kiss and Ginny winked.

And then there was a collective "ooh" and she turned. May May, gorgeous in her gown, was at the doorway with Daddy in his handsome new suit that actually fit, clutching hands and wearing smiles as bright as the new sun. Veronica joined them, taking her place between the two of them.

As the priest, dressed in black and holding a Bible in the palm of one hand, beckoned them from the other end of the patio, the three Mays descended the back steps and down the makeshift aisle. The guests were assembled on either side; the balloons wafted in the breeze, none the worse for wear. The sun shone, the grass glistened. Perf.

Veronica settled Moose and May in front of the priest, joined their hands and kissed them both.

"Dearly beloved," the priest began as Veronica took her place off to one side. "We are gathered here today . . ."

Change was good, she thought. Scary, thrilling, head-lightening, nausea-inducing, but good, definitely good. She glanced over at Ginny and Val, who would soon be in L.A., following her dream with her, and at Philip, who wore a contemplative smile as he watched the nuptials.

She wouldn't run away again, she told herself firmly; she would run *to*.

And although she didn't know, couldn't know, just how much her life might change, there was someone who did. He was listening to her answering machine back in L.A., his furry ears pricking up at the gruff voice leaving a message.

"Yeah, hi, Veronica, this is Harvey from the Santa Barbara Rep. We'd like to offer you a place in the company for next season."

Max barked once.

"We figured out a way to give you an Equity card, but you'll have to start as an understudy. If you're still interested, give me a call and we'll start the paperwork."

Max cocked his head and appeared to nod, as if he thought Harvey was an okay guy.

"And we also figured out how we got your resume. One of the Rep's former members forwarded it directly to us, a guy named Philip Caton. A friend of yours? Anyway, have a good holiday and we'll talk to you after the New Year."

BEEP!

Max lowered his head and rested them on crossed paws. She would be back, he might have been thinking, and the walking would continue. Or running or jogging or biking. Whatever, it didn't matter to him.

No one could say he was not a dog willing to change.

Acknowledgments

My sincerest thanks go out to my editor, Kristen Pettit; my agent, Faye Bender; and my manager, Adam Peck. Their talent, support, and dedication continue to make my dreams come true.

A very special thank you to Ben Schrank, Razorbill's publisher, and to all of the amazing people at Penguin who work so hard to design, print, and promote my books.

And finally, thank you to Mom, Dad, Jay, and Maurice for all of your love and encouragement.

I wouldn't have been able to do this without all of you.